Body Check

Also Edited by Nicole Foster

Awakening the Virgin: True Tales of Seduction
Electric: Best Lesbian Erotic Fiction
Skin Deep: Real-life Lesbian Sex Stories

Body Check erotic lesbian sports stories

Edited by Nicole Foster

alyson books
los angeles | new york

ALL CHARACTERS IN THIS BOOK ARE FICTITIOUS. ANY RESEMBLANCE TO REAL INDIVIDUALS—EITHER LIVING OR DEAD—IS STRICTLY COINCIDENTAL.

© 2002 BY ALYSON PUBLICATIONS. ALL RIGHTS RESERVED.

MANUFACTURED IN THE UNITED STATES OF AMERICA.

THIS TRADE PAPERBACK ORIGINAL IS PUBLISHED BY ALYSON PUBLICATIONS,
P.O. BOX 4371, LOS ANGELES, CALIFORNIA 90078-4371.
DISTRIBUTION IN THE UNITED KINGDOM BY
TURNAROUND PUBLISHER SERVICES LTD.,
UNIT 3, OLYMPIA TRADING ESTATE, COBURG ROAD, WOOD GREEN,
LONDON N22 6TZ ENGLAND.

FIRST EDITION: APRIL 2002

02 03 04 05 06 a 10 9 8 7 6 5 4 3 2 1

ISBN 1-55583-738-7

CREDITS
- BRIDGET BUFFORD'S "WORKING OUT" FIRST APPEARED IN *PILLOW TALK II: MORE LESBIAN STORIES BETWEEN THE COVERS*, EDITED BY LESLÉA NEWMAN, ALYSON PUBLICATIONS, 2000.
- ANNE SEALE'S "THE TABLE" FIRST APPEARED IN *SET IN STONE: BUTCH-ON-BUTCH EROTICA*, EDITED BY ANGELA BROWN, ALYSON PUBLICATIONS, 2001.
- COVER DESIGN BY MATT SAMS.
- COVER PHOTOGRAPHY BY YVETTE GONZALEZ.

to A.B., for showing me the ropes

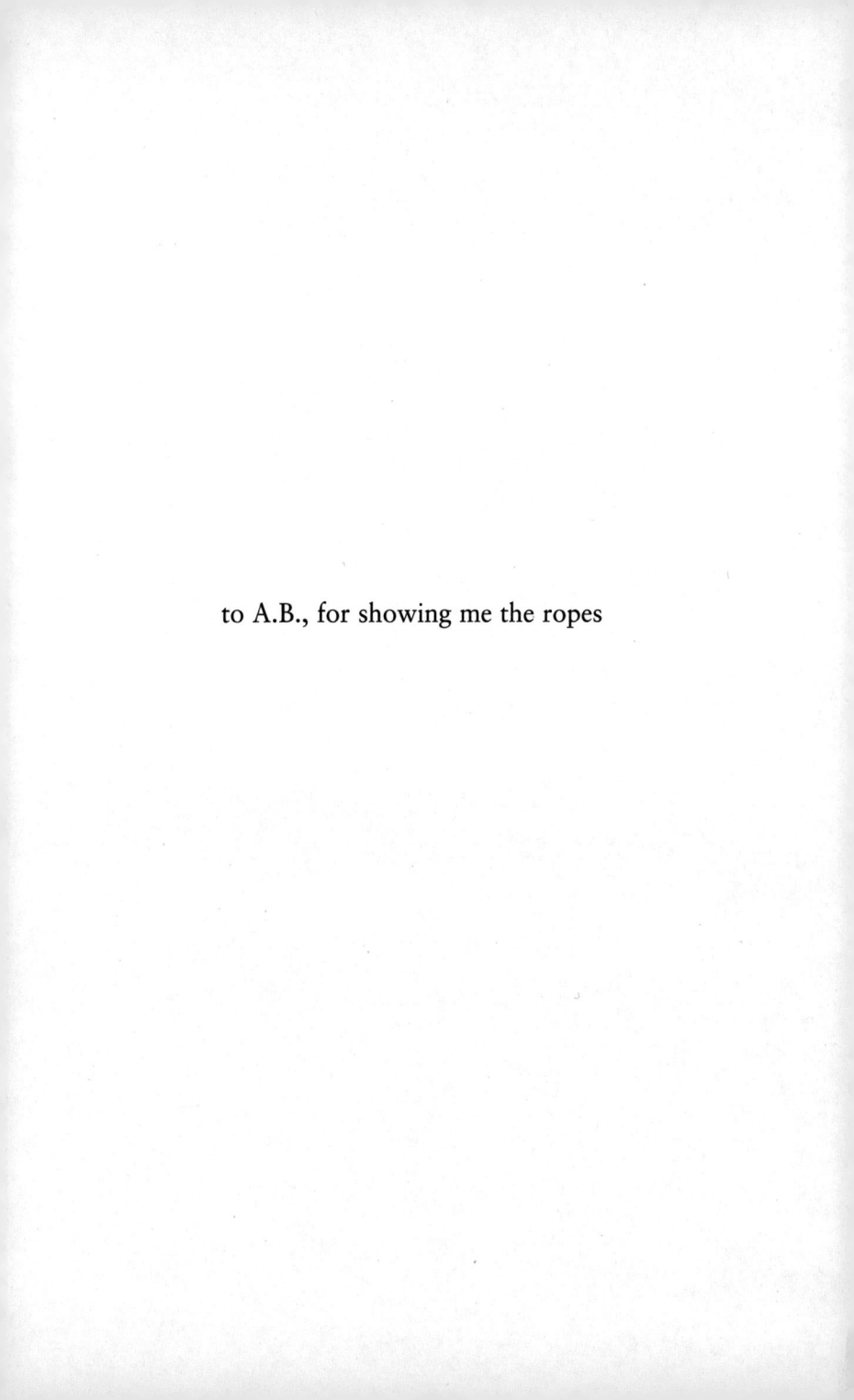

Contents

Introduction xi
The Legend of Teddi Jo • *Gina Ranalli* 1
Thin Ice • *J.L. Belrose* 16
Working Out • *Bridget Bufford* 31
The Art of Running • *Rosalind C. Lloyd* 41
The Table • *Anne Seale* 50
Black Belt Theater • *Catherine Lundoff* 63
Rivals • *Yolanda Wallace* 75
The Basketball Diaries • *M. Christian* 86
Spiked! • *Laurel Hayworth* 99
Mulligan on the Green • *Trixi* 113
Bull Rider • *Sacchi Green* 122
Turned Out • *Kirsten Imani Kasai* 139
Going Up • *Anne Seale* 148
Spurred On • *Debra Hyde* 161
The Fencing Tournament • *Sarah b Wiseman* 171
Naiad • *M. Christian* 182
Sports Dyke • *Dawn Dougherty* 192
Touchdown • *Ren Bisson* 206
Blue Ball Passion • *Shannon McDonnell* 218
Roller Ball • *Thomas S. Roche* 235
Contributors 246

Introduction

Recently I was chatting online with my dear friend Jane about a very attractive young lady in my beginners tennis class.

"She's so hot I can't keep my eye on the ball," I wrote. "She's totally muscular yet lithe. She's got the body of a pro, but she's a complete klutz on the court."

"Sounds perfect for you," Jane quipped.

"Ha, ha," I typed back. "And guess what? After class she asked me if I wanted to 'rally on the back courts' with her. What do you think that means?"

"That you're imagining things again," Jane wrote. "How do you even know she's gay? Is it a gay girls' tennis class?" Sensible, sensible Jane.

"I don't know," I told her. "My gaydar is whacked on the tennis courts. To me, all women in tennis outfits look gay."

Now, dear reader, I don't have to clarify that remark, do I? How many times have you wanted to spend a little "athletic time" with Mia Hamm as you watched her break international scoring records—and the hearts of lesbians around the world? How many of you have yearned for just one kiss from that sexy Anna Kournikova (then curled up into a little ball and cried for hours when you learned she had eloped)? How many of you can say Lisa Leslie hasn't ignited a "spark" in your heart (and other places)?

Of course, I'm not implying that any of these women are gay—I'm just saying there's something inherently lesbian about *all* female athletes. The strength of their bodies, the

INTRODUCTION

power of their muscles and self-confidence; the potent sexuality exuded by a woman giving her all on the field, court, and, at least in my fantasies, in the bedroom, where all that athletic energy is transformed into the workout of a lifetime. Why do you think I joined a women-only gym? It certainly wasn't for the nail care tips!

So with my dyke-jock fantasies running rampant and forcing me out of bed at 6 A.M. to an estrogen-laden gym for a little eye candy (and maybe a bit of work on my triceps), it's no wonder I decided to pull together an anthology that would put hot girl jocks "in touch" with each other. With that in mind, I asked writers to concoct original, explicit, highly charged stories of female athletes and their fans working each other's muscles and stamina in unexpected, super-hot ways.

Of course, no book of lesbian sports erotica would be complete without a softball story (from the submissions I received, I could have created a 25-volume erotic encyclopedia). But in this book I included just one. I wanted to show the breadth and depth of lesbian athletics, so reader beware, even though this book contains stories featuring some pretty popular sports—football, basketball, volleyball, etc.—there's also some pretty fringe stuff in here: Roller Derby, bull riding, dogsledding, and arm wrestling, for example. Let's just say I'm trying to test the limits of your fantasies, force you to expand your sexual horizons, and, community-minded gal that I am, perhaps get you to start your own local Dykes on BMX Bikes League.

In addition to exploring and celebrating the sensuality of the lesbian athlete, I hope this fiery collection inspires each and every one of you to get out there on the court and in the bedroom and give it your all. At the very least, deck

INTRODUCTION

yourself out in a helmet and kneepads and tell that special someone you'd like to get sweaty with her tonight! Even if you can't "Just do it," at least "Do her."

I'd like to end by thanking the very talented, first-string erotic writers who have helped to make this book a knockout. Special thanks also go to Terri Fabris for her excellent editorial assistance and unceasing wit; Trixi for cheering me on from the stands; Alan, Jon, Melissa, Lisa, and Redsie for their unwavering friendship and humor; and, finally, my relentless workout partner, the inimitable Angela Brown.

Now, players, get ready to go for the burn. I myself am hitting the showers.

—Nicole Foster

The Legend of Teddi Jo Gina Ranalli

"Lucy or Ethel?"

I scratched my nose. "Definitely Lucy."

Colleen nodded without looking at me, observing the softball game with a look of helpless disgust. "Same here."

The dugout was the perfect place to watch the Red Eyes dust the field with Colleen's Racers under a crisp blue September sky. I was only along for the ride, suited up under the guise of relief batter even though I hadn't played any ball for quite some time.

"Wilma or Betty?" Colleen asked, snapping her gum.

"Well, I guess we know when *you* realized you were a lesbian, huh?" She shot me a look, so I said, "OK, OK...Wilma."

Colleen had called at the last minute and begged me to join her, more for moral support than anything else. She'd been feeling dejected about this game, knowing her team would get their asses kicked because they *always* got their asses kicked when they played the Red Eyes.

I hadn't played ball in a long time and was reluctant until she promised to buy dinner and a few rounds of cold ones after the game. It was just one of those lazy autumn days where there wasn't a whole lot going on anyway, so I accepted, thinking, *How bad could it be?*

So there I sat, feeling ridiculous in a uniform that was too big, and playing Who Would You Do? with my old friend Colleen.

"Xena or Scully?"

"No contest. Scully."

Colleen glanced at me skeptically. "I'd pick Xena any day, but I'm a sucker for leather."

I laughed. "Different strokes."

We sat in silence for a while, watching strike after strike, while the large crowd hooted from the bleachers. I kept my gaze on the Red Eyes' perfect weapon, a pitcher named Teddi Jo Bell. Their team had been the league champion for three years running, and she was the only reason why. No one could get a hit off her.

"She's sort of cute," I said, pointing my chin at the pitcher's mound. "Vicious but cute."

"Yeah, like a pit bull." Colleen fanned her face with her cap. "I swear I don't know where you get your taste, Anne."

"I love all women," I smiled. "Even sore losers like you."

The comment earned me a swat on the arm before Colleen laughed and said, "The game isn't over yet, wiseass. Besides, you're supposed to boost my confidence, not ogle the enemy."

I looked at her. "I could hum the *Rocky* theme if you want, but it won't make a damn bit of difference. That woman has a shotgun growing out of her shoulder."

Colleen nodded her blond head helplessly, her apple cheeks even more flushed than usual. "I told you, Teddi Jo is infamous. I've even heard some of her own teammates can't stand her because they get so bored just boiling in the field all day. She's very antisocial too—won't go out with her team after a game, shit like that."

I leaned forward, elbows on knees, and studied the notorious pitcher. She was dressed like the rest of her team, in a black T-shirt with red trim and matching shorts. Her cap obscured the upper half of her face, but the lower half was clearly visible and was tanned a golden brown, the lips pink and pulpy. With each minute movement, muscles rippled over every part of her lean body, while a fiery ponytail rested between her shoulder blades, glinting in the sun.

All day I sat on that bench, wincing as the Racers got pounded deeper into the ground. Finally, in the top of the ninth, I was asked to step up to bat. After a quick warm-up, I stood over home plate with no particular nervousness or expectation. I just assumed I would strike out as I'd seen the rest of the team do over and over, especially since I wasn't much of a ballplayer to begin with.

When Colleen yelled a few words of encouragement, I threw her a quick grin over my shoulder, and when I looked back at the pitcher, I was surprised to see she'd adjusted her cap back on her head, exposing her entire face for the first time all day. She looked down at the ground and tilted her head left and right, maybe to loosen a tight muscle in her neck. Finally, she became perfectly still and looked straight at me. I saw a sharp, sunburned nose and high, freckled cheekbones. She wound up for the pitch, and I sucked in air through clenched teeth. One side of her mouth curled up in an unmistakably flirtatious little smile. I blinked in surprise and heard the ball smack hard into the catcher's mitt, the loud bark of, "*Strike!*" ringing in my ears.

I stood frozen for several seconds, staring at her. She'd already gone back to her stretching and kicking at the plate routine, ignoring me completely.

"I'll be damned," I muttered. I gave my head a quick shake before raising the bat again.

She took less time preparing for the second pitch. Our eyes locked for the briefest instant, then the tip of a rosy tongue snaked provocatively across her upper lip. Again, the unquestionable sound of ball in glove. "*Strike!*"

"*Shit!*" I hissed, and dropped the bat, pacing around home plate for a few seconds. I dared a glance in Colleen's direction, but all she could do was shrug.

Eventually, I regained my composure and picked up the bat, determined not to allow the pitcher the satisfaction of distracting me again. I no longer gave a damn about the actual game. I was being teased and toyed with, probably for the amusement of all her teammates, and though her tricks had obviously worked wonders for her so far, I knew I could be equally tenacious. I wouldn't permit myself to be the butt of anyone's jokes.

Rigid with concentration, lips pressed tightly together, I mentally challenged her to try her games on me one last time.

She prepared for her wind up, lifted her chin slightly, and stared hard at me. Then the smile came again, sweeter and wider than before, followed by a quick wink. My fists tightened on the bat, every muscle in my body tensed, and I began my swing at the same millisecond I looked down to see the ball still in her hand. My eyes flicked back up to her face just in time to catch the seductively pursed lips as they blew me a kiss so inconspicuous it could have been a smoky shadow cast by imagination.

The ball whizzed a hair's breadth over the bat and exploded into the catcher's mitt like a firecracker.

"*Strike three! You're out!*"

I was dumbfounded. I stood at home for what seemed like a long time but was probably only seconds. Then I walked back to the dugout, dazed, glancing back at that Teddi Jo Bell as if I'd been hypnotized and made to cluck like a chicken. She, of course, paid me no attention whatsoever, already engaged in her next breathtaking display of magical wonders.

"Nice try," Colleen said as I took my place on the bench beside her.

I ran a hand through my short cinnamon hair and sighed. "Hey, thanks for the warning. Appreciate it."

"Huh?"

"Doesn't that shit she pulls get old? How the hell do you guys fall for it every time?"

Puzzlement creased her brow. "I don't know. She's just fast, that's all. *Really* fast."

"Yeah, she's fast all right. Are those kind of stunts even legal?"

Colleen hesitated, then asked, "Who's on first?"

"What?" I frowned. "What are you talking about?"

"What are *you* talking about?"

"*Her!*" I pointed at the pitcher's mound. "Her and her cute little bag of tricks." When it became clear that Colleen didn't have slightest inkling of what I was referring to, I lowered my voice and told her of Teddi Jo's pitching antics. "Doesn't she do that to everyone?"

"No, all she usually does is glare. If she acknowledges you at all." Colleen paused, became thoughtful for a moment, then smiled. "You're doing that thing again, aren't you? That 'let's see how gullible Colleen is today' thing, right?" She laughed as if she'd just figured out a particularly amusing punch line.

I could only gape at her in disbelief until I shook my head and said, "Never mind."

Turning my attention back to what had to be the most pathetic ball game in history, I eyed Teddi Jo once more.

There she posed on her mound, alone in the center of the diamond as if she were the sun itself, dwarfing the stars and moons and planets that spun around her, for her, for as long as she willed them to.

Behind her, the western sky had darkened to a deep indigo with a thin ribbon of fire blazing just above the horizon, a fire the exact same shade as her hair.

Hours later, Colleen and I sat at a table in a little dyke bar called The Lesser Evil, nursing our third beers and still bemoaning the Racers loss.

"Zero to 4 isn't that bad, really," I said.

Colleen giggled. "That's right. Last time we played them it was zero to 5, so we're improving."

"Well, there you go."

We tapped the necks of our bottles together and drank to all the losers of the world, then she gestured for me to lean forward across the table and whispered, "There's a fine-looking daddy-type sitting at the bar, and she's been sneaking peeks over here for the last 20 minutes."

When I turned around in my seat, she cried, "Don't look! Jesus, Anne, does the word *casual* mean anything to you?"

I faced her again. "Sorry, I just wanted to..." And then Teddi Jo Bell strolled into The Lesser Evil. "Fuck!"

Sitting with her back to the entrance and her eyes on the woman at the bar, Colleen said, "You just wanted to fuck? Oh, that's nice, Anne. Very ladylike." Then she saw my expression and glanced behind her. "Fuck!"

We both watched in stunned silence as Teddi Jo walked over to the bar and ordered a drink, then carried it over to the pool table where she proceeded to rack 'em up. She had changed out of her uniform and into jeans, boots, and a New England Patriots T-shirt. Her flame-colored hair was now loose, falling in untamed waves across her shoulders.

"This is too weird," Colleen said. "She looked right at us!"

I nodded. "Have you ever seen her in here before?"

"Never." The pool table was behind Colleen, so she eventually had to stop staring at Teddi Jo and look at me again. "I didn't even know she was gay."

"Even after all that crap she pulled today?"

She rolled her eyes. "God, don't start that again."

I scowled at her, then glanced back at Teddi Jo, who was looking right back. She winked.

I softly yelped something unintelligible and slammed my bottle down. "Shit!"

Colleen lifted an eyebrow. "That damn Tourette syndrome, huh?"

"She did it again," I hissed.

"What?"

"Winked at me!"

"Oh," Colleen laughed. "Well, maybe she really likes you."

"Right, and I'm Angelina Jolie." I downed the rest of my beer and said, "I'm gonna go talk to her."

Looking past me, she replied, "Yeah, why don't you? I just made some serious eye contact with Miss Thing, and I think she's about to come over."

I wished Colleen luck and marched over to the pool table just in time to see Teddi Jo miss her shot. "Looks like you're not as good at pool as you are at softball," I said.

Teddi Jo didn't look up. Instead she studied the balls, moved around to my side of the table and said, "Looks like." Then she bent over and took another shot. This time she sank it and paused to glance at me before returning her attention to the table.

"Interesting pitching method you have, by the way." I tried to glare. When I received no response, I added, "You can't really pitch a ball very fast. You obviously need to distract the batter in order to make her think you're pitching bullets."

She smiled. "Obviously."

"Are you being sarcastic?"

Finally, she stopped looking at the balls and gave me her full attention. Luminous green eyes flashed with amusement. "Not at all. If you want to believe that I can't pitch, then you go right ahead and believe that. I don't see what the big deal is. Weren't you just a relief anyway?"

"That's not the point. The point is, I know I could have gotten a hit off you if you hadn't pulled that shit."

"You know that, do you?" She shrugged and smiled again. "OK."

Her nonchalance was infuriating. "You know it too," I snapped.

She had begun to make her way to the far side of the table once again; now she circled back to where I stood. "I don't know any such thing."

We proceeded to have a mini stare-down for probably 10 seconds, until she said, "Let's go back to the field then."

I blinked. "What? You mean right now?"

"Sure. I have bats and balls in my Jeep, and you can prove to me what an outstanding hitter you are."

"It's nighttime," I protested.

Teddi Jo shrugged again. "There's a full moon. Plenty bright enough." She watched me carefully. "Unless, of course..." She trailed off, letting the rest of the sentence reveal itself in her bright jungle-green eyes.

She was challenging me again, just as she had done that afternoon. I knew it and knew it was stupid and knew I should say no, but instead I heard myself say, "Fine. Let's go."

While Teddi Jo polished off her drink, I went over to tell Colleen I was taking off for a bit. She barely glanced up at me, already deep into her flirting session with the butch from the bar.

Outside, as Teddi Jo led me to her Jeep, she asked, "Who are you, anyway?"

I frowned, puzzled, until I realized I hadn't introduced myself. "I'm Anne," I said lamely.

Teddi Jo laughed and quickened her step. She told me her name over her shoulder and tucked a lock of flaming hair behind one ear.

"I know," I mumbled, my eyes suddenly drawn to the graceful rolling of her perfectly round ass. "I know."

I was a nervous wreck, certain Teddi Jo's driving would be the death of me. Weaving around other vehicles at breakneck speeds, barely pausing for traffic signals, her hair whipping around her head like a brushfire halo, Teddi Jo quickly convinced me I'd inadvertently caught a ride with Hecate, the goddess of the underworld. I was in seriously deep shit. Between the rushing of the wind and the Hole CD splintering my eardrums, conversation was impossible. All I could do was pray my seat belt held and recite what I could remember of the Lord's Prayer, which is really saying something since I'm not even religious.

Only when the Jeep stopped, when Courtney Love's guitar ceased its screeching, and when the engine finally cut did I dare open my eyes. We were at the field, and Teddi Jo was staring at me with a pleased expression. "We're here."

I released my breath and said, "You owe me new undies."

Teddi Jo grinned and jumped out of the Jeep. "Grab the bat, will ya?"

We took the equipment out of the back seat and trudged across the deserted, moon-dappled field to our respective positions. The night was cool and quiet and breezy, an early autumn masterpiece.

Swinging the bat a few times, I called over to Teddi Jo, "Get ready to duck." The soft sound of her chuckle drifted over to me, so I added, "I'm serious. You might be decapitated."

"Yeah, OK, killer, get ready. Here comes your first strike."

Teddi Jo wound up and let the ball fly. I swung and heard a solid whack before I felt the vibrations rush through my hands and up my arms to my shoulders.

I stood stunned and watched the ball whiz its way through the sky and land with a hard thunk out in left field. Teddi Jo, hands on hips, watched it soar as well, her head tilted back and cocked to one side.

"Ha!" I cheered and jumped up and down ecstatically. "I *knew* it! I *knew* I could get a hit off you! I *told* you!"

Teddi Jo stood on the pitcher's mound washed in moonlight, her radiant hair burning. I could see her smile. "Beginner's luck," she called, and bent down to retrieve another ball from the bag. "Bet you a beer you can't do it again."

I told her she was on, and sent the next ball chasing after the first. And the next one and the next one and the one after that. She was probably pitching the seventh ball when I realized she was just feeding them to me, tossing them slow and easy, right over home plate. Only the most athletically challenged couldn't have hit those balls, but at that point I didn't care. I was having fun, giddy with adrenaline and what I eventually realized was attraction. An attraction like I hadn't felt in a very long time.

Teddi Jo appeared to be having a great time as well; she laughed almost constantly and particularly enjoyed teasing me about my batting technique.

Inevitably, the time came when there were no more balls to hit, and we had to tromp around the field gathering them up. I was stunned when I looked up at the sky and saw stars, the moon having spun away to nestle behind a distant stand of trees.

"Crap!" I exclaimed. "What time is it?"

Teddi Jo consulted her watch. "Wow. Late. Or early." She laughed and scooped up another ball.

"I told Colleen I'd be back in an hour."

When she smiled, her teeth shown brightly. "I guess you lied."

"Damn, she's gonna be pissed. Not to mention that she drove." I began pacing a patch of center field in search of stray balls.

"Oh, she'll recover, and I'll give you a ride home. Besides, it's not like she was sitting there all by her lonesome. She was busy doing the same thing as us."

I looked up quickly. "What do you mean?"

But Teddi Jo ignored my question and plopped down on the grass, lying back with a heavy sigh. "It's really clear tonight," she said.

I took my cue and sat beside her. For a while neither of us spoke. We just stared up at the black sky admiring the shimmering stars.

One question had been nibbling at my curiosity all

evening. "Why aren't you doing something with your talent?"

"Hmm?" Her voice sounded dreamy and faraway.

"I mean, you're good. You should be...I don't know...playing in the Olympics or something."

Teddi Jo shrugged. "I don't know. I guess that scene isn't for me."

"What?" I exclaimed. "How can you say that? You're too good to just be playing in some crappy city league."

For a while I didn't think she'd respond. I was beginning to wonder if I'd said the wrong thing, when she finally replied, "Not everyone who's good at something wants to do it in a big way. Sometimes just the satisfaction of doing it at all is enough."

I lay back in the grass and thought about that. Then she giggled. "You laugh a lot," I said.

She proved it by giggling again. "So?"

"Today you seemed so serious. Tough and sort of scary. And tonight...it just surprises me that you're so quick to laugh."

Suddenly she sat up and gently kissed me, her lips surprisingly warm in the cool night. Leaning over me, she said, "Boo." Then she smiled. "How's that for scary?"

I wrapped my arms around her neck, pulled her facedown, and pressed my mouth hard against hers. Her lips parted, eagerly accepting my tongue, and she rolled herself on top of me, effortlessly placing a thigh between my legs.

Groaning, I reached up with one hand to finally feel the silky texture of that thick flame-colored hair I'd been admiring all day. My other hand roamed south, exploring the exquisite curves of her taut ass.

The kiss seemed to last a lifetime, gradually becoming

more intense until I forgot we were virtual strangers outside in a public place; place and time and circumstance ceased to have any meaning or purpose. Only she and I existed in that immediate moment, in that astral space.

Slowly I became aware of the sound of our ragged breathing, the fierce reckless rocking of our bodies, and Teddi Jo's mouth leaving mine to press into my neck with desperate sounds of need. I raised my body off the ground, crushed my thigh into her crotch, and seized her ass for leverage. She cried out, shuddering uncontrollably, then collapsed against me.

I stroked her hair, feeling her rapid heartbeat on my breast, wondering how I could have been intimidated by this woman.

A few minutes later she propped herself up on her elbows and looked down at me with a sheepish expression. "Sorry."

"Don't be," I whispered, and kissed her again, expecting only a peck but finding it quickly developing into another fevered frenzy of hot tongues and roving hands.

Eventually, Teddi Jo's lips made their way to my sensitive ear while her left hand cupped my breast, her thumb massaging the puckered nipple until my breath caught and I let out a low primitive growl.

Encouraged, she deftly rolled my T-shirt up to my chest, swiftly releasing the clasp at the front of my bra. I gasped as the brisk air hit my body, goose bumps quickly dimpling my skin as Teddi Jo lowered her head and took a nipple into her gloriously warm mouth.

I moaned and shivered wildly, as every inch of my body melted magically into an electrified nerve ending, my pussy drenched, swollen, aching.

As Teddi Jo flicked teasingly at my nipples, alternating between the two with obsessive attention, she maneuvered her body slightly away from mine and slid her hand slowly beneath the waistband of my shorts.

I bucked and whined, begging for the fingers I knew would send me into orbit the moment they made contact with my flesh.

Abruptly she froze and stared down at me as if she were thoroughly enjoying my torment, her face framed by that wild mane of fire, green cat-eyes blazing. I swallowed hard and tried to still my gyrating hips. Then she flashed a mischievous smile and tugged my shorts down in one fast motion, panties and all. I pulled out one sneakered foot, leaving them to dangle from my right ankle.

Again the chilly air shocked me, but only for an instant. Then Teddi Jo's warm velvety tongue tickled my inner thigh, moving down, down with excruciating laziness.

"Please..." My voice cracked with frustration. *"Please."*

I closed my eyes and lay spread-eagled, grabbing fistfuls of grass and yanking them out of the earth with vicious little jerks until I finally felt her engulf me. I howled, opening my eyes and seeing brilliant pinpoints of light spattered across the smooth black glass high above me. My hips rose off the ground, meeting her, inviting her, trying desperately to absorb her.

Teddi Jo clamped herself to me. She drove deep into my core and bloomed there, filling me with the fire of a thousand suns and breaking something deep within me, something I hadn't known existed.

My eyes fluttered, and I caught a glimpse of the vast black sky overhead. The glass had fractured; thin fissures now connected the beaming specks of light to one another, and I heard myself whimper with fearful anticipation and quickly closed my eyes again.

The heat had become unbearable. In spite of the brisk air, sweat beaded up on my forehead, and I dug my fingers into the ground, hips rising and falling uncontrollably. I pressed my lips tightly together, knowing that if I released any sound at all it would be a loud primal wail.

Suddenly there was a moment of utter stillness; I heard crickets and distant traffic and someone's soft gasping breath.

And then the sky exploded.

Hot black glass rained down on top of me, sizzling my skin and causing sparks to dance behind my eyes like tiny lightning bolts. I shrieked, released the ground, and clasped my hands to Teddi Jo's head, close to crying without knowing why.

Sometime later, when everything had grown quiet again, I felt her move out from between my legs and curl up beside me on the cool grass. She adjusted my clothing some, then slipped an arm around my middle. We lay there for a long time, not speaking, watching the stars until they faded and finally disappeared.

Thin Ice J.L. Belrose

I squinted at the glowing red numbers: 6:54. Gentle sporadic snores from within our pile of down-filled duvet signaled that Nadine was still sleeping soundly. I disentangled my arm, reached into the morning's gray chill, and located the alarm's shut-off button. There was no reason to wake her so early, especially on a Sunday.

Beyond our lace curtains the sky was sagging with snow-heavy cloud. The icicles, hanging outside the window like fangs from the eaves above, told me our January mini-thaw was over. The deep freeze of our northern winter was back on. I wanted to stay, all warm and drowsy, snuggled in against Naddy. I knew how she'd stir in her sleep if I burrowed my hand down past her belly and cupped the sweet-centered mound between her legs. Our morning lovemaking was always so deliciously slow and rambling.

But I'd agreed to meet Kendra on the trail by Snakehead Rock at 10. I pushed back the duvet and blankets. "Shhhhiiit," I hissed as cold air assaulted my bare flesh.

If Naddy and I were sensible, we'd wear jammies in winter. Flannel ones. But we're not sensible. We're in love and still reveling—even after three years—in the intimacy of sleeping skin against skin.

I jerked the covers back up over my head and spooned in against her. "Are you awake?" I whispered.

"Mmmmmm..."

"It's fucking cold in here. That damn fire's out again."

"Mmm…"

"We have to get more of that good firewood, that seasoned oak, from Sandy."

"Hmm hmm…" She yawned. "I called him yesterday."

I pushed my hand in under her arm. She shifted obligingly, giving me access to her breasts. "Mmm," she hummed in response to my fondling.

I love it when she's on her side and her soft, full breasts mound together. My hand circled lazily from one to the other, cherishing their luxuriant weight and warmth. I spread my fingers and thumb, spanning both nipples, and pinched them together. She says she almost comes from tit-play alone, but she seemed to decide in favor of more sleep. She wrestled the sheet and blankets, and rolled onto her stomach.

I cuddled in against her side. I kissed her shoulder and nuzzled her neck, while my hand explored the familiar contours of her buttocks. My fingertip strayed down the crack of her ass and feathered through her back pussy hair.

"God, you're *bad*," she mumbled into her pillow.

I stroked teasingly down the back of her thigh, then up the inside of her leg. She twitched and giggled. "Weren't you going to race today? Didn't you want an early start?"

"Are you trying to get rid of me?" I asked.

I knew she wasn't. Only my own guilt made me say it. I sometimes trained with Kendra; Naddy knew that. But she didn't know our history. I'd never found the right way, or perfect time, to tell her. Anyway, it hadn't seemed necessary. As soon as I met Naddy, I'd have sworn nothing would ever happen with Ken again. And it hadn't. For almost three years. Nothing. Then suddenly the old desires had resurfaced, the same way a fire lies dormant in dull darkened embers until, stirred by a certain breeze or touch, it flares into brilliant devouring flame.

"Of course not, silly. Why would I want to get rid of you?" Naddy tented the sheet and blanket so she could reposition herself on her side facing me. Then she angled her leg up over my hip to make her cunt accessible.

"I was teasing," I said. "Looking for a reaction."

"Uh-huh. And did you get what you wanted?"

I snorted laughter into her neck, as my hand rippled over her back and around under her smooth, rounded belly, before delving into the slippery fold of her cunt. "Yeah," I said, still grinning as I pushed my fingers farther into the warm yielding flesh, and pressed my fingertips forward, targeting her G spot.

She drew air into her lungs and arched her head back. I felt her clench and release my fingers again and again, every release offering my hand a deeper cavern. I withdrew my hand enough to slide my thumb up beside her clit. She opened her eyes and frowned, but as soon as I located the tiny shaft and started massaging into the side of it the way she likes, she closed her eyes again and relaxed into the sensations.

"Oh, yes, that's good," she confirmed.

My clit reacted like it always does, as if we were twinned, our pleasures magically duplicating.

She moved her hand to her breast and tweaked at her nipple. Maintaining a rhythm in her pussy, I put my lips to her hand and ran my tongue back and forth between her fingers until she freed the swollen knob and offered it to my mouth. I took it between my teeth, nipping lightly, then sucking. "Oh, yes, that's good," she repeated, flushing, coming in a series of stifled gasps.

She grabbed my arm, immobilizing it. When she loosened

her grip, I moved my hand to her reddened cheek and placed my thumb tenderly on her lips. I gazed for a moment into the gold-flecked dark-rimmed hazel of her eyes, aware of how much I truly loved her. I inhaled her scent from my hand, then skimmed my tongue over her dry lips, then over my thumb, tasting it for traces of her girl-cum.

"It's hot enough in here now, isn't it?" she panted. She tugged an edge of sheet up to wipe the sweat from her eyes and forehead.

Usually we would have continued our lovemaking. I know how her orgasms build, one on the other. But there wasn't time. I rearranged the duvet around her shoulders and tucked it in. "Don't get chilled," I told her.

I scrambled into my fleece tracksuit and sprinted barefoot over the cool carpet to the bathroom with its built-in heat lamp. Then, while my gut-fortifying oatmeal cooked and my coffee brewed, I tended the wood stove, raking live coals out of the night's ash bed and laying on kindling. When it caught, I added logs, some of the hard maple left from the year before, so the place would be toasty for Naddy when she got up.

With my toe, I nudged the wolf-like dog curled in a corner of the kitchen. "Come on, girl," I said. "Let's do it."

Kendra would sneer if she knew we allowed one of the sled dogs to sleep in the house. To stay in top condition, huskies, particularly working sled dogs, should sleep as nature intended: outside, in snug dens of snow. But it was hard not to make an exception for Solo. She was the eldest, the foundation of my kennel. And she had, for a few lonely years, been my only companion. She deserved TLC.

I zipped up my suit. Insulated and waterproof, with my felt-lined boots, ski mask, hood, gloves and fleece-lined mitts, it's ample protection even in sub-zero temperatures.

Solo had stretched out beside the stove to savor the increasing warmth. "Hey!" I snapped. She yawned, rose languorously to her feet, and went through a series of stretching rituals before joining me at the door.

We stepped out into the deep silence of trees and snow, the sun lancing valiantly through layers of heavy cloud. It was even odds the weather would hold. I hauled the sled off its storage rack, and instantly the outside dogs shattered the stillness with the excited yaps and yodels distinctive to huskies. They bounced with pent-up energy and spun into frenzies, the rattle and clank of their chains adding to the din as I laid out the sled's gang line.

I hooked up Kimo, my lead dog, and put Solo behind him, then attached Taiga, another female and a hard worker, beside her. I placed two strong young males at the back as wheel dogs. Solo lifted her muzzle to the sky, giving voice to an ageless lament. The others joined in. Their song wavered, faltering and rising again, in harmonies as elemental as the land.

As the group howl scaled down, I lifted the snow hook, the anchor for the sled. "Hike!" I shouted, and we were off, careening across the open field. The dogs blew off their first burst of energy and settled into the smooth steady pace they can sustain for hours, mile upon mile.

We cut into the forest and picked up the trail. Gliding through the hushed woods is like sliding through time. The embracing silence offers kinship to the earth, to things more ancient than machines and schedules. The trail roughened when we reached the shoreline. We picked our way along the ridges of ice tumbled in from the bay. I saw Kimo was hunkered in, strong and steady, and left most of the mapping to him. I knew I could trust him to instinctively follow the shore and keep us on solid ice.

I've heard stories of how Inuit culled their litters, back when their lives depended more on their dogs than on gasoline engines. They'd take the youngsters out and let them romp near thin ice. The ones that fell through were left there. The others, the ones with smarts, were kept. I asked Kendra once if she'd heard the story. I didn't ask her if she practiced it. Not that I wouldn't have understood why. I've only been out on thin ice once, but that moment of awareness, when you realize what looks solid is actually in flat slow-motion undulation beneath your feet, is a terror you never forget.

Kimo swung wide when I called the turn onto the Nottawasaga River. I knew he was avoiding the deep part of the river mouth where currents weaken the ice from below. We skimmed past Snakehead Rock and the dogs settled in for a long smooth run, the frozen river like a highway luring them on. I scanned ahead for the scarlet trademark flash of Ken's suit.

It wasn't until we rounded the bend at the old bridge that we came up on her. I urged my dogs forward until our teams were abreast. "You're late," she shouted in a crystallizing cloud of breath.

How can I explain my history with Ken? There isn't much choice of partners in small northern communities. Was that it? No, there was more to it than that. Much more. If I'm being honest, I have to admit that in some slightly perverse way her toughness attracts me. But one thing's for sure—when Naddy appeared, all girly girl, brought in as an assistant by the dentist in Petawatik—I'd dumped Ken, and not very gently.

"Do you think your crips can make it to Anderson's?" she challenged, and hiked her team without waiting for my answer.

The race was on. My lungs ached, and frost mustached my mask. I helped my dogs as much as I could by pumping with my leg until it felt like a rotten log ready to crumble. But of course Ken won. Hell, she's a pro. She says she's building a team for the Iditarod, the most challenging dogsled race in the world, and I believe her. But at least we stayed on her back most of the way.

At Anderson's we unhooked the dogs and staked them out. Some sat subdued, while others curled into the snow to sleep. Solo lay down, nosed a paw, then began licking it with exaggerated care. I checked the paw and saw nothing wrong.

"You should dump that one." Ken flipped a hand in Solo's direction.

I didn't try to explain how other things can sometimes be more important than winning. I returned to my sled and dug through my pack for my thermos and sandwich.

"Will we need a fire?" I asked her.

Anderson's cabin, deserted decades ago by someone presumably named Anderson, contains a table, a couple of chairs, a cot, and a wood stove, and is left open and stocked with firewood for anyone in need. The only requirement is that people replace whatever wood they use.

Ken didn't answer me about the fire, so I glanced toward her. She'd climbed onto the cabin's small ramshackle veranda and was appraising me, her eyes calm and centered as a hawk's. Then, as if she'd satisfied herself about something, she pulled off her mitts and hood, shook her head, and raked her fingers through her short raven-black hair. "We might as well be comfortable," she said. "You don't have to worry about the wood. I've already added more than we'll use."

She wrenched at the wood-plank door until the stubborn, creaking hinges yielded, and left it for me to follow her in. She was adding a log to the stove when I entered, but the place was already warm. She must have gotten there earlier to tend to the fire, then mushed back to Snakehead to meet me. Since she'd never been one to put herself out for anyone, much less me, it surprised me she'd gone to so much trouble. She clanked the stove door shut then stripped off her suit.

She's attractive in a rough, angular way. There's something about ruffled dark hair, dark heavy-lidded eyes, and strong, wide cheekbones that's compelling. Combine those features with a lanky lean body, denim and plaid, and a kick-ass attitude, and that's Ken. That's my nemesis.

I removed my boots, then worked my zipper from my chin to my groin and on down the leg of my suit, all the time willing my hands not to shake and jam the damn thing. I didn't want to signal how eager I was. I finally stepped out of the suit and draped it, like hers, over a chair near the stove. She slipped her hands flat into her jeans pockets and swaggered over to stand, legs spread, eye-to-eye in front of me.

She asked, "Are we going to waste time?" Then she smirked and added, "You know you want it."

I swung at her. Even though the ache in my groin was clawing up into my chest, I didn't want to admit how needy she made me. And she was so damn smug, standing there. I swung at her before I knew I was going to. She easily deflected the blow, her hand like bands of rawhide around my wrist. I stumbled back against the rough logs of the wall, remembering why she was arm-wrestling champ at the Anchor Inn.

She pressed into me, so sinewy and hard it made air spiral out of my lungs and pre-cum seep into my pants. Her mouth bruised my lips. Her teeth jarred against mine. Her tongue invaded my mouth until I was groaning, trying to breathe, making noises I couldn't believe were mine. She was reducing me, like she always had, into a whining whimpering idiot. And I liked it. Hell, I liked it so bad I was sniveling.

She backed away.

"Damn you!" I grumbled. I wiped the back of my hand across my mouth and checked for blood.

She pursed her lips, trying to contain a lopsided grin, but it broke loose; and suddenly I was laughing too. She's wild and greedy. But in my own way, so am I.

"It's been too long," she said, and opened her arms.

Our embrace took us swaying around the small cabin in a weird shuffling bear-hug dance until she pinned me in a corner beside the cot.

"I've missed you," she said. "Tell me you haven't missed me too."

"Not much," I answered, and we both knew I was lying.

She struggled with the layers and folds of my sweatshirt and undershirt, finally getting her hands under them and onto my small hard breasts. She squeezed, seeking to trap my nipples in pincers of thumb and finger. Part of me wanted to stop her and shove her away, but instead I grabbed her ass, pulling her into me, shifting position to get one of her legs between my thighs.

"Have you done any online shopping?" she asked.

"What?" It took me a moment to convince myself I'd heard right. "What the hell's that got to do with anything?" I asked, trying to connect dots that seemed as distant as the sun and moon.

"You should. It's wonderful what you can find and receive through the mail these days—in plain brown packages."

The pinch she gave my nipple would have sent me reeling backward if I hadn't already been wedged in the corner. Then, with a wicked grin, she pulled away, walked over to the wobbly bent-twig table and picked up one of the boxes I'd assumed was her lunch. With her back to me, she fiddled with something, and I resisted the urge to rub the lingering pain out of my breasts while she wasn't looking.

I opened my mouth to ask her what the hell was going on, when she turned and faced me. The mushroom-like head of a dildo poked from the zipper of her jeans. "Oh, god! That is sooo gross!" was out of my mouth before I could stop it.

She looked genuinely puzzled. "Why? Because it's a white man's dick?"

I shrugged. I couldn't stop staring at it. I'd never imagined that a fake penis would interest me, but I'd never actually seen one before.

"That's close enough," I said as she came toward me.

"OK. But remember the candle? You didn't say no to that."

Yes, I remembered that night. The power had gone off, and we'd tiered candles on every horizontal surface in her bedroom. She'd bagged a big white one, and I'd let her slide it lengthwise back and forth between my legs. She'd angled it to thrust more insistently against my cunt hole until the wet noise I made and the raggedness of her breathing suffused every square inch of the room. I remembered how I'd shuddered as it entered me, the incredible fullness, and the sweetly satisfying domination and pain it bestowed.

Ken detoured toward the cot, loosening her jeans as she

went, pushing them down to ride around her hips. The cot's rusty joints screeched as she sat and lounged back against the cabin wall. She stroked the dildo, like jerking off, then left it jutting from the fly of her thermal long johns while she dug a condom from her shirt pocket. She was enjoying herself, whether I was part of it or not. She positioned the rubber carefully on the cock head before rolling it down the thick, veined shaft.

"The harness too?" I asked. "You got that online?"

"Do you want one? I'll order it for you."

She anchored the cock with one hand and held her other hand out in invitation. She said, "Are you sure you don't want to..." indicating with her free hand that I could use her in some way. I didn't know what she expected. Maybe she didn't either. But I went.

Desire flowed through my body and eroded whatever pride I had left. My hands went to the button on my jeans, and I let her watch as I took them and my thermals off. I stood there naked from the waist down, except for my work-wear socks.

The cot's squeaks crescendoed as I got onto it, a knee on each side of her. I half-expected the old metal frame to collapse as I balanced above her, finding finger holds on the log wall. She aimed the cock toward my cunt and I eased myself down onto the shaft, grateful for the lube on the condom and the gush of my own juice. I took it in slowly, inch by inch, relishing the delicious stretching and exquisite pain, until the head nudged a place deep inside me.

Involuntarily my muscles contracted, and I thrust down at her, driving the cock's base into her crotch. Her groan ignited me, and within seconds I climaxed. But when she told me to lift my weight off her, I did. We clung together as the spasms in my groin subsided. Then, in a chorus of grunts and curses, we levered away from each other.

"Wow!" she said and, laughing, fell over sideways, face down on the scratchy gray blanket.

"We're crazy," I told her, doing a one-legged jig to get my thermals and jeans back on.

"All we need is a bit of practice."

We ate mostly in silence, both of us aware the other's mind had strayed to thoughts of weather and time. She got into her suit first while I stayed at the table, finishing my hot chocolate. Her best route home was upriver, then east, whereas mine was to return the way I'd come.

Before she left she strode toward me. She twisted her fingers into my hair, pulled my head back, and kissed me hard on the mouth. "Let's not make it another three years," she said.

"No," I agreed, "let's not."

I got out soon after she did, pausing on the veranda to study the sky. The dogs set a good pace down the river, but it was rough going along the shore. Wind had come up, sweeping in over the frozen bay, and we had to drive into it, snow swirling into our faces while the sky lowered onto the land in numbing gray palls. The trail became bleak as the early darkness spread out from the timberline to our left and pooled around the ridges of ice to our right.

Solo's line went slack. "Solo! Get up there!" I yelled. She responded, but I didn't know how long she'd keep moving.

Distances become deceptive in fading light and whirling snow. I hoped we hadn't missed our turn in to the forest. Figuring the woods would at least be protection from the gnawing wind, I gave the command to turn in. "Kimo!

Haw!" I shouted and he obediently veered left. But we'd lost the trail. The dogs floundered in chest-deep snow.

We labored slowly forward. I pushed the sled, while ahead of me the dogs plunged up and down through enshrouding drifts. Finally, we came out onto the packed main trail. The dogs stopped to shake snow out of their coats, and I slumped forward over the sled, exhausted. But we had to keep moving. "Home!" I shouted, and Kimo moved us out.

"Go for home!" is the musher's signal to the team that they're near the end of a run. It tells them food and rest is just ahead, and it's no longer necessary to hold back any reserve. Even Solo found buried energy. We did the last half-mile in a sprint, me anticipating a cozy evening by the fire and wondering what Naddy was cooking for supper.

The team hit the open field near the kennel at a fast trot, tongues lolling, tails waving. I rode in pumping a fist in the air. It wasn't the Iditarod, but for us, it had been a damn good run.

I was also riding high on the afterglow of my fuck with Ken, but it was Naddy I thought about while I fed the dogs and stowed the gear. I loved Naddy, and I didn't want to lose her or hurt her. I didn't want to deceive her either. But I didn't know how to explain to her how it was with Ken and me, how Ken filled a certain need in me. Would she understand it was something separate from how I loved her?

On my way to the house I noticed snowmobile tracks looped through the snow out front. *Good*, I thought, *Sandy's been here. We'll get our wood.* But I forgot all about firewood when I detected the smell of pork roast in the air. It's my favorite meal, and I was starving.

Naddy was in a bathrobe, as if she'd just taken a shower,

and was towel-drying her hair near the fire when I walked in. "I was worried," she said. "They've been giving warnings of pressure cracks near the Point. I hope you weren't out there."

She draped the towel over her shoulder and came to me, reaching for the zipper at my neck to help me out of my suit. "It's OK," I said. "I can manage. I think I'll jump right into the shower, though, before we eat. My back's going to kill me if I don't get some heat on it."

What I wanted, of course, was to wash away any sign or scent of sex.

"A warm bath would do you more good. And a massage. How about one of my backrubs?"

That was an offer I couldn't resist. I loved Naddy's backrubs, but I usually had to wheedle them out of her.

"Is there time before supper?" I asked.

"We can make time. Or later maybe? After supper? Then we wouldn't have to rush. We could take as long as you wanted."

I couldn't figure it out. Naddy was normally good-natured, but it was suddenly like she couldn't do enough to please me—which made me feel even guiltier about the stuff with Ken. Then, while we were eating, she said, "Did you have a good time with Kendra today?"

"Yeah, it was a good workout for the team. They really needed it." I hoped I sounded natural.

"So what all did you talk about?"

I shrugged. "Oh, you know—guy stuff."

I changed the subject by asking about one of the damn TV shows she's addicted to, some soap opera thing, and we got through the rest of the meal with that.

The backrub was glorious, but with my full stomach and the day's fresh air and exertion, I plummeted into a sound dreamless slumber before it was half over. I didn't rouse again until the mattress bucked under me as Naddy settled in for the night. Her breath smelling of toothpaste, she asked, "Did I wake you?" then took my hand and guided it to her breast.

I played drowsily with her nipples until she kissed me good night and turned onto her side for sleep. That's when I remembered the firewood. "Did Sandy come by today?" I asked.

There was a moment's hesitation before she answered. "Was he supposed to?"

"I don't know. You're the one that phoned him. I saw snowmobile tracks out front and thought maybe he had."

"No. I guess those were Amber's."

"Amber?"

"Yes, you know, Kendra's new girlfriend. We met her at the Orillia races. Don't you remember?"

"I remember a blond girl asking Ken if she wanted coffee."

"That's her. She's here doing some kind of environmental study for the government, monitoring deer herds or something."

"I didn't know she was Ken's girlfriend."

"I guess I was talking to her longer than you were. You and Kendra were tending the dogs."

"So, like, what did you talk about?" I asked.

Naddy yawned as if she couldn't stay awake a moment longer. Then she said, "Oh, you know, girl stuff."

Working Out Bridget Bufford

Too bad it's still cold at night; I'd like to put the top down. The Mustang's five years older than me and of a vintage too common to be classic, but it's a red convertible, almost irresistible. Holly had succumbed on the third date. "Terry," she said, "let me drive." I parked and walked around to the passenger door. Holly took off a little fast, popped the clutch, and barked the tires. I slid to the middle of this great bench seat and got more intimate than a bucket seat would ever allow.

We met at my favorite club, Minerva's. Tuesday night the place was moribund, and this tall strawberry-blond goddess strolled in. Long legs, long hair; I flew to her like Icarus, circled that golden radiance. We danced four dances, and the goddess barely broke a sweat. I run and lift weights, and I was winded. I asked if she worked out and got her card: Holly O'Brien, Certified Aerobics Instructor, The Body Zone. "Come by and see me sometime," she said. I took her free introductory class three times.

The Body Zone is the biggest gym in St. Louis, a converted textile warehouse. I pull into the parking lot, get a spot near the entrance. It's Saturday, an hour from closing. Everybody's already gotten their workout in; those hard-earned buns of steel are garnering admiration in other venues, perhaps embarking on a different type of exercise. Not me—my night is just beginning. I grab my gym bag and bound into the lobby.

The Zone is also the most expensive gym in St. Louis. I

joined a year and a half ago, during a three-month trial offer over the summer. When that expired, I quit. I can't afford the regular monthly charges, much less the initiation fee. Holly's been helping me out: I just say I forgot my ID when the gym is busy, and Holly lets me pass through. Tonight Holly's behind the counter, but so is Dave, the beefcake trainer. He's grinning, practically drooling; he never takes his eyes off her.

I conceal my driver's license in my hand and run the card through the scanner, which just beeps. "Still not working?" Holly asks, all innocence. I hold out my license, and she palms it. "Maybe we should just make you a new ID, Terry." She turns to the keyboard, enters someone else's code.

Excellent. I'm in the system. Holly's been letting me in with the driver's license ruse for two months now. It's risky, though; if caught, she could lose her job. We'd talked about making me a fake ID, but neither of us could figure out a way to falsify the payment. Last night I hit on a plan: Holly could go through the attendance records of lifetime members and find one who hasn't been in for a few months. Then she'd make a new ID for that account, with my name and picture on the card. The time is paid for; no one is using it. Nobody loses.

I pose for my picture with a big victorious grin. "I'll have this ID for you by the time you're done with your workout," Holly says.

"I'll do it," Dave says. "You're closing. I don't mind." This is great: Holly doesn't even have to make the card herself.

Before I change into my workout clothes, I take a quick shower. I want to be relatively fresh when Holly gets off.

WORKING OUT

She leads two aerobics classes four evenings a week, and lately she's been working the desk until closing. I work days, painting houses; if I didn't lift, I'd never see her. It's been nearly a week since we spent the night together.

Hot water flows over me, the evening's first caress. Holly and I took a shower together at her place last Sunday. I ended up on my knees in front of her. She pressed her shoulders against the tiled wall, arched her hips forward; by the time she was done, the water on my back had turned cool. I shiver, in memory and hopeful anticipation.

Someone's humming over by the sink, a sweet familiar song I can't place. When I emerge from the shower in my towel, though, I find only a flushed young woman, sweaty from her racquetball date, and generic jazz on the sound system.

I put on my shorts and tank top, go upstairs to the weight room. Two Herculean red-faced men are at the squat racks. They bellow and exhort each other through, "One more, push it!" The inclined abdominal board is hooked on the third rung; I climb onto the pad, secure my feet under the strap. The behemoths are reflected in the mirror, rising and falling as I curl my trunk, raise my torso again and again till the muscles burn and sweat gathers behind my knees. I fall back, take a few slow breaths. By the time I'm through with my abdominals, the guys are gone. I'm the only person here.

The lat pull-down machine has the wrong attachment. Since I'm short I have to stand on the seat to undo the clasp and suspend the longer bar from the cable. I hop down, take a wide grip, and sit. From arm's length I draw the bar slowly down, working the broad muscles of my back. I've always liked this exercise, the deep stretch as the weight pulls my arms overhead. Between sets, I find Holly's reflection in the mirror before me. She's still at the desk, flipping through an aerobics schedule, bored; I'll take care of that soon enough.

Bar dips next: I hoist myself onto the parallel bars of the rack, my body suspended between extended arms. I lower myself, controlled, then exhale and press up. Most women can't do dips. I crank them out like pushups, keeping time with the canned music. Panting, I jump down, wiping my sweaty forehead with the back of my hand.

Holly's reflection again, this time close. "Hey, girlfriend," I say and turn the wrong direction, disoriented by the mirrors. "You here by yourself?"

"Yeah," she says. "I'm closing, but I'm almost done. Hey, did you see those guys doing squats?"

"Couldn't miss 'em."

She tells me that they're linebackers; they play for the St. Louis Rams. Holly loves football; she was a cheerleader in high school.

"Looks like it's been busy," I say. "The windows are completely steamed up."

"It was a total zoo all afternoon. Everyone came in at once." She snags a leather jump rope from the floor and hangs it from the proper hook.

"You want to go out?" I ask.

"I don't think so; let's just go to my place and chill."

"Fine with me." I'll show her a better time that way. "Hey, can you spot me on the bench?"

"As soon as I'm done."

I grab a pair of dumbbells from the rack and face the mirror, curl the weights to my chest and lower them slowly, my elbows tucked to my sides. My biceps bulge, then lengthen. The sound system goes off; the sudden silence is eerie. My breath becomes loud. I can hear the switches snap as Holly turns off the overhead lights by the cardiovascular platform. I set the weights down like they're made of crystal.

That tune is in my head still, the one from the locker room. I do another set of curls to the slow meter, try to put words to it. "Amazing Grace, how sweet the sound / That saved a wretch like me…" That's it. Haven't heard it in years; I don't know if I could remember all the words. The melody permeates my brain; I'm in for an evening of it.

My workout is done, except for bench presses. An Olympic bar sits on the two uprights that form the rack of the weight bench. The bar alone weighs 45 pounds. I thread a ten- and a five-pound plate onto each end of the barbell, then sit and wait for Holly, feet up on the bench and my arms across my knees. A glance in the mirror confirms that the position displays my deltoids admirably.

Holly surveys the room. I picked up weights as I went, so it's already straightened. She shuts off the lights at the near end. "You don't mind, do you?"

"No, I can see." I point to the emergency lights by the exit.

"All right, let's get these done." She takes her place at the head of the bench. I lie down, whip out a quick set of ten. Holly scoffs. "Intensity, girl! You're working too light."

"I'm saving my energy for later."

She laughs. "How much can you bench?"

"More than this. Put 20 on either side." I hook my wrists behind the uprights and let gravity stretch my pecs. My legs fall to the sides, a provocative arrangement. I've always had a fantasy of making it on a weight bench.

Sprawling on the narrow support, legs spread, the grunt and thrust and sweat; it gets me hot.

Holly slides 40 pounds of plates onto the bar, then steps close. The hem of her gym shorts just touches the top of my head. I wrap my fingers around the knurling, a little in from my normal grip. Tighten the muscles behind my shoulder blades, take a big breath, and lower the bar to just above my nipples. Thrust it up with a grunt.

Holly helps position it on the rack. "Damn, Terry! That's more than I weigh. That's way over what you weigh."

"I weigh more than you'd think, for being short. We're probably about the same."

"Little as you are?" She looks dubious, but I'm not going to get into an argument over weight.

"Put on 30 more; I'll try again." That will be 175, more than I've ever done. Can't hurt to try it with a spotter.

Holly puts on two ten-pound plates. "Try this first. You want a lift-off?"

"Please."

She steps up to the bench. My attention is diverted-what I'd taken for a leotard is just a Spandex top tucked into shorts so loose I can almost see they cover nothing but flesh. I wasn't the only one thinking ahead. Holly grips the bar and tenses. "Ready?"

"Not yet."

She nods, eyes on the bar. My hand on her thigh startles her. Holly's definitely not wearing panties; curls brush against my knuckles. "Shit, Terry, what are you doing?" Her voice is edged with panic, low, but she doesn't move away.

"There's no one here." I cup my palm over that provocative little juncture where all the seams of her shorts converge, press gently upward.

"We're right in front of the window." Now she's whispering.

"No, we're not. Besides, it's steamed up. Nobody can see in." My thumb strokes the seam, persuading. "We can both get a workout."

Holly leans on the bar, takes a wide stance that brings her tantalizingly near. I slide my hand to her hip, draw her closer. Propped on my elbow, I can barely bring my face to her. I breathe against her shorts, then draw the cloth away and kiss the soft inner thigh. I reach for her breasts. Spandex restrains her nipples; a light persistent circling of fingernails brings them forth.

Half-reclining is a strain right after a workout. I hate to stop, but a tremor of fatigue wracks my left shoulder. I fall back onto the bench. "Come around to this side. I can't reach you there."

Holly looks to the window again. "You're crazy. I'm going to lose my job."

I knew she'd be like this. "Holly, we can't stop now. If I'm crazy, it's because of you." Holly gives me an "Oh, please" look, but I'm not giving up. She's stalling, twirling a lock of red-gold hair around her finger. "Just sit here in front of me a minute. At least give me a kiss." I sit up and lean back against the cold barbell.

Holly straddles the foot of the bench, places her hands on my shoulders. Is she going to reason with me, kiss me, or just hold me at arm's length till my passion falters? A drastic response may dispel her doubts. I stand, step close. Holly's hands fall to my waist. I entwine my fingers in her hair, dig my nails into her scalp until she shivers. Holly sits down, and I nip her neck, tarry at the soft spot behind her ear. Tip her head back, kiss her until her lips soften and her hands knead my hips and neither of us can breathe. Ardor prevails.

She lifts my shirt. Warm lips caress my nipples; her soft touch brings a sweet ache to my groin. I take her hands. "Stand up."

She does, and I kiss her once again, slide down to the bench beneath her. Caress her thighs, urge her closer. Holly grips the barbell; I hope it is secure.

Her musky scent compels me. I slide two fingers inside her, curl them slightly, nuzzle the front of her shorts with my lips. "Wait," she says. She steps over me, takes off her top, her shorts, and sneakers. Gloriously nude, she straddles the bench again, shifts her stance to meet my eager tongue.

Her labia glisten, rich and swelling. I part the lips, point my tongue, find her clit. Her knuckles are white; she's gripping the uprights, her triceps taut. I relax my neck, the muscles of my jaw. My rhythm is established now; I realize that song is still in my head. "I once was lost, but now I'm found…" It almost makes me laugh, but that would be a crime right now. No point in fighting it; the tempo is right.

Sweat from Holly's thighs wets my shirt. Her breasts obscure a full view of her face, but I can tell she's looking up. Watching herself in the mirrors, I think. Ex-cheerleader, aerobics instructor—what else would she be doing? Back in high school, the cheerleaders sometimes practiced at the same time as the girls soccer team. I would look at them and dream of this very thing, even before I knew the finest feeling in the world is having some red-headed woman about to climax against my upper lip.

I can't stand it. I reach beneath my shorts, match the stroke of my finger to that of my tongue. "How sweet the sound…" Holly's breathing hoarsely. Each caress elicits a jerk of her hips. I try to lighten my touch, diminish the pace, but that crazy song compels me. "The hour I first believed…"

The weights rattle on the barbell; Holly shakes from her foundations. Her hips grind into my face. A spasm rips through me, but when her left knee buckles, my hand gets pulled away, and I have to grab Holly to save myself. We tumble to the floor, me on top. She clutches my shoulders and bursts out laughing, tears rolling down her face. "Holly?" Now I'm whispering. "Are you OK?"

She wipes her eyes and laughs again. "You sucked the sense right out of me," she says. She's limp now, sprawled, arms outstretched. I curl against her side, stroke her beautiful bare torso, soothe her till her swollen eyelids flutter open. She smiles at me and starts to speak, then shoves me away. I hear it too—the elevator's moving. It stops at the lobby. In the mirror I can see the doors slide apart. A faint sweet song emerges, the same voice I heard in the locker room. "When we've been here ten thousand years / Bright shining as the sun…"

Holly leaps to her feet, then crouches. I grab her tangled clothes, throw them at her, untie the laces of her sneakers so they're ready to slip on. A middle-aged woman is pushing her cart of cleaning supplies into the lobby. By the time the woman shakes out a new trash bag, Holly is disheveled but dressed. Her eyes are huge, and her weird smile is just this side of a grimace.

"Lie down," she whispers.

"What?"

She shoves me onto the bench, repositions herself as spotter. "Ready?" she says loudly.

I start to laugh. Her glare pins me to the bench. I grab the bar, but there's no way. I wasn't sure I could lift this much the first time. "Holly, for crying out loud, I just got off."

She starts a lift-off. I tighten up in self-defense and manage to lower the bar to my chest without killing myself. Limp with laughter, I can't budge it. I can barely breathe. Holly's ineffectual jerking bounces the 165-pound bar on my sternum, squashing me.

The cleaning woman runs past Holly, yelling, "Grab onto the end of it!" Together they raise the bar to the uprights. I sit up, rub my chest, and erupt in another surge of giggles.

"You're lucky, miss," the woman says. "I came in a little early tonight."

"We were just going," Holly babbles. "I didn't think...I was closing tonight, but we were just...thanks so much."

"Yes, ma'am," she says. "You're welcome." She squats and reaches beneath the bench, retrieves my new ID and Holly's car keys. Looks at the picture, then holds the card and keys out to me. "Here you go."

Holly grabs them before I can react. "We appreciate that, Irene." The woman's name is on her badge. "We've always been happy with your company. Thanks again. I'll write a note to your supervisor, tell her what a help you were." I've got to get her out of here; she's trying to stuff everything into the pocket of her shorts, but they're on backwards.

"You were lucky," Irene repeats. "God was looking out for you tonight."

Saved a wretch like me. I need to get my giddy self out of here too; the giggles overtake me once again. "Good night, Irene," I say, then wish I hadn't. Holly's hand tightens on my shoulder, and we head to the nearest door.

The Art of Running Rosalind C. Lloyd

It was 1:30 A.M., and I stood alone on the well-lit campus track field, intent on training for the NCAA Track and Field Indoor Championships. Even though I was excited about making the cut, I was also nervous about being the only freshman sprinter on our team who had made the finals.

About ten minutes into stretching, I noticed a figure in the distance coming toward the field. Although she was wearing a hooded sweatshirt and blazing red short-shorts (crimson and gold being our school colors), Brigitte Tanner's tight, muscular gait was a dead giveaway. I pretended I didn't see her and continued my stretching routine, fully aware of her image and her very existence, which made me weak. To watch Brigitte run was an auspicious event. She was lightning personified, her speed a mere blur in one's consciousness. The inherent design of her body, delicately curved with dramatic contours embodying strength, speed, and agility, defined the type of physique runners envied.

Yes, you'd be correct in assuming I experienced some degree of hero worship for her. In fact, I was embarrassed by it. But the way she ran was poetic, nearly spiritual. I would watch her sprint, lusting after her infinite energy, her muscles bulging and flexing, expanding and contracting. With the squint of unadulterated determination always in her eyes, the hunger for pure competition deep in her soul, Brigitte Tanner was athletic artistry at its finest.

She was a senior and Olympic hopeful who was counted among the university's athletic elite, her record in the 100-meter sprint and 100-meter hurdles still unmatched by anyone in our school's history. Making the Olympic trials was no small feat; still, she was quite modest about all the attention.

As a lanky little shorty with skinny legs on the south side of Detroit in a single-parent home with four other siblings, I'd never dreamed I'd be courted by major universities offering full scholarships. Once I got out of Detroit and witnessed how the rest of the world lived, I realized how poor I really was. Even in the face of urban poverty, my mother, a factory employee who worked 16-hour days to make ends meet, was one of the most caring and supportive yet strict parents a child could have. I was the first in my family to attend college and remained personally committed to ensuring the academic futures of my younger sisters and brother. With my background, it was natural for me to participate in campus activities such as Black Students United, Third World Feminists, and, of course, the Gay and Lesbian Student Coalition.

Brigitte's life was quite the opposite. An all-American student allowing her impending Olympic career to temporarily eclipse the prospects of medical school, she came from a long line of physicians. Her parents were upper crust Ward Connelly–Thomas Sowell Black Republicans, with affiliations at exclusively private clubs such as the Links and Jack & Jill; her mother was high in the AKA hierarchy. Our obvious class differences had no effect on my deep-seated desire for her.

Brigitte didn't appear to feel the same about me. Distant and detached, she wasn't really friendly with anyone on the team. We were proud of her accomplishments but frustrated and even embarrassed by her lack of team involvement. Brigitte was more a loner who didn't care about social skills when it came to the team, nor did she care for being in the spotlight. It didn't help when the rumor mill identified her as a dyke jock, she neither denying nor admitting any affiliation.

I found myself getting defensive when certain teammates talked badly about her. The most outspoken was high jumper Denise Patterson, a junior of humble beginnings like me who detested Brigitte with a nauseating kind of passion. My replacing Brigitte on the 440 relay kicked her down several notches, making us automatic adversaries despite my freshman status.

"Bougie redbone closet case," Denise spat while reading a special feature on Brigitte in the sports section of *The Detroit Times*.

"Bet her parents are pissed she never made the cut on the polo or tennis team. Instead she's out here slumming with us on the *field*." This brought nervous laughter to certain teammates. I called them Denise's fan club. What angered me more than anything were the constant homophobic comments Denise made. To top it off, some of her "fan club" members were lesbians! I knew who they were, but Denise, a tragic heterosexual, acted like even she didn't know some of her closest friends were dykes. I believe it had everything to do with her good looks. Some of the women thought she was the hottest thing on the team and would swoon all over her. But she did nothing for me.

"What do you know about closets anyway, Denise?" I asked, only half-humorously.

"There you go, Hightower, defending Ms. Crossover. Sounds like you know a thing or two about closets yourself."

"Yeah, I know I don't like them."

These exchanges didn't win me any popularity contests, but I didn't care. I was focused on the championships, my strenuous training program, and struggling through classical languages.

That night I continued my workout, somewhat amazed to see Brigitte continue toward the track, right in my direction.

"Hey, Hightower," she called, standing about five feet away. She began her stretches.

I was at a loss for words. This was probably the most she had ever said to me. Ever.

"What's up, Tanner?" I tried hard not to stare.

"Strange hour for training. What, can't sleep? Or just committed?"

"Probably both. And you?" How could it be true that our university's track star, an athletic celebrity, the woman of my dreams, was here stretching in front of me on this moonlit night? Why, all of a sudden, was she socializing with me?

"I know this is going to sound crazy—well, probably not to you—but I love training," she said. "Running—it's in my blood, girl. The adrenaline is my high. The feeling doesn't compare with anything else I know...well, almost anything." She blushed. I couldn't believe Brigitte Tanner was actually blushing in my presence. Where the hell was this going, and where was she coming from?

I needed to switch gears fast.

"So when do you go down to the training facilities for the trials?"

"Next week. I'm psyched. It's a dream come true."

"Mine too," I said.

"You're a talented runner, Hightower. In fact, you're the most gifted freshman I've seen since I've been here. You'll be at the trials soon enough. You're a natural." All this coming from a prospective Olympic sprinter. It was far too much to bear. "What's your best time for the 100?" she asked.

"Uh, about 12:07."

"Really? I didn't hit 12 until I was a sophomore. Come on, let's see what you've got!" Brigitte got up from the ground, lifting her knees high in the air, preparing for a race.

"You've got to be kidding!" I replied. We'd raced hundreds of times during training, but never alone at 1:30 A.M. And never under the stars.

"No, I'm not kidding. Isn't that what you came out here for? Come on, Hightower! Let's see what you've got!"

"I haven't warmed up my hamstrings yet."

"I don't wanna hear it." Brigitte was already in position at the starting line. She looked so sexy in crouch position. Of course there was no resisting her.

I crouched beside her in the next lane.

"On three," she said.

Then we were off in the wind. We ran so fast and so close to each other I could hear her every breath. Our footsteps synchronized perfectly, digging lightly but swiftly into the field. I imagined Brigitte's every muscle rippling like water. She was like an apparition on my left. I kept up with her about halfway down the track. Suddenly she disappeared—she wasn't ahead of me. I stopped, looking for her while trying to catch my breath, when unpredictably I heard sharp footsteps heading straight for me at full sprint! Before I could jump out of her way Brigitte grabbed me with her strong, full arms, knocking the wind from my lungs, pressing herself against me. For a second we were airborne. I thought I might faint as we stumbled together, arms, legs, bodies flying wildly. Defying gravity, we desperately attempted to find our footing on the field without causing each other serious injury. As soon as we did, Brigitte's lips were all over me, her arms, her hands roaming my body as if it were the most natural thing in the world.

There was no time for words or to act surprised. This was the moment I'd been waiting for all year. Her wet kisses were hungry and sensual as she twirled her tongue round and round, in and out, between my lips until I was dizzy. There was so much longing in her kiss, like she'd wanted to do this for some time. Her hands felt so good, sliding, rubbing, squeezing, roaming, and ravishing me. Her tongue darted along the side of my neck, causing me to catch my breath. Then, moving slowly behind me, Brigitte tongued the back of my neck with soft, steady strokes that made my knees buckle—only she was right there behind me, steadying me with a slow grind against my buttocks, gripping me tightly around the waist. Then we just couldn't stop kissing. Her hands went beneath my sports bra, taking subtle but meaningful handfuls of my breasts, kneading them while I answered by slipping a finger into those fiery red shorts. She was far wetter than her kisses. She moaned sweetly as I entered her, then pivoted her pelvis and rammed her pussy on my finger with a desperate jerk.

In a swift attempt to move our tryst off the field and away from the bright lights, Brigitte and I stumbled along without separating lips, mouths, and tongues—her hands in my shorts, mine in hers—ending up on a soft cushion of grass near some trees. Her body collided on top of mine, pushing me deeper into the reality of what was happening. Her hips ground against me as she attempted to bury the thick hardness of her clit as deeply between my legs as she could. Her breathing quickened as she rolled her swollen button around mine until they both twitched and trembled. The crushing sensation was almost unbearable. Despite the repressive heat of the late July night, despite our sweaty selves, despite the wetness of her kisses, I wanted to feel her entire essence. Brigitte read my mind as she wiggled out of her shorts, peeled her sweatshirt and sports bra off, then shifted to quickly disrobe me. Touching her bare clit to mine, I got to feel just how silky, soft-moist-thick, and large she was as she rotated herself round and round until the heavens opened up above me and the earth moved and shifted beneath me. Her body felt like only love could feel, as her beautiful firm breasts, her slick, hot, sweaty femininity, and her strong hips pressed down against mine. Her muscularity moved fearlessly like a powerful warrior princess. Those muscles I'd been lusting for were now merging with my own.

My moan was low and pornographic. Her heavy breathing filled my ears, making me want her even more—which I thought could hardly be possible. In response, she spread my legs and tried to push her clit as deeply as she could inside me. My body exploded with orgasm, as did hers, saturating me, flooding me. Brigitte whispered my name over and over until the throbbing between her legs and the rippling of her tummy calmed down. But she didn't stop there. Politely she rolled me over, sliding her lean body across me, grinding against my buttocks so the tip of her clit brushed the rim of my ass. I couldn't control myself as the incredible sensation sent a harsh rumbling through my thighs and something unintelligible from my lips. I assumed she felt the same way, because both of us were working very hard to ensure this very sensation was repeated over and over until our knees were burned from grass and dirt and we were drenched in each other.

We stood up, a bit worse for the wear, from our grassy bed. Then I guided her so her back was pressed against a tree. I kissed her lips as gently as I could, then moved to plant tiny sweet kisses about her face. She stared through me with unrelenting desire. It felt like the very first time we had looked into each other's eyes. I teased the well of her neck with my tongue, lightly brushing her shoulders and the center of her chest before letting my lips settle on her succulent nipples. She moaned as I tongued one of them with quick tiny twirls of my tongue before pulling it between my teeth, squeezing the other between my thumb and forefinger. I sucked gently at first, then as hard as I could, while a finger from my free hand jabbed her between her legs. She was all liquid love. I wanted to taste every inch of her. I moved to stop fingering her, but she didn't permit me to stop. I bit her lip. She let out a groan. Removing my finger, I continued my trail of kisses down the center of her chest to her lean hips then lower, to her very core.

The combination of both our scents heavy in the air, I gently stroked my tongue between her lips. It wasn't hard to find her clit; it was so huge. Taking it into my mouth, I sucked it and teased it while Brigitte's body rocked against my face. She tasted divine. Gently and carefully, I massaged her clit with the very tip of my tongue, careful not to go too hard, too soft, too fast, or too slow. Her silky clit danced with my tongue, darting, rolling, vibrating, hiding, poking out, and poking in. When I slid my tongue inside her, she grabbed my head with her hands, feeding herself to me like a fiend. Hers was the honey pot of life, and I leaned my tongue into her as far and as deep as I could, savoring her sugar walls. We were on that field till daybreak. Once Brigitte started tasting my love, I couldn't pull her away. Have you ever tried doing 69 at 4 A.M. on a bed of grass? To this day, nothing has ever topped that night.

■ ■ ■

Our affair was a private one. Brigitte and I barely acknowledged each other in public, especially during training. When we were alone together, no one or nothing else mattered. I tried to convince myself that our feelings went beyond passion. She took comfort in the aloofness of our public personae, which ultimately made it easy for her to slip out of my life just as easily as she had slipped in.

■ ■ ■

The Olympic trials were painful to watch. Brigitte missed making the team by one spot. This was to the joy of Denise and others who were total player haters. Sending a teammate to the Olympics would have elevated our university's standing, but they were too blind with jealousy to care. I couldn't help thinking Brigitte didn't want to make the U.S. team.

The next semester I shattered all the university's records for the 100-meter, including Brigitte's. I was on my way to the Olympic trials, a first for a sophomore, when I learned Brigitte was attending an Ivy League medical school on the East Coast. They say she's studying either psychiatry or gynecology. I prefer to keep my suspicions to myself.

The Table Anne Seale

They take their arm wrestling seriously at Dar's Bar. Every Tuesday evening, women sign in on the blackboard on the west wall, and at 7 P.M. sharp Tank McCloud takes her massive self to the side of the table that's reserved for the reigning champion, which she always is, and jams her elbow in the pad.

It isn't that Tank never loses. When she does, however, she turns to the board and prints her name in giant letters at the bottom of the list. Then she orders a draft and stares into it until her name is called, at which time she takes the challenger's spot, looks her opponent right in the eye, and snorts loudly. This time, she always wins.

I'm an arm wrestler too, a good one, and I have a couple of trophies to prove it. But I'm a different kind of wrestler than Tank is. My body type is thin and wiry. I have to use my brains as much or more than my brawn.

I used to live in Orange County, California, but moved to Chicago a few months ago to be with a woman I met in a chat room. By the time we broke up three weeks later, I'd found a good job busting tires at a suburban Pep Boys, so I got myself a little apartment and settled in. Soon after, I saw a notice in *Outlines* for the Tuesday tournaments at Dar's and decided to check it out.

I haven't added my name to the challenger list yet. I'm not ready. Every Tuesday evening I sit in the shadows at the far end of the bar, sipping Pepsi, watching the drama unfold between Tank and her rivals.

Some like to pull her fresh, before she hits her stride. Others figure their best bet is to wait until she tires, but this strategy never works (Tank's arm *improves* with use). In the first match her bi- and triceps barely swell. After ten minutes or so, the muscles start to bulge and shine with a layer of perspiration that by the fifth match begins to run, pooling on the table so that Dar, who serves as referee, has to blot it with a bar towel. Soon Tank's whole shirt is dark with sweat. It's beautiful to see.

Tank doesn't seem to have a lover. At 9 or so when the tourney ends, women hang around, flirting and buying her beers. She talks and laughs and spends time with each of them, especially the blazing femmes. When she leaves, however, it's always alone.

This observation takes root in my head and blossoms into a scheme. If I want to become the reigning champion at Dar's, and I do, I'll have to spend time with Tank McCloud, get to know her inside and out without showing my cards. I've already seen her strengths, but what are her weaknesses, her Achilles' heels?

I have the following Tuesday off, so I use it to become a different woman. My hair is washed and blow-dried by a stylist named Ginger, who was recommended by the wife of one of the guys I work with. Ginger can't believe I'd appeared in public the way I looked before.

I tell her I need some makeup too, so she applies some and doesn't even charge. She says it's a mission of mercy. Then she sends me to another booth, where a woman glues ten very expensive long red fingernails over my own.

I stop at the mall on my way home and buy a frilly yellow blouse and a pair of tight black jeans. I finish the outfit with a pair of two-tone cowboy boots from when I used to line-dance and a wide chain-metal belt I'd bought to give the chat-room woman for Christmas, but she'd thrown me out on Christmas eve. Her loss.

I arrive at Dar's at a quarter to 7 and pause inside the door, looking for Tank. I don't see her, so I sashay over to the bar. Instead of retreating to my usual end, I take a stool as close to the wrestling table as I can get. After ordering soda water with a maraschino cherry from the bartender who shows no sign of recognition, I turn and lean back against the bar's edge, crossing my legs in what I imagine is a sexy pose.

A few minutes before 7, Tank strides in, waves to a few acquaintances, and assumes her rightful place at the table. She squares her shoulders and puts her elbow on the pad. Then she nods. This is Dar's cue to call the first challenger.

Tank's in great form tonight. She conquers each of the other wrestlers once, and some twice, which is the maximum number of times they can challenge in one evening. After she's shaken the final hand, she turns and grins at me like she knows I've been watching. I smile and mouth, "Congratulations." After exchanging a word with Dar she heads in my direction. When she's less than two yards away, one of the blazing femmes grabs her arm and pulls her across the room.

Dang! I swivel to face the bar and pound on it with my red-nailed fist. The bartender jumps to attention and points to my half-empty glass. I nod.

A $20 bill is placed on the bar in front of me. "I'm buying," says one of the better wrestlers, who has taken the stool on my right. (She'd be a real threat to Tank if she'd build up her back with some hammer curls.)

"Thanks, but that's all right. I'll get it."

She doesn't pick it up. "Haven't seen you here before. I'm Patsy." The bartender brings my drink and grabs Patsy's 20 before I can stop her.

"Look, Patsy," I tell her. "My girlfriend just went to the bathroom, and you'd better not be here when she gets back." She doesn't even wait for her change.

An hour and several come-ons later, I admit defeat and head for the door. Tank pulls herself from the booth where she and the femme have been chatting and intercepts me. "You're new here, aren't you? Haven't had a chance to introduce myself," she says. "The name's Tank McCloud."

"Pleased to meet you, Tank." It's hard to sound seductive while yelling over the jukebox. "I'm, uh…Betty." So far, so good. Now, how am I going to finagle a date?

"Nice to meet *you*, Betty. I've been trying to get over to say hi," she says.

Sure you have. "I really enjoyed watching you arm wrestle. You're so-o-o strong," I gush.

Tank's ears turn red. "Thanks, Betty. Hey, would you like to meet me sometime for coffee?"

Well, that was easy. "Won't your girlfriend mind?" I glance toward the booth, where the femme, wearing a fake smile, sits watching us.

"I don't have a girlfriend."

Good to hear. I've been worried there might be a little gal waiting at home.

"OK then, sure," I say.

"How about tomorrow?"

"I get off work at 6."

"Six-thirty then, at the Wiener Kitchen down the block? We can grab a dog."

"Sounds great."

Tank returns to the booth.

Later, while I'm scraping gunk off my face, I realize there's no way I can be ready tomorrow at 6:30. I'll never get the 'do back without Ginger's help, and I'll have to buy some different clothes (Betty wouldn't wear the same yellow blouse on Tuesday *and* Wednesday).

I look in the phone book for McClouds. There's no Tank or T. McCloud, so I start with the A's. I wake only three of them before I hear, "Hey, hi, this is Tank. I'll have to get back to you," followed by a beep.

In a throaty voice I say that this is Betty and I'm sorry, but I'd forgotten I have a previous engagement on Wednesday and would she please call me. I leave my number and hang up.

Tank doesn't call until Friday, by which time I've given up on her. The phone's ringing when I come in from work, and I answer it with my usual "Yeah?"

"Betty? Tank McCloud. The arm wrestler. We met at Dar's."

I raise my voice half an octave. "Yes, I remember. Of course. You're the one I was supposed to meet for coffee. I'm so sorry."

"That's OK. Thanks for letting me know you couldn't make it. How'd you get my phone number?"

I laugh cutely. "I'm a woman of many resources."

"I'll bet you are!" she says. "Say, I was wondering if you're, by any chance, free tomorrow night. We can go bowling or something."

"Gee, sorry, I don't bowl," I say. The truth is, I bowl too well.

"Oh, OK. Do you like movies?"

THE TABLE

"Sure. Can I meet you there?" Can't have her coming to my door and getting a glimpse of the bench press.

The first thing I do after hanging up is call the salon. Ginger says she's booked up Saturday, but if I come at noon, she'll try to work me in. The next morning I call in sick and run to the mall to buy another blouse. I really like this coral one with little pearls sewed on, but decide it might clash with my red nails. I settle for a plain soft blue. I also buy a lipstick. That was the only part of the new me that didn't last the whole evening.

Tank and I meet outside the lobby of a theater that shows several dozen movies at a time, only two of which are ever worth seeing. After ten minutes of deliberation she buys tickets for a romantic comedy, though I'm sure we'd both prefer the action flick. Halfway through she eases her hand around the seat divider and takes mine. I let her.

After the movie we go for pizza. While it bakes she tells me she works in construction, then asks what I do. "Oh, you know, office," I say, then quickly ask her to tell me about arm wrestling, explaining that I don't know a thing about it. She loves the subject. She runs through all the rules, followed by her philosophies on the sport and the way she trains. Then she invites me to come to her place the next afternoon to see an arm-wrestling video she bought on the Web. When I accept, she takes a napkin and draws a detailed map of the south side of Chicago. She circles the X that is her apartment and adds little hearts.

The pizza finally comes. I almost choke on a piece of pepperoni when I realize that Tank will soon be dropping me off at my tricked-out GMC in the theater parking lot. I should have rented a Volvo. But all she says when she sees it is "Nice truck!"

Since I'm sure Ginger doesn't work on Sundays, I leave the makeup on and sleep sitting up so as not to flatten my hair. So in the morning all I have to do is brush my teeth and apply fresh lipstick. I decide to wear the yellow blouse and black jeans again. Betty can't afford more clothes.

Tank's apartment is in an old brick building. She hugs me warmly when I arrive and says she has the video cued. I look around for a chair, but there isn't one. There's a large entertainment center that holds the TV, VCR, and a stereo system to die for. There are bookshelves lining every wall, filled with trophies, photos of Tank holding trophies, and videos. But there's only one place to sit-a well-worn green plaid sofa. So I take a seat on the sofa.

Tank sits next to me, on the very same cushion, in fact, and hits the remote. I've seen the film before at a training session in California, but I don't mind watching it again. It's filled with how-to's and helpful tips.

While the video's rewinding, I ask if I can see her training equipment. She leads me to a spare bedroom where, along with the usual grippers and weights, she has a pretty nice rowing machine and a cherry arm-wrestling table she built herself. It has generously cushioned leather elbow pads and is rigged with surgical tubing that she can pull at much the same angle as she would an opponent's arm. I don't have to *act* impressed. "Go ahead, show me," I say.

"Really?" she says. "You want to see me train?"

Do I ever!

She does ten minutes of warm-ups then rows for a while. Sweat runs down her cheeks. After a few wrist curls, she works each hand with an IronMind gripper, then moves to the bench and lifts weights. I don't dare spot her, but I keep my eyes open.

Next she goes to the table and takes hold of the tubing. She does 50 pulls with each arm. Her shirt becomes soaked, and I can't help noticing that her nipples are erect.

She stops and mops her brow. "Want to try?" she asks.

"Sure."

"Start with some warm-ups."

Dang. What I really want is a go at that table.

I do a couple of stretches and move to the rowing machine. Tank adjusts the Velcroed foot straps and gives me a short lesson. As I row and my knees move up and down, I see her eyes dart from my breasts to my crotch and back again. This woman is hot for me! After a few minutes I feign fatigue.

Tank suggests I lift weights for a while. She helps situate me with one foot on either side of the bench and gives me a pair of hand weights to work. Now, of course my legs are spread wide open. Under the guise of realigning my hips, Tank manages to stroke the inside of my thigh, and I feel an answering thrill. I gasp and sit up, thrusting the weights at her. "Done already?" she asks, then takes them.

I'm realizing with horror that I'm not immune to this woman's charms. Have I *become* Betty? If I didn't want to try the table so badly, I'd leave right now.

Shaking a little, I cross to the near side of the table, place my elbow on the pad, and take hold of the tubing. "Like this?" I ask.

"That's right," she says, "It may be a little tight for you. Let me help."

Tank stands behind me and curls her right fist around mine. In tandem we do 20 reps. I start to heat up, and the odor of my exertion blends with hers. The moisture of her shirt seeps through the thin fabric of my blouse. Her other hand slides around and presses on my abdomen, pushing me back against her. Pebbly nipples dig into my shoulders.

Ten more reps. I'm breathing hard now, but it's not all from exercise. "That's enough, Tank," I say, my voice trembling.

"Got to do your other arm. Don't want to get lopsided," she says, and leads me to the other side of the table. She presses into my back again and slides her free arm around me, but this time her hand lands lower. Hot fingers slip into my crotch. After a couple of pulls I feel her blow in my ear. *I've got to put a stop to this,* I think lazily.

Soon she whispers, "You know, Betty, exercise makes me real horny."

"Yeah?" I say weakly.

"Yeah. How about you?"

What I should do is tell her I'm not that kind of girl or something. I've been lying to her all week, so I don't know why it's so difficult now. I can't tell her the truth—that my underpants are becoming as wet as her shirt. Oh, well, since her fingers are where they are, she'll soon discover that for herself. A couple more reps, and she does.

"OK!" she whoops, and lets go of me so abruptly I almost fall over. Unhooking an exercise mat from the wall, she throws it on the floor and points to it, eyeballing me like she does her opponents at Dar's. I stare back as I move slowly toward her, unbuttoning my jeans on the way. They and the sopping Fruit of the Looms are down to my knees by the time I reach her.

Like Betty would, I raise my face for a kiss, but she lowers me to the mat and pulls off my boots, followed by my pants, adding her own clothes to the pile. I raise my arms like Betty would so she can pull off the blouse. Instead,

THE TABLE

grasping my hips firmly, she pulls me flat, flings me on my stomach, spreads my legs, and jams a couple of fingers into the source of my wetness.

"Tank!" I gasp. This isn't in Betty's script. Betty likes to have it done slowly. She likes to have her clit played with and nipples sucked. I should know—I've been with many Bettys in my time.

Tank, however, is beyond foreplay. She puts her body weight behind the thrust of her fingers. I'm pinned beneath a hot, pulsing, grunting mountain of flesh. Sweat starts dripping, then running, from her body onto mine. Her mustiness combines with the old gym-shoe smell of the mat, and I feel an overwhelming rush. Betty wouldn't like this, but I'm amazed to find that *I* do. My body sends a gush of fluids to meet her fingers, drench them.

Tank pants and shudders. Her fingers plunge again and again. My clit stiffens and with each thrust of Tank's body rubs across the sodden mat. It soon becomes the only part of me that I'm aware of. "Tank, yes!" I cry.

When I'm just about there, Tank's body starts quaking. She stops grinding on me, holds her breath for the duration, then gives a final monumental grunt and rolls off. "Tank?" I say. She doesn't move. I continue rubbing against the mat, but without her weight there isn't enough pressure. I sit up and look around for a pillow, anything. The arm-wrestling table!

"Tank?" I say again. She opens one eye. "Will the table hold my weight?"

"Sure. Why?"

I jump up and lift my body backward onto the table so that my clit lands smack on an elbow pad. The table rocks as I rub on the pad across and forward, then in little circles.

My fluids run off the leather pad and onto the table, making it slippery.

"Come here," I tell Tank. "Hold me so I don't slide off." She pulls herself to her feet, wearing a puzzled frown.

So, wearing nothing but the yellow blouse and hanging on to Tank for dear life, I erupt into the deepest, strongest, strangest climax of my life. It's all I can do to dry off, get dressed, and go home.

The following Tuesday evening I'm myself again, lurking in the shadows of Dar's Bar. The only difference is that on my way in, I wrote my name on the west wall blackboard.

"Missed you last week. Where were you?" asks the bartender.

"Busy," I say.

Tank arrives, takes her seat, and the matches begin. She wins the first four without half trying. The fifth takes a little longer, but Tank again comes out on top. Dar looks at the board and calls "Gerry Slater." That's me.

Tank is talking with someone and doesn't look up as I approach. In any case, I've got my baseball cap pulled way low on my forehead. Tank squares her shoulders, and we get into position. When Dar signals the start of the match, I raise my head, and for the first time Tank looks at me. Her brow furrows. She knows me, she's thinking, but from where? I try to slam her in her moment of indecision, but she doesn't fall for it. Her fist squeezes mine and pushes it, millimeter by millimeter, toward the table. I push back, but it's no use, she's too dang strong.

At the last possible moment, when I'm at the edge of the point of no return, I whisper through clenched teeth, "Betty says thanks."

Tank freezes. She peers into my face again, and the light

dawns. Her arm falters, and I slam it to the table. The spectators give a great cheer. They like to see Tank dethroned once in a while, even though it's only temporary.

Tank is still staring at me. I can see her mind running backward through the events since last Tuesday, wondering where things went wrong.

Finally, she exhales, shakes my hand, signs at the bottom of the list, and disappears into the crowd.

I move to the champion side of the table and await my first challenger. It's Patsy, the drink buyer, who doesn't recognize me at all. I take advantage of her weak back and win easily. It's the same thing with the four others whose names lie between my name and Tank's. Using a hook or top roll, depending on what weakness I've observed, I come out the winner each time.

"Tank McCloud," calls Dar, "you're up!" Tank doesn't appear. Dar calls her name again. Maybe she went home, I think. Maybe she'll default. Maybe I'm already this week's champion! I'm about to check the board to see if there are any more challengers when Tank appears, dispiritedly pushing through the ring of spectators. She approaches the table like it's a coffin.

Wow! It's going to be a shoo-in! I won't even have to resort to my trump card, which is that I know from the phone book that Tank's real name is Amber.

She finally gets to the table. I put my arm into position, but Tank continues looking down. Then she puts the first two fingers of her right hand on the elbow pad and gently rubs it. The crowd starts whispering, and Dar shifts impatiently, but Tank keeps rubbing the elbow pad.

I try to look away, but I can't. I watch, fascinated, as Tank's fingers tease the pad, rubbing across and down, and in little circles. My breathing quickens. My pelvis heats up and my clit swells. Prickles flow through my blood. A tiny moan escapes my lips. Tank snorts, slams her elbow in the pad, and grabs my hand. Dar says, "Ready, go," and Tank flattens my arm on the table like it was a stick of butter. The crowd cheers.

My face burns with lust and humiliation. Who'd have thought Tank would resort to such a dirty trick? I leave the bar, drive home, and start packing. I hear they have some real good arm wrestling in Canada.

Black Belt Theater Catherine Lundoff

That whole day would have been different if I hadn't gone to the movie before class. I mean, nothing would have happened without the tae kwan do classes and my huge crush on Leslie the black belt either. But the movie was the first thing that happened that day, and if I hadn't been there, I never would have met Crystal.

The movie was *Wing Chun*, and I was there watching my favorite Hong Kong actress, Michelle Yeoh, kick some guys' butts. I love Michelle; she's gorgeous. The film is sort of based on the life of Wing Chun, the woman who developed the Wing Chun fighting style. They play it like it's a romantic comedy, even though I think she was a Buddhist nun, but it's a lot of fun anyway and kind of feminist. I've seen it four times.

If nothing else, I was hoping this time it would give me some inspiration before I went down to the Flying Dragon for my afternoon class. The Dragon is the women's *dojahng*, my tae kwan do club. I got my green belt there, worked my way up from white belt and all. I'm not too bad, but what I really wanted was to be as graceful as Michelle. She used to be a dancer, and you can really tell in the fight scenes.

There's this one great fight where she spins up in the air in a series of graceful twists and kicks. Her opponent drops like a stone when one little foot connects with his jaw. You can almost hear his head snap back when he hits the ground. Then he just arches his back and bounces right back to his feet just as she lands. Then she does this fierce chopping blow at his neck, but he blocks, and then...well, let's just say it's poetry in motion and all that.

Right about then, my mind started to wander. I wondered what it would be like to spin around in the air like that. After I watch a bunch of martial arts movies, anything seems possible: flying, running over rooftops, the whole bit. OK, maybe not the flying parts.

Learning tae kwan do is the closest I'll ever get to that. To me the terrific thing about martial arts is learning to be centered in your body, knowing where everything is all the time and how to control it. The learning to defend yourself part is also pretty cool. Notice I'm not talking about *my* body specifically but about martial arts-honed bodies in general. Anyone who watched me at the club would know that I'm barely in control of my body, unfortunately.

Times like this I think that getting into martial arts by watching the movies left me with this huge overblown fantasy about what's possible. It was hard for me to get past that to all the really hard work and discipline you have to develop to get good at them. But that's not to say that the films aren't fun. The '90s Hong Kong films are the best because they have a bunch of really strong women in them. Once they started showing those at one of the little theaters, I went almost every week.

One thing led to another, and my mom found out about my martial arts fantasy life and signed me up for classes. From what she mumbled about helping me "realize my potential," I guessed it was part of her dealing with me coming out last year. She wouldn't say it one way or the other, but why else would she pick The Flying Dragon

Women's Dojahng over Bob's Karate Club? I may never know. She has a hard time talking about stuff like that.

When I tuned back in to the movie, Michelle was perched on a big spear stuck in a wall, taunting the bandit chief. He was giving her this look that did a nice job of combining lust and amazement. I wanted someone to look at me like that. Well, not just anyone: I wanted Leslie to be the one doing the looking. She was one of the instructors at the Dragon. The midnight blackness of her new belt matched her hair and the velvet of her eyes. She had muscles in places that I couldn't imagine having, and, of course, a girlfriend.

The girlfriend and I had two things in common: We both wanted Leslie, and we were both named Pam. When I wasn't dying of jealousy, I thought Pam-the-girlfriend looked pretty nice, in an "I wanna be your friend" kind of way. But most of the time I just wanted Leslie. It was one of those deep-down burning-achy kind of wants. I quivered every time we sparred. It made me worthless to practice with, but she was nice about it.

I drifted back to the screen. Michelle had freed her friend from the bandits, and now they were outside the bandit fort. The guy that Michelle loved was there too. She spat up some blood and rode off heroically, leaving the guy with her friend because she thought they were in love. I knew just how she felt. Well, sort of.

If I closed my eyes, I could see a similar scene starring me and Leslie. I'd save her from some fate worse than death, and she'd be awed by my fighting skills and great love. Of course, I wouldn't ride off then. No way. I'd stick around, because then Pam-the-girlfriend would be history.

The fact that I could barely break a board in class with

repeated snap kicks made a little dent in the fantasy, but not too much. I promised myself that I'd practice my forms again when I got home. All that hero stuff took work. For incentive I pictured Leslie's fingers rubbing my sore back, digging their way into my muscles, sliding lower and lower.

Then they dug their way inside me. Ooh, my favorite part. They were nice long fingers, long enough to even find my G spot, wherever that was. I'd been looking, mind you, but I just hadn't found it yet. The way I pictured it, it was a pretty big deal. Especially with someone else's fingers instead of my own. My hips rocked against the seat, and I felt my underwear get a little damp.

For a split second I thought about sliding a hand down my pants to rub my clit where it ached for the imagined touch of Leslie's fingers. No one would notice me quivering silently in my seat for a few minutes, right? But the screen got bright again, and I glanced around: too many people, and I was too uptight. Damn. I squirmed against the seat and tried to watch the movie.

Michelle was riding away, headed for her teacher's home. I just love that her teacher's a woman in this film, and an androgynous one at that. She heals Michelle then teaches her some metaphorical martial arts lesson to demonstrate how Michelle's character should bend against force until she can throw it back. I wasn't really sure how you did that, but it did set me to thinking again.

The bending against force thing and some of the blocks and strikes I was learning seemed like they might go together. I loved the way the words sounded in Korean, like *gudro makki*, the helping block or *doongjoomuk chigi*, the back fist strike. They had a kind of martial arts poetry sound to them. Thinking about them got me thinking about Leslie again. It was a circular kind of day.

I tuned out the old upholstery and stale popcorn smells of the theater, and imagined the sweat of a good workout: Leslie's sweat and mine, mingled together. Pam-the-girlfriend probably never sweated. I was sure she could never relate to the Zen-like feeling of doing the forms, the *pal-gwe*. Turn, block, kick, punch, turn again to repeat on the other side: These were what warriors would use to prepare for battle. When you did them just right, it was a high.

Back up on the screen, Michelle headed back to go and retrieve her beloved. He was a dimwit, but hey, she loved him anyway. Maybe Leslie could get to see me in that light. Bumbling but good-hearted clown, that's me. When I remembered the last time I sparred with her, it was pretty appropriate.

It had been just last week, as a matter of fact. Her block knocked my punch aside, sending it sliding along her arm. She made a quick strike to my ribs, just hard enough to get my attention and I fell back. We circled, and I made a pathetic attempt at a roundhouse kick up at her safety helmet. She sidestepped and sent me flying with a kick of her own. So there I was, lying on the mat and thinking, *She touched me! Wow! Goddess, I'm such a dork!*

She stood over for a minute, waiting for me to get back up. I had this flash of me curling snakelike around her calves. My tongue gliding, lapping its way up her thighs. My fingers wrestling with the drawstring of her pants until she reached down to do it herself. Her strong, capable fingers untying her pants so I could bury my face in her pussy, its sweet-sour scent filling my nose and mouth.

In my mind, she spread her legs, strong neck arching

her head back while the motion of my tongue on her clit tore deep groans from her throat. I'd slip my fingers inside her wetness and feel how much she wanted me. My tongue would find that magic spot to coax her into coming, her strong thighs shaking against my ears until she had to collapse into my arms.

Of course, that wasn't what happened. "Hey, Pam, you all right?" The words rode over the pleasant dream I was having until I had to wake up and look at her. There stood a Leslie fully clothed and pissed because I wasn't sparring the right way. Oops.

Thinking back on that moment, I was perfect for the lovable, faithful buffoon role. Pam-the-girlfriend had actual fingernails and hair that stayed styled. There was no way I could compete with that. I studied Michelle up on the screen. I tried to imagine her in Leslie's place in the same fantasy. It just wasn't working for me. She just wasn't a substitute for a flesh and blood someone who I could touch three classes a week, at least when I could get near her.

I got really lucky last Thursday night and got to the Dragon just as Leslie was changing from her street clothes into her *dobak*. It was the first time I got to see her shirt off. Rrrowrl. She was wearing a black sports bra, and it was hot enough that I could see the beads of sweat sliding down into her cleavage. My eyes followed them the way my tongue wanted to. The way it wanted to roam over her entire body, taste every single hardened muscle, and sample all the nooks and crannies. Especially the crannies.

She flexed, stretched out, and flexed again, her mind on something: class, tae kwan do, Pam-the-girlfriend. On just about anything but me. So I just stood and watched her as I slowly unbuttoned my blouse. Then, for a moment, she glanced up, and those big dark eyes seemed to take me in, to really see me as I slid off my shirt. She smiled, and goose bumps appeared all over my arms.

Then she pulled on her tank top and reached for her *dobak*, her eyes sliding past me as though I was part of the locker room. I watched the muscles in her calves ripple as she stood on one foot then the other to pull her pants on. Her eyes were still far away when I glanced back up at them, but I could tell she was starting to focus. For the first time I wondered about showing her some of the poems I was trying to write. Maybe she'd understand them.

I'd forgotten about that idea until I was sitting in the theater remembering how strength quivered through her arms and legs. For me, it wasn't so much that Leslie was beautiful, although she was, but that she was powerful too—like a real-live version of the babes in the martial arts films. If I thought about it, I could easily picture her doing the kinds of things they did, except maybe for the magical parts.

In fact, thinking of her as a movie star was probably the best way for me to think about her, especially if I had to keep sparring with her. Dreaming about her just before I went to sleep sure wasn't helping me in daylight hours, even though she was mine, all mine for a few blissful moments.

Or I was hers, depending on my mood at the time. In my dark bedroom, I could almost feel her strong fingers inside me, probing all my secret places until I had to come, groaning into my pillow. They would slip deeper inside me than my own fingers could possibly reach, filling me and easing that ache that filled my pussy whenever I got near her. Then if I moved my fingers just right, I could feel her tongue circling my clit in long, slow strokes until I came again and again.

Ah, well, it was a nice dream. Maybe I could superimpose someone else's face over hers, and then I wouldn't be all quivery every time she came near me. Ha.

Michelle was working out her own romantic troubles when I opened my eyes again. For some reason her beloved doesn't recognize her until toward the end of the movie because she was going around dressed in men's clothes. OK, so it had been a few years since he saw her last, but he was still dumb. She wanted him back anyway. The thing that gets me is that she had the bandit chief to fall back on, and he's smarter and cuter than the true love. He just wasn't the right one.

Oh, joy. Yet more drivel about true love and finding the One. I wondered how you knew which one the One is. I thought about that while Michelle had her big showdown with the bandit chief. He gave it his best shot, but she won by taking her teacher's advice and turning his force away instead of trying to absorb it. In a way, that was the essence of a lot of martial arts. Maybe there was a lesson here about unrequited love too. I tried to picture my feelings about Leslie as a snap kick to my heart.

I knew I should turn it aside to wait for someone who was available instead of trying to absorb it and hide it. But the question was, who? None of the other women at the Dragon or at school was as hot as Leslie, not even close. Michelle wins and gets her guy at the end of the movie, but when would I get a girl of my own?

The thought probably would have gotten me pretty down if I hadn't been at this particular movie. Despite all my teen angst, I always leave *Wing Chun* feeling like I can take on the world. Or at least do flying spin kicks that keep me airborne longer than gravity allows and maybe beat up a bandit chief or two. If it had been another movie, what happened next might not have happened.

The theater is in kind of a rundown part of town, just off a big street where the tides of espresso bars haven't come in yet. It's a few blocks away from the Dragon. and there aren't many people there on a Saturday. That was why I noticed the girl and a couple of guys on the other side of the street. Her voice cut through my martial arts fantasy haze.

"Hey, Cliff, get lost. You're an asshole, and I'm not going out with you again."

I looked up. She was blond, on the big side, with lots of nice curves, pretty femmey in an I-used-to-be-Goth-but-I-can-wear-colors-now way. You know, lots of black, kind of low-cut green shirt, a pink streak in her hair, a little too much blue eye shadow. She was about my age, and something about her tripped my gaydar. Of course, that might have been wishful thinking; I hope I get to find out.

The guy she was yelling at looked like a refugee from an old James Dean flick, late '90s style. His brown hair was slicked back; he had on baggy jeans and sported a couple of not so great tattoos. One hand was holding on to the blonde's arm, and even from across the street I could see that it hurt.

"Asshole! Let go of me!" The blonde tried to yank her arm away, but he just gave her an evil smile, like a shark.

"What's the matter, baby? You know you…hey, what are you looking at, dyke?"

Oh, goody, that was meant for me. Without even realizing I'd started doing it, I was crossing the street. I could feel my walk slink down in something like Michelle's catlike stride.

A voice rasped out, "You need a hand?" It sounded so studly I almost looked around until I realized from the blonde's stare that it had come out of my mouth. I watched her like he wasn't even there.

She looked at me, then down at his white knuckles on her arm. "Yeah," she glared at him, "maybe I do."

Cliff dropped her arm and tossed his cig away. He sneered at me, and I gave him the death stare right back. I was a little scared because he was bigger than me, but mostly I was just mad. We locked eyes for a long minute. I felt my face turn itself into my best imitation of Lucy Lawless's stare of death. You know the one: vintage Hong Kong, but she makes it all her own. The look must have made him realize I was serious because he balled his hands up into fists. His friends were laughing, and I saw the blood rush up into his face as I dropped into my fighting stance.

He punched out hard, and I turned it with a quick block, using the opening to land my other fist in his stomach. I was Michelle all over for that instant. If I wanted to, I could fly. Cliff didn't know that, though. We circled around a little and drew back for a strike. I wasn't fast enough, and he managed to punch me in the jaw. The pain exploded into white light for a second, but I fought it to pull my leg back for a really solid snap kick. One in the thigh, followed by one in the balls. OK, the second one was lucky, but it would have snapped a board for sure.

Damn, I wish someone from the Dragon had been there to see it. Here I was, rescuing a babe and all, just like Wing Chun. Cliff was at my feet, curled into a little ball. I looked at his friends and rubbed my jaw; I was ready for them. Hell, I was ready for anything, with the possible exception of chewing. They looked back for a couple of seconds. Then, "Hey, Cliff, you wuss—you got beaten up by a girl.

Loser!" They lit some more cigs and wandered off. I let out the breath I hadn't realized I'd been holding.

The blonde looked like she wanted to kick Cliff herself when she looked down. So she looked up instead. Her dark blue eyes met mine. Ooh. My stomach did a little flip. "How's the jaw?"

I could move it, so I hoped it wasn't broken. "I'll live. Can I walk you somewhere?" I was ten feet high. Wait until I told them about this down at the Dragon. Hell, I wondered if I should ask for her number. I gave her my best butch-in-training smile: the little one that said I knew what I was doing. I'd been practicing that one for a while; it looks good on me.

She gave me a big, pretty smile right back. "My hero. How about walking me to the bus stop?" One high-heeled boot then the other stepped over Cliff like he was trash, and she tucked her arm into mine.

I tried not to blush. We headed up the block watching each other from the corners of our eyes. What the hell did I do now? The glow of the fight was fading, and my face was killing me. I looked at the little Xena lunchbox purse she was carrying. It wasn't big enough for a portable ice pack, so I didn't ask. Oh, well, at least it wasn't Hello Kitty.

We wandered to the bus stop. When she spoke, her voice was deep and husky. "So what's your name?"

I should have thought of that. Duh. "Pam. Yours?"

"Crystal. Where'd you learn how to do that stuff?"

The Flying Dragon was just down the way. For a minute I was so proud of my little *dojahng*, I almost bowed to it. Instead I just pointed to its red dragon sign blowing in the spring breeze, "At that tae kwan do club over there. You should check it out."

She gave me a mischievous grin. "Maybe I will. You hang out there a lot?"

"Every Saturday afternoon, and Tuesday and Thursday nights from 7 to 9." I looked up. The bus was coming. Time to make my move. "Um..."

She saw it too. "Tuesday, Thursday, and Saturday, huh? OK, I'll remember that. Thanks for the Cliff thing." Then it happened. She leaned over and kissed me. There was the brush of lipstick wings on my mouth, and she was gone. Butterflies danced in my stomach, and my lips burned while I gaped after her. Smooth. She did wave from the bus, though.

My first kiss. Ever. Well, except for that time in third grade. They were never going to believe this down at the club, but hey, I had the bruises to prove it. I started toward the red dragon sign. That was when it occurred to me that maybe Pam-the-girlfriend could give me some dating tips. And an ice pack. It was going to be a long wait until Tuesday.

Rivals Yolanda Wallace

Standing outside the doors of the soccer team bus, Leah Whitlock greeted each of her teammates by name. She had something positive to say to each one.

"Good game."

"Way to defend."

"Thanks for the assist."

"Nice sliding tackle in the first half."

It was obvious why she was the unanimous choice for team captain year after year. Her leadership abilities made the coaches think she would sport a whistle and clipboard of her own one day.

To the surprise of no one, Nicole Webb was last to disembark.

"You're just waking up, aren't you, Nic?" Leah asked. Like a child, Nicole could sleep at any time in any position no matter what was going on around her. "You missed Coach's heartwarming speech."

"The one thanking us for all our time, effort, and sacrifice?" Nicole slung her oversize gym bag over her shoulder. "That's the same spiel he gave us in the locker room before the game."

"Hey, let's face it, the man only has two speeches."

"There's my dynamic duo." David Parsons draped his arms across the shoulders of his two star players as they crossed the parking lot. "Great game, you two."

"Thanks, Coach."

"Yeah, thanks, Coach," Nicole seconded, aware he was working up to something more serious.

"I know you both will be traveling with the national team this summer, but you *will* be back here next fall, won't you?"

Leah and Nicole looked at each other, both waiting for the other to answer first. They had grown up in the same town but attended rival schools. After competing against each other all their lives, they'd decided to attend the same college. They had just led that college to the national championship over perennial power North Carolina. Leah was a striker with dazzling speed, great field vision, and magic in both feet. Nicole was a rangy goalie with a savant-like sense of where the ball was headed at all times (though her frequent forays to the offensive end of the pitch drove her coaches crazy).

"Well," Leah began, "with all their firepower, they certainly aren't hurting for offense. I think they can survive without me for another year."

Leah and Coach Parsons turned to Nicole. Her decision was tougher. The national team's best goaltender had retired, and the backups were proving to be more porous than expected. "We'll see," she said with a shrug.

Leah's stricken expression matched that of her coach. "I think you just put a serious wrinkle in his recruiting plans," she said to Nicole after Coach Parsons had left to confer with his assistants. "If you decide to stay, let me know, OK?"

"Want to make it a package deal?"

"We've done pretty well together so far, don't you think?" Leah smiled.

Nicole eyed the MVP plaque tucked under Leah's arm.

"That should be mine, you know. Yeah, you scored twice, but I haven't given up a goal in 15 games."

"So, what's your point?"

"When in doubt, give it to the straight girl."

"Yeah, I'm sure you'd love to give it to the straight girl, wouldn't you?" Leah laughed. "No, you can't do that. Your girlfriend might get upset."

Nicole looked at Leah quizzically. "What girlfriend?"

"Jennifer."

"Jen's my new roommate, not my girlfriend," Leah said.

"Well, you're together all the time. Who can tell?"

Nicole knew what Leah was doing but didn't let on. Her easygoing, laconic manner made her seem like the quintessential dumb jock, but she had a lot more on the ball than people realized. Leah was always dipping her toe in the water but was too afraid to jump in. "That's what roommates do, unless they hate each other."

"Then I guess that explains why I'm never with mine." Leah tossed her bag into the trunk of her car. "I think it's time we decided which of us is actually the better player."

Nicole leaned against the side of Leah's battered blue Accord. "And how do you propose we do that?"

"Penalty kicks. Best of five."

"That's not fair."

"I make three and I win. You stop three, you win. Sounds fair to me."

"No, I mean it's not fair to you," Nicole said. "I'm the PK queen."

"Then let's make it interesting." Leah stuck the MVP award into a side compartment of her bag and slammed the trunk shut. "For each goal I make, you lose a piece of clothing."

Nicole laughed. "Strip soccer. I love it."

"For each goal you stop, I lose one."

"Does equipment count?"

"Hell, no," said Leah. "Otherwise you'd show up wearing shin guards, kneepads and your entire winter wardrobe."

"Shirt, shorts, bra, underwear. In that case, let's make it best of seven."

"So you're game?"

"I'll meet you on the practice field in ten minutes." Nicole turned to leave then stopped. "I'm going to make you my bitch, you know that, right?"

"In your dreams."

"In your fantasies."

Leah was dribbling the ball off her head when Nicole drove up 15 minutes late. "I was beginning to think you weren't going to show up."

"I was born late. When have you ever known me to be on time for anything?"

"True." Leah passed the ball to herself and rocketed a shot into the empty goal. "What took you so long this time? Did Jennifer give you a kiss for luck and the two of you got carried away?"

"No, I was picturing you naked and I got distracted."

Blushing, Leah turned to retrieve the ball. "Need some time to warm up?"

"No. Let's do this." Nicole tightened her keeper's gloves.

Centering the ball, Leah positioned it 12 yards in front of the goal and tried to decide which shot she should take first. Her right foot was slightly better than her left, but she decided to set up on the left side to throw Nicole off. Nicole knew her better than any other goalie, so she would have to break her usual patterns.

Leah's best left-footed shot was her high chip to the far post. Nicole anticipated it but slipped on the dew-covered grass and watched the ball float past her outstretched hands. "Shit," she said, pounding on the pitch.

"There goes your shutout streak," Leah gloated. "Now show me some skin."

Sighing, Nicole pulled her USA Soccer T-shirt over her head and tossed it aside. "Happy now?"

"Ooh, nice abs."

"Has it occurred to you that I could be letting you win?"

"No."

"Don't savor this too much," Nicole warned, tossing the ball back. "You're going to be pulling a Chastain in about ten seconds."

Leah went for her right-footed power shot, one that started low and rose as it picked up speed. Most goalies instinctively duck out of the way rather than try to defend it. Nicole batted it harmlessly over the crossbar. "Now show me some skin," she said.

Leah stood with her hands on her hips, and her mouth gaped open. Once she recovered from the shock, she pulled off her Lakers jersey and dropped it on the manicured grass.

"Ooh," Nicole teased, "nice abs."

"Did we decide on best of five or best of seven?" Leah was suddenly serious.

"Oh, it's not as much fun when you're not winning, is it? We'd better make it five. Get caught doing the full Monty and the campus police might haul you in. I'll let you flash me instead."

"We'll see about that." Taking advantage of the slippery

conditions, Leah went for a low shot. The ball lost some speed as it skidded on the wet grass but still had enough juice to slip through Nicole's hands and trickle into the goal. "Yes!" Leah shouted. She pumped her fists.

Nicole stepped out of her Umbros, revealing black compression shorts that matched her sports bra.

"Damn," Leah said, eyeing Nicole's chiseled legs, "I was hoping for a thong."

"Sorry to let you down, but I'm about to disappoint you even more because that was your last score."

"We'll see about that."

Leah went for the same shot on the opposite side, but Nicole anticipated and managed to get her body in front of the ball. "Let me see that thong," she sang with the ball tucked under her arm.

Leah brought her hands to the fly of her denim cutoffs. "Do you realize how stupid this is? If we get caught, we could get suspended, lose our eligibility, or both."

Nicole bounced the ball impatiently. "You're stalling."

"Can't blame me for trying."

Nicole whistled as Leah dropped trou, revealing zebra-striped bikini briefs. "Nice ass."

Leah playfully slapped one cheek. "It's nothing you haven't seen in the locker room a million times." She waved for the ball.

"Maybe, but I can't tell you there how much I appreciate the view."

Leah swallowed. It wasn't easy with such a large lump in her throat. "Now you're trying to throw me off."

"Is it working?"

Leah spun the ball between her fingers with an air of nonchalance. "No."

"Then why do you look so nervous?"

"Because this is the deciding shot," Nicole said.

"Admit that I'm the better player and you won't have to take it."

"Fuck you."

"Would you like to?" Nicole grinned.

Leah dropped the ball, retrieved it, then gave her undivided attention to positioning it. "What about Jennifer?" she asked, staring at the ground.

Nicole abandoned her ready position and stepped out of the goal mouth. "She went home for the weekend. She won't be back until tomorrow."

Leah pondered for a moment, then backed away from the ball. "I'm not saying you're the better player or anything," she said, shakily gathering her clothes, "but I think I'd rather kiss you than beat you."

Nicole smiled wide. "I'll meet you at my dorm in five minutes."

Leah called over her shoulder as they sprinted to their cars, "This time, don't be late."

Nicole flung everything off her bed. Throw pillows, books, boxes, and an assortment of soccer gear landed on the floor with a series of thumps and thuds. Too late, she remembered her downstairs neighbors. They voiced their displeasure by banging on the ceiling. "Sorry," she called out, though she doubted they heard her apology over the sound of the music blasting next door.

Someone knocked on the door. Through the peephole, Nicole saw Leah anxiously glancing up and down the hall. "Who's late this time?" Nicole teased, after letting Leah in.

Leah rushed in, then closed and locked the door behind

her. "Just because I finally know what I want doesn't mean I know what I'm doing."

"I'll show you." Nicole leaned to kiss her, but Leah backed away. "I know you're scared," Nicole said. "I was nervous my first time too. But I'm not going to throw you on the bed and take you. You're going to have to come to me."

"I think it'd be easier if I didn't know you," Leah explained, running her hands through her hair. "Then I wouldn't have to worry what you think about me if I suck."

"I'll still love you even if you suck."

Leah's eyes widened. "You love me?"

Nicole winced. "Oh, damn. That slipped out." She flopped onto her bed. "Now I bet you're even more nervous."

"No." Leah sat next to Nicole. "Actually, that helps. It helps a lot." She slid closer. "I love you too."

Nicole grinned. "Because I'm the better player?"

"Hell, no."

Nicole's strategy—make Leah laugh to make her relax—worked. When she slid her left hand under Leah's basketball jersey, Leah didn't push her hand away. So Nicole replaced her hand with her lips. "Nice abs," she said, kissing Leah's stomach.

"Mmm, that feels good."

"Do you want me to go up or down?"

"Up first, then down," Leah gasped, breathing through clenched teeth. She hadn't allowed anyone past second base since high school. She had done it to silence the whispers, because she was supposed to, not because she wanted to. But Leah wanted this.

Slowly, Nicole pushed Leah's jersey up higher and unhooked her bra. She kissed one of Leah's nipples while she teased the other with the palm of her hand.

Leah reached for something—anything—to hold on to. For Nicole. "Take your shirt off," she directed. "I want to feel you."

Nicole lifted her arms. "You do it."

"So I can't just lie here and enjoy myself anymore?"

"No."

"I have to work?" Leah asked.

"Yes."

Sitting up, Leah pulled Nicole's T-shirt and sports bra over her head. "You work out too much," she teased, cupping Nicole's small breasts in her hands.

"You're not exactly Dolly Parton yourself."

"You know, you got to second before you got to first," Leah pointed out. "Isn't that against the rules or something?"

Nicole kissed the side of Leah's neck. "Are you going to call me out?"

"Not if you tag up and go back to first."

Nicole kissed Leah, parted her lips with her tongue, and slid it into her mouth. Leah met Nicole's expert tongue with her own. "I like the way you call a game," Nicole said. "What do you want me to do next, Coach?"

"Kiss me again. Slower."

Nicole kissed her again. Slower. But after six years of foreplay, she was anxious to dispense with it and get to the serious friction. Kissing her all the way down to Leah's shorts, she unbuttoned the cut-off Levi's and drew the zipper with her teeth. "I've been dreaming about your legs," she said, sliding the faded denim over Leah's hips. Because of her height—6 foot 1 and growing—Nicole had the long, lean lines of a basketball player. Of the two, Leah looked more like a soccer player—low center of gravity, thickly muscled thighs, cut calves. Running her hands over those calves and up those thighs, Nicole pushed Leah's legs apart.

"What are you…Oh, god." Leah bucked as Nicole sucked her clit through her zebra-striped panties.

"Can I take these off?"

Leah nodded furiously. Nicole removed them and used her tongue to tease Leah's clit even wider awake.

"Is that why your hair's so wild?" Leah grabbed two handfuls of Nicole's spiky, razor-cut hair. "Because girls are always doing this to you?"

Nicole came up for air. "No, because I'm always doing this to them."

"Should I be jealous?"

"Not anymore." Nicole lay on top of Leah and positioned herself so that they were straddling each other's legs. "I've been dreaming about your legs," she repeated. "Riding them. Riding you. Watching your face as I grind on you. As you come for me."

Leah moaned, uncertain if she were affected more by what Nicole was doing or what she was saying. "Nic," she whispered, trying to hold herself at bay.

The muscles in their legs quivered with effort, coiling and uncoiling, clenching and releasing. Their hips twisted and turned like a bed of thrashing snakes. Nicole rose up on her elbows to add more pressure.

"Nic," Leah said. And again, with an air of desperation and wonder, "Nic!"

Nicole bit her lip to keep from screaming. Then she remembered the blasting stereo next door would provide sufficient cover. Then she didn't care, and she let go.

"That was worth the wait," she said once her breathing slowed to a rate resembling normal. She brushed a stray

strand of hair out of Leah's satisfied face. "Are you OK?"
Leah nodded.
"What are you thinking?"
Leah sat up. "Wanna go best two out of three?"

The Basketball Diaries M. Christian

January 12

Well, I finally decided to exert myself. No, the New Year had nothing to do with it—OK, not much to do with it. Fact was, I shuffled out of bed one morning and realized two important things. One, I had forgotten to close the closet door—you know, the one with the mirror on the inside? I hated the mirror but could never really deal with that, so rather than smashing the son of a bitch like I secretly wanted, I always made sure the closet door was closed. And two, I realized I was definitely, positively, no denying it, getting...well...chubby.

Not that I really cared. No, scratch that—I was fucking depressed. I don't mind a little...plushness in a girl. Doesn't bother me in the least. In fact, I kinda like it—it gives you something to hold on to, and face it, gals, there's nothing worse than a sharp hip in the middle of some late-night friskiness. Am I right? Nothing wrong with a little upholstery, not at all...if it's on someone else. There's also that delightful moment as you watch your date padding off to the bathroom in the middle of the night and think, *Fuck, she's a hottie*, then right behind it add, *but my ass is a LOT smaller*. The thought of being on the receiving end of my own sneer was just too much.

So, with the rest of my resolutions either dearly departed to the trash—only a slight whiff of bourbon marking their passing—or ground out in an ashtray, I resolved to do something. Since liposuction is too expensive and no one, certainly no mirror, can keep me from my Hostess Chocodiles, I did the only sane thing left: I joined a gym.

Not just any gym, of course. I mean, think about it: 70 bucks a month to stare at some guy's cellulite hypnotically undulating as he tromps up a Stairmaster? Hell, a lava lamp's cheaper, and it doesn't sport sweat stains in revealing places. The Gyn Gym is my kind of place: squeaky-clean floors, Ikea lockers, soft towels, a Jacuzzi, and—just like San Francisco itself—a place where the men are pretty and the women are strong.

So I went in there and signed up. It might mean a few less empty containers on the nightstand, but what the hell. A new century, a new resolve, and a new ability to look at myself in the mirror without wincing—OK, not wincing as much.

There was just one problem. I mean, I could dig the clean floors (Jeez, what was the alternative?) the snazzy lockers, hot tub, and big, fluffy towels, but what was the rest of that junk? I could identify the bench press, because it had a bench, and the Stairmaster, because it had steps. But what the fuck was that chrome-and-rubber medieval torture device? Sure, I wanted to lose some pounds—but not by getting my leg chopped off.

I wandered around the place for a few minutes, then ended up at the main desk. A delightful brunette with sparkling green eyes, who (in spite of her Spandex body suit) looked like God's gift to womankind, smiled and asked, "Found everything you're looking for?"

Boy, had I ever. I coughed to cover my sudden flush of embarrassment as I felt a twinge of lust. *Work first*, I reminded myself as I smiled right back, *then play*.

"Oh, I just love this place. I mean, it seems to have all the right equipment" *(in all the right places!)* "and everything. I was just wondering if you have something a little more basic and not quite so..." *(Quick, don't say "hard." You'll look like a wuss! How about...)* "...not quite so boring."

She smiled again, and I was in love, right then and there. She said something, but I didn't catch it because I was melting, dissolving into a warm puddle. Before she could get a mop and bucket, I shook my head and tried to focus—and that's when she said the word: "Basketball?"

I don't have a lot of good memories of high school: my first kiss—with Mary Jane Lawson, my sophomore crush who reciprocated by going, "Ewwww...that was icky"; my oral book report on *Fried Green Tomatoes*, at the end of which Miss Hampton said, "But we all have to be tolerant of relationships like that. Right, class?"—meaning dykes, meaning me; and when my mom caught me gawking at a copy of *Playboy*. But there were, surprisingly, some good times. But basketball hadn't really been any of them. Probably the best time was when I finally got my hand down Mary Jane Lawson's panties. Still, there was something neutrally nostalgic about bouncing a ball on the court. *Besides*, I thought, *being ten years older, lots stronger, and hopefully a bit smarter, I'll bet I can be a mean-ass player in no time*. I didn't have any options left—and that cutie behind the desk definitely deserved a return visit.

"Sounds perfect," I said with what I hoped was my winning smile. "I'll be back tomorrow."

So here I am, bags from the Gap and Sport Chalet by my bed—some sweats, new high-tops, even a Lisa Leslie headband—with thoughts of that girl behind the desk running through my head. Tonight I'll think of her some more as I buzz myself to delirious ecstasy with my favorite Hitachi magic wand. There's just one problem: Mary Jane Lawson's underage quim, the flushed embarrassment at Miss Hampton's homophobia, my first look at *Playboy* pussy—all that has pretty much burned into my noggin, but all I can remember about basketball is the ball—which is orange, I think—and the object of the game—which is to somehow put it in a basket. The rest is a haze of embarrassment and hormones.

Oh, well, how hard could it be?

January 13

I HATE basketball.

Of all the pointless, frustrating things to do on a Tuesday night, basketball has to be the winner. Not that I didn't try. No sirree, I certainly gave it a shot. I showed up at the gym all puppy-dog eager right after work (hoping to see that luscious receptionist again—but no such luck). I marched into the locker room, crawled out of my stiff work clothes and into my brand-new workout duds, picked up a ball, and stepped onto the wide-open court.

I had acquired a little knowledge of the game, having rented a couple of inspirational flicks on the way home the night before. Not that they were a lot of help. *The Air up There* and *The Basketball Diaries* did nothing to help me figure out what to do with the ball. They only confirmed something I already knew. After watching Kevin Bacon and Leo DiCaprio till midnight and not getting even a little steamy in the panties, there's no doubt I'm definitely a fag girl.

I mean, get this, not only do you have to throw the damn

ball—which refuses to obey the most earnest entreaties and screeched profanities—but you can't even haul the stupid thing around. You have to do this "dribbling" thing, and no, I don't mean practicing poor lip control. Dribbling means you have to bounce the damn thing up and down while simultaneously moving your feet. I barely got the bouncing under control, hitting myself in the nose a couple of times. But every time I tried to take a step, I ended up kicking the ball all the way down the court. Argh!

Like I said, I gave it a shot. Mom didn't raise no stupid girls, but after three frustrating hours I flung the fucking ball at the far wall and crawled back into my street clothes. I was bound and determined to get my deposit back and never darken the Gyn Gym's towels again.

However. On my way out, whom did I see but that tasty bit of girl-flesh, that melt-in-your-mouth bit of honey from the night before. Incurably perky, she said, "Have a good workout?"

"Oh, yeah," I mumbled, amazed at the sweet shape of her tits under that black spandex workout bra and imagining how much fun it would be to discover if she was a natural brunette or just San Francisco hip. "I haven't sweated this much since that girls' rugby team gang-banged me last Easter."

She laughed, and I almost threw her down right there. Tongue down her throat, hands down her pants...but there were too many people around, and none of them were anybody I'd want to join in.

"Well," she said with a smile both hot and noncommittal (Don't you just hate that?) "some exercises are better than others. See you tomorrow?" Just then an old queen in a towel walked up and demanded her attention—something about a hair clog in the Jacuzzi.

"Wild horses couldn't keep me away," I called out, walking toward the front door.

Basketball definitely sucks, but as the (hot, hot, hot) girl said, there's more than one way to work up a tasty sweat.

January 14

I LOVE basketball: the beauty of movement, the way it reaches every part of your body and exhilarates you in ways you never knew existed, the poetry of dribbling, the song of the ball on the polished wood floor, the pure beauty of a shot sunk straight through the net (or so I hear). It's a divine sport…no, not just a sport: an art form.

My pits are rank in a way that's anything but sexy, my arms are stuffed with lead, and my neck feels like a giant just used my head as a twist-off—but I still love basketball.

Her name is Stan.

It happened like this. It was right after work. I was grouchy and *not* looking forward to another lesson on the laws of gravity telling me I was flat-out too old for this shit and should just surrender to the inevitable sags and cellulite. All this just to try and impress some patronizing gym bunny who I couldn't even talk to without swallowing my tongue? All because I couldn't stop dreaming of swallowing hers?

So there I was in the locker room, popping my tits into the new sports bra, trying to figure out one more damn time which hole was for which leg in my crotch-huggers, when I realized that me, my cellulite, and gravity weren't alone.

Be still, my thudding lesbo heart. Sure, soft lips and nice tits get my heart a-pumping.

A pair of righteous gams gets my internals all a-flutter. But deep down in my heart, I love them good, hard…and stone-cold butch.

And butch she was. All stone and pretty damned cold. Not like that'd stop me, you understand, but it's tough to turn on the charm when your tongue is lolled out on the floor.

She was about 5 foot 8 and a muscularly packed 140-or-so sexy pounds, with a white sports bra and neon blue nylon shorts painted on incredible muscles. Bright pink hair buzzed down to a nasty quarter inch. Eyes like cobalt and…very firm lips. Her tits were small beneath that white bra, and as crisply defined as her bare belly and thighs.

OK, so I fall in love all the damn time. But this wasn't love: It was raw, real, pussy-melting lust. Just watching her walk into the locker room, each step like the action of a pile driver, was like a hand down my crotch. Fuck love, this was pure desire. She nodded toward the basketball I'd wedged under the bench. "You playin'?" Her voice was like rolling thunder.

I should've said something like, "Basketball's just one of the games I play" or "With you, anytime" or "Only when I'm not playing with myself," instead of drooling and saying, "Yeah, sure—yeah, I mean…I, uh, yeah…"

"Well, come on then." She looked down at me with this Clint Eastwood smile. "Name's Stan. Let's shoot some hoops."

I said something stupid and tripped over my shoelaces.

Getting up off the floor, I caught sight of her tight perfect ass as she walked toward the court. I was smitten. Who cared if the game was stupid, frustrating, and too damned hard? I was in the throes of pussy-pounding lust.

And I absolutely adored basketball.

"You play much?" Stan stood at the far end of the court, absently drooling the ball. No, wait—that's not what it's called. Dribbling—that's what she was doing. And so was I, as I watched the way her muscles flexed and rolled as the ball bounced up to meet her so-strong hand. It was all too easy to imagine that hand stoking my swollen labia, dipping deep into my well of hot stuff. Fuck that romantic crap, let's be honest—I wanted those four strong fingers and that thumb deep in my cunt, pounding, pounding, pounding me till I took the Lord's name in vain and endlessly repeated the word "fuck."

"Me? Oh, um, sometimes, you know—every while and a once," I mumbled, hoping I wasn't leaking pussy juice...or, if I was, that she just thought it was sweat or something.

"Well, come on," Stan said, a wicked smile on her steel-hard face, "try and take it from me."

OK, I thought, biting my lip, *this is where Leo and Kevin prove their worth. Time to put it all on the line. Time to shoot for the prize. Time to jump through the hoops...er, that was right, wasn't it?* What the fuck. It was time to take it from her—and I didn't mean the ball.

"Sure," I said, hunkering down into my serious kick-ass pose (which wasn't all that kick-ass as I glanced down and realized my gym shorts were on backwards). "No problemo," I finished, turning a lovely shade of magenta.

"Then let's do it." Her voice was a tiger, a lion, a lovely, lovely pussy (I hoped) growl. Then we were at it.

Or she was, at any rate. God above, I didn't think a person could move so fast. *Don't they have laws against this kind of thing?* I thought, as she ducked, wove, sprinted, and generally ran circles around me—doing that perfect dribbling thing and smiling the whole time.

First I was amazed, then I was tired. Then I couldn't get over the image of someone that quick, that strong, that…sexy, naked, and gleaming with good sweat, nipples firm and tasty, quim all wet and steamy. Then I was tired again. Then I was thinking of what it'd be like to haul this bitch into the locker room, yank down her gym shorts, bury my face into her slick, slick twat, and lick to my heart's content. Then I was thinking of licking her while she grabbed my hair and pulled, hard. Then I was tired. Then, chasing her down the court, backward shorts riding up my ass crack, I was thinking, *Boy, my ass crack hurts, AND I'm tired*. And then I was thinking of what it'd be like to have my face buried in her hot pussy while she said something nice and romantic like, "Lick it, bitch. Lick it good." THEN I was thinking about how my legs hurt, my arms hurt, and my feet ached. Man, I was tired.

"I win," she said—not panting, not heaving, not even the slightest bit nauseous, and even sexier than before. I stood there and just looked at her…well, that's not quite true. I went from hands on knees—panting, panting, panting—to sitting on the hardwood floor and obviously staring at her with unbridled lust. (I'd read about unbridled lust in trashy novels but had never really understood until that night when I sat on the gym floor wanting nothing but to fuck this gloriously hard dyke.) "…since you didn't score once." There was a wicked turn to that lovely mouth. "It was a lot of fun kicking your ass, though."

Oh, yeah, I thought, still looking at her, *and there's a lot more I want you to do to my ass than kick it*.

Then she walked up to where I lay sprawled and panting like the beached whale I was, and she knelt down, way too close to me with her tasty body. It was all I could do to keep myself from just tackling her, throwing her tight lusciousness to the floor, and doing her.

"Make you a bet," she said. "I'll meet you here on Friday. You beat me, and..." Oh man oh man oh man oh man oh man oh man oh man oh man, that wicked, wicked smile. I felt my body heat kick up at least a thousand fucking degrees, and all I wanted in the world was her mouth on my mouth, her nips in my mouth, my hand down her pants feeling her hot wet quim, her face between my thighs licking, licking, licking. I closed my eyes, feeling her so close and so damned hot, pushing myself forward to meet her lips that I knew were so close, all the time thinking, *Do me baby do me hard do me fast do me nasty take me down and hold my wrists while you bite my neck, pound my puss with your knee and make me cuuuummmm!* "It's yours," she whispered throatily, tongue-wetting her tight lips.

Then she stood up, turned around, and waltzed those wonderful buns into the locker room.

January 15

Insert "Eye of the Tiger" music here. You know, pure *Rocky* shit: fast montage of our heroine (me, silly) punching the bag, skipping rope, running up and down the stairs, waxing the floor, doing the windows...waitaminute...well, you know what I mean.

Got to the gym, jumped into my workout clothes (shorts on right this time), grabbed a ball, and hit the court. *It's you and me, ball,* I thought, holding it in my hands. *We win, and it's endless ecstasy with the dyke of my dreams. We lose, and it's night after night of* Xena *reruns and the Hitachi wand. Let's do this thing.*

Da-dum-dum, da-dum-dum...I was in the groove, I was rocking and rolling, I was there, I was in the zone, I was a finely tuned athletic machine. I was "The Man." The ball and I were one. I raced up and down the court chasing the damn thing; I hung air...I think, as I am still fuzzy on the concept.

Till the place closed I ran up and down, dribbling and shooting, all the time keeping my eyes on the prize: Stan. Her smile, the promise of a night locked around her, lips to lips, lips to nipples, fingers to clit, mouth to clit... I was slick with sweat, but not all of it was from working out.

I was there, I was done. Stan would be mine. I knew it, could feel it as I tossed up one last shot. It hit the rim, rattled around a bit, wobbled, and finally fell in.

Yeah, man! Sly Stallone ain't got nothing on me, and my tits are bigger than his. Look out, Stan. You're going get your ass kicked all the way to my bed.

January 16

"Ready?" Stan dribbled the ball. She wasn't even looking at it.

I felt a lead weight in my belly. "Anytime you are, babe," I shot back, clapping my hands hard. "Let's do this thing."

So we did this thing—that thing—well, we did *a* thing, at least. Stan started off, the ball magically dribbling right where she wanted it, not bouncing all over the damn place. My job was to get it away from her. *OK, girl*, I thought to myself as 140 pounds of hard-core, pink buzz-cut bulldyke roared toward me. *This is it, this is where I prove to the whole world I'm not just a Chocodile-eating, Hitachi-wand-abusing girl, but someone who, through dedication, hard work, and a gym membership, could earn the mad passionate lesbo love of someone like Stan.*

That one night of training really paid off. I stuck to Stan like...like some kind of mad, passionate glue. I wove, I blocked, I flailed, I spasmed, I jerked, I made all kinds of other fancy basketball moves. The game and I were one…mostly. I was a well focused, very well lubricated (ahem) machine as I took her on so that I might take her on later. My mind was a beam of intensity, and I never once let my concentration slip into fantasies of Stan growling, "Come for me, bitch," as her fine, strong hand hammered time and again into my slick, wet cunt. There were no thoughts at all of her dipping her hand down between her legs, coating two fingers with Stan-juice, and painting my lips till they glistened, all the time purring, "Taste my cunt." Not once for a second did I imagine Stan with the biggest damn plastic cock I'd ever seen fucking me as those silk-wrapped vice grip lips worked and worked and worked again at my so-tight, so-hard nipples. Not even briefly did I daydream of Stan in a leather miniskirt and metal breast-plate locked in a passionate clench with me in my bilious green sports bra and leather hot pants—lips and tongues in a mad dance of passion, hands roaming over each other's hot bodies. And I never, ever entertained the idea of Stan and me showering off a night of sweat and juice, feeling our lust rise again to culminate in a liquid fuck under the pounding, steaming water. OK, I admit that for a fraction of a second I slipped into a reverie of us picking out a china pattern as we decided whom to invite to the wedding.

Then Stan, standing at the far side of the court, said, "I win," and I realized that the eye of the tiger might be one thing, but the cunt of a dyke is much more powerful. "Sorry about that, babe. Maybe some other time," she added, meaning exactly the opposite, as she tossed me the ball.

I was crushed, I was devastated, I was totally bummed. Pathetic and alone, I chased down the ball and picked it up, wanting nothing more than to curl up around it and cry my eyes out. I was a failure, and a chubby one at that.

"Hey," said a voice from the door to the locker room, "I saw you out there."

Sweat trickling down my back and thighs, I turned around and just stared.

"You were pretty damn hot. Wanna go for coffee?" said the cute receptionist, her eyes gleaming with more than simply admiration.

Well, dear diary, we did just that—and much more—till early in the morning. And after all this I learned three really important lessons. One, a cunt beats a tiger's eye any time; two, I HATE basketball; and best of all, three, there's losing, but then there's winning even after losing, which is just the very best there is. Believe me.

Ah, the doorbell. Now for my new nightly workout!

Spiked! Laurel Hayworth

I hate her. I really do. And her team is up 20 to 19. That bitch Marta thinks she's so fucking tough, talking shit at me through the net. I'm taking her down.

"Set," my teammate Claudia yelled, charging through the sand, dropping to her knees, and lofting the ball up in a perfect step two of the ultimate triangulation—bump, set, and now me, SPIKE!

I took three running steps toward the net, blinking the sweat out of my eyes, and jumped, my body rising effortlessly as the ball descended. I kept my eye on the ball, but I wanted to look at Marta, watch how her face would screw up when she realized what I had in store for her on the court—and maybe off it as well.

My hand met leather with a loud crack as my breath left my body in a howl. Like a meteorite, the ball hurtled downward. I landed and took two steps back, watching as Marta launched herself at the ball, her strong body arcing through the air, plowing arms outstretched into the sand, and—Fuck! She got it, scooping the ball from the sand, making it look like she wasn't even trying. It grazed the top of the net and trickled straight down, just out of my grasp. Shit.

A cocky look of self-satisfaction flashed in Marta's hazel eyes as she smirked at me then went to the cooler to grab another Coors. Claudia, Peggy, and I all went to the net to shake hands with our foes. Julia, beaming as if she'd only ever won at checkers and hopscotch, took my hand limply, the way a girlie girl or the guy with the mustache at work does. "Great match, Tyler," she said. "Man, you nearly took the life out of me. You're terrific, babe." Her hand lingered on mine a little too long, and Leslie, her girlfriend of six years, squished up her face, then quickly looked down when I caught her eyes. She brushed a golden lock off her forehead. Leslie didn't have anything to worry about, though, since I had no use for prissy femmes with nails that could tear a hole right through a volleyball—and a heart.

My teammates, Claudia and Peggy, left, making some excuse about being tired, but I knew the two were going off to their minivan to have sex. They were the biggest horndogs in town, and any kind of sport only made them even hotter for each other. So now I was alone with my "rivals."

I looked over at Marta, who was sitting on the Igloo, downing her beer and watching two bikini-clad beauties near the shore. She was definitely a babe, with nearly black hair that swept across her shoulders; toned, tanned arms; tight six-pack abs; and an ass that just about screamed, *Let's play!* But I could never actually be attracted to another jock... Or could I?

Julia sidled up to me as soon as Leslie's back was turned. "Marta's hot, isn't she? Probably could even make a stud like you go weak in the knees."

I turned toward her. The smell of her sweat was like sweet perfume. I felt the heat of her lithe body against my arm. It was distracting and it pissed me off.

"Yeah, whatever, Julia," I said, running my fingers through my sweaty, sandy-brown flattop. "You know I don't play that side of the court. But if Leslie catches you sniffing around her, she's gonna rip your head off."

She laughed. "Tyler, you are so funny. You act like it's a

crime to look at a beautiful woman. Just because you look doesn't mean you touch."

"Yeah, well, sometimes it does."

"Oh, Tyler, get off it. Jenna was Jenna. Not all women are like that."

"I don't wanna talk about it." I looked down and kicked a little at the sand beneath my feet.

"Good. Don't. But don't keep reliving it either. There are plenty of other fish in the Gulf." She shot a pointed glance in Marta's direction.

I lowered myself onto the sand and stared out over the rippling water. The Sarasota sun was sinking behind me, and I smelled the smoke from the fire Marta and Leslie were lighting. But I felt distanced from it all somehow, Julia's comments still ringing in my ears.

Jenna DiAngelo. The bitch from Palm Beach. Tore through town like a tropical storm, wrecking friendships and breaking hearts, before barreling north to Savannah, leaving skid marks a mile long on my hopes for happily ever after.

Jenna. Jenna of the raven hair and full lips, whose golden body rode the waves of pleasure as my hand found her center of ecstasy. Whose catlike growls and purrs spurred me on to forget myself and remain focused only on the sensations I could provide her. Jenna of the 14 orgasms one night after a party at Julia and Leslie's, when we drank just enough to think it was cool to drive down to the water and fuck under the moon, not caring if anyone saw us. Yeah, that Jenna.

The same one who went down on my best friend Rachel under the table at Barlowe's. And snuck out of our tent up in the Smokey Mountains to fuck Barb, the only other friend I had who liked camping, damn it. Yeah, that same Jenna, and me none the wiser, following her around with one eye glued to her leather miniskirted ass, the other scanning the room to see who was admiring us. Shit, they weren't admiring us, I found out later; they were looking at me, thinking *Poor Tyler, what a pussy-whipped schmuck.* But of course they kept their traps shut.

Then Rachel announced she was moving to Savannah to run the Citibank office there, and after her going-away party, I got home to a note and all Jenna's shit gone.

Yeah, Julia was right. Jenna was Jenna. I should have seen it coming, just like everyone else. But even though it had been more than seven months since that night, the night I broke my hand punching a hole through the bedroom wall and smashed out the living room window with one of Jenna's lame-ass Precious Moments figurines, I still hated women. Don't get me wrong, I wanted to fuck them, but then I wanted to leave them gasping and bruised by the side of the road.

But of course every time I got near one, I went all to pieces—drinking too much, talking too much, and imagining Jenna's pretty clipped pussy between their legs. I'd wrap myself around some tight babe, swaying to Paula Cole's "Feelin' Love," my hands sliding down over her back to the sweet curve of her ass, my heart pounding in my cunt, and feel myself wanting to cry.

It was all bullshit. My friends were sick of me, but no more than I was sick of myself. I barely ate, and I threw myself into work, taking on more clients and teaching extra aerobics classes, and on the weekends I'd play volleyball, basketball, softball—whatever sport I could find to blank out my mind and heart—until my muscles screamed and all I could do was hurl myself at my bed. My body was in the best shape of my life, tight and hard, but for what?

"Wanna beer?" Marta had come up behind me and was offering an ice-cold, dripping, long-neck Miller.

"Sounds good," I said, my heart missing a beat. When I reached for the bottle, her fingers grazed mine for what seemed a moment too long. Or was I just imagining things?

With a popping hiss, Marta opened a beer of her own, then flicked the cap like a bullet toward Julia.

"Ow!" Julia squealed, jumping.

"You were great out there. You play a lot?" Marta returned her attention to me, while Julia flounced and pouted minus an audience.

"Pretty much every weekend."

Against my will, I found my eyes drifting over her generous chest as she tipped her head back for a hefty swallow. Her brown arms were tight with muscle, a bicep bulging slightly as her arm raised the beer to her lips again. A drop escaped and coursed down the tendon of her throat, before traveling below the edge of her sports bra. What was I thinking? Was I that hard up that I'd be lusting after another jock? What was coming over me?

I quickly took a swallow of my beer before my trembling hands betrayed me. I felt her eyes on me, and my control returned in an instant. "Hey, what are we talking about here?" I laughed. "*You* were amazing. That last save, I was sure I had you, but you pulled that out like you were pouring punch at a party. Man, it pissed me off."

"Thanks, but it wasn't easy. I thought my arms were on fire afterward." She held out her forearms; I could still see the red marks.

"Are you guys ready to eat?" called Julia.

We sat in the sand, paper plates balanced on our knees, and ate and laughed into the darkness. The fire flung sparks toward the stars and cast flickering amber light on the faces of my friends. Maybe it was the beer, maybe it was the Gulf breeze at my back, or maybe it was the pleasant ache in my muscles, but I felt better than I had in months. Maybe, just maybe, time was working its magic.

I learned that Marta was in town from Charlotte for two weeks checking out Sarasota for a possible move, that she and Julia had gone to UNC together, that her MSW meant less to her than being outdoors, so she worked as a foreman on a road construction crew.

"It's kind of weird," she said. "Usually the women just pull flag duty, but I started doing construction work while I was in college, and they liked me. I get along really good with the guys, and they know I'm not some bullshit power tripper."

"Do you get to drive that big equipment?" Julia giggled.

Leslie reached out and put her hand on Julia's knee. I knew that motion. Julia was cool, and she didn't screw around on Leslie, but put her in a group of women and she turned into Sarah Michelle Gellar. Leslie's hand was all that was needed to bring her back to Earth. Julia scootched her butt across the sand and settled into the curve of Leslie's arm. As I watched them, my heart broke a little.

"Yeah, yeah, Julia," Marta laughed, deep and warm. "I run that big equipment. I drive them dump trucks and graders. And I stand around with a mouthful of chewing tobacco, leaning on a shovel and scratching my balls." Just then Marta grabbed a fistful of her crotch, causing Julia, Leslie, and I to keel over in laughter. When I looked up, Marta shot me a wink and a sexy grin. That's when I felt a familiar but long overdue sensation between my legs—my own personal Gulf of Mexico.

It was getting late, so we picked up and headed for our

cars. Marta and I trudged through the sand, carrying the cooler between us in amicable silence. Our competitive tension from earlier had evolved into something a little more pleasurable and a lot less uncomfortable. Up ahead, Julia's laughter drifted back to us through the shadows, her body pressed close to Leslie's from shoulder to hip.

"I'm really glad to see Julia so happy," Marta said quietly.

"You guys were pretty close in school?"

"Yeah. Actually...well, never mind." Something in her voice told me that not only had they been more than friends, but that Julia still held a piece of Marta's heart.

"It's a bitch, ain't it?" I said.

"What's that?" She turned toward me, eyebrows lifted.

"They hurt us, and we still love 'em."

"That is so true," she laughed. "But it's worth it."

"You're nuts."

"Bad one, huh?"

"Bitch outta hell."

"Bride of Satan?"

"Whore of Babylon."

"Cunt of Cthulhu?"

I cracked up, and so did she.

"Been there, ate that," Marta said.

I lost it. Dropped my end of the cooler and fell against my car laughing.

Marta grinned at me, her teeth flashing white through the darkness. "We can't take this shit so seriously, Tyler."

"What shit is that?" asked Julia, her head buried in the trunk of Leslie's Corolla as she shoved crap around to make room for the cooler.

"Women. Evil, bad, nasty women," Marta snarled at her.

"What-ever." Julia rolled her eyes and flapped a hand at the cooler. "Hey, Tyler, slide this in here." But before I could help her, Leslie whipped around from the driver's side of the car and eased the cooler into the trunk.

"Hey, Marta, listen: Julia and I are kind of wiped out," Leslie said. "I think we're gonna stay in tonight. You still want to go out?"

"Yeah. If you think I wanna hang around watching Lifetime with you guys, you're crazy."

"Well, why don't the two of you go out?" Julia pointed vaguely in my direction. "You could show Marta around town…right, Tyler?"

Leslie's smirking face and Julia's wide innocent eyes were all I needed to understand what they'd been giggling about as they walked to the car.

What the hell, I thought. It had been a while since I'd been out dogging around. I only hoped I wouldn't make a fool out of myself, like two weeks ago when I got so drunk I made up a poem about a chick's eyes and recited it to her while she fed quarters into the jukebox and tried to ignore me.

"Sure, why not?" I smiled. "In fact, Marta will probably never want to leave Sarasota after taking my deluxe tour of our fair city." Fuck Sarasota! As much as I hated to admit it, by this point I was hoping she'd never want to leave my *bed*.

Julia and Leslie exchanged knowing glances. "OK, then," Julia said. "Marta, you have my extra set of house keys, right?" Marta nodded. "All right, be good, then. We're probably going to bed early tonight, so just watch out for the kitties on your way in. They sleep like logs. See you in the morning."

Or early afternoon, I thought.

As Julia and Leslie started up the car and barreled off toward home, Marta turned toward me with a devilish grin. "Ready?"

"As I'll ever be," I told her.

"This is where the Sarasota Red Sox play," I said, pointing toward Ed Smith Stadium. "They're our minor league team. I go to all their home games."

Marta, looking out the window of my beat-up Ford pickup, said nothing. So, of course I had to say *something*.

"Yeah, the stadium has a seating capacity of 7,500..." I trailed off.

"That's great," she said.

I could tell she wasn't really interested. Especially since I'd been driving around Sarasota for nearly two hours, describing all of its four landmarks. Maybe I'd read her signals all wrong—which, by a long shot, wouldn't have been the first time.

"You want a tour of the go-cart track where I set the Florida speed record last summer?" My repertoire was definitely dwindling.

Out of the blue, Marta placed her hand on my thigh. "I'd rather have a tour of your apartment."

I didn't need any clarification. I put pedal to the metal and said nothing else until we pulled up to my one-bedroom off Bee Ridge Road. Marta's hand stuck to my thigh like glue the entire time.

Inside my sparse but clean apartment, I was about to offer Marta some coffee, but we didn't even make it to the kitchen. Immediately she pinned me to the foyer wall, her strong hands roving under my light blue muscle tee. "What a fucking excellent body you've got," she said. But before I could answer with a modest reply, she had her luscious lips on mine, her tongue fervently exploring my mouth. I was so hot it felt like someone had cranked the heat up in my apartment 90 degrees.

What little strength I had I used to maneuver Marta to the living room sofa, which was covered with some back issues of *Sports Illustrated* and *Girljock*. I quickly flung them to the floor and eased Marta onto her back. Straddling her, I helped her pull off her thin green tee. "Come on, babe, let's get that sports bra off," I told her. Like a pro, Marta whipped off the bra, and I zeroed in on her breasts, which were amazingly full for such an athletic woman. My tongue circled a dark brown nipple; my teeth bit it gently as I teased her with my hungry mouth. I was like a baby at the bottle—I couldn't get enough.

As I've said, I've never been attracted to other jocks, but this girl was definitely different. There was a certain sadness in her eyes; something told me she'd been hurt just as many times as I had, and that made her seem a little vulnerable, a little softer. But I could tell she was also a tough egg like me, and it would take a lot to make this one cry or even let her guard down. Maybe with some time…

I pulled off my muscle shirt to expose my own chest (I don't need to wear a bra at all), and soon we were breast to breast, our hot skin rubbing against each other. I slid a hand down Marta's nylon shorts—I could tell she wasn't a girl who needed a lot of foreplay—and eased a couple of fingers between her legs. Jesus Christ, it was like the Everglades down there; she was so wet I thought I'd need a paddleboat just to get around.

"Damn!" I whispered in her ear. "You are so fucking hot."

"Not half as hot as you, Tyler," she said, and pulled my face to hers. Our tongues did a wild, urgent dance. She playfully bit my lip as I eased two fingers into her wet, wet hole.

"More," she whispered.

I eased in one more.

"More," she groaned.

I slipped in another.

"Another," she cried.

Well, all that was left was my thumb, so I got down on the floor and kneeled. I'd never fisted a woman before, but if I was going to learn, it might as well be from this hot, athletic babe. As Marta pulled off her shorts and underwear, with my left hand I gripped the edge of the sofa cushion for balance, then squished up my fingers and pushed up far inside her. "Ball up your fingers now," Marta said.

"I've never done this before. I don't want to hurt you," I told her.

"Don't worry, baby. I'm a pro. And I never cry."

I balled my hand into a fist. I'd never been inside a woman this far before, except with a dildo. I couldn't believe how warm and wet she was inside. I eased back and forth inside her, my arm feeling like a giant cock or a snake, deftly exploring her and twisting inside her. With each gentle turn and thrust, Marta's face contorted, and a slew of curse words and religious terms came out: "Jesus fucking Christ Tyler holy shit you're so motherfucking hot sweet Jesus fuck me fuck my brains out fuck me hard shit Mother Mary fuck shit Jesus Christ." Then all of a sudden she screamed, "Harder!"

Cautiously, I increased my force a bit, my arm covered

with sticky girl-cum. She was like the freaking bottomless well of horniness. I felt her hot, silky cunt walls contract around my arm like they were holding onto me for dear life. Beads of perspiration trickled down her neck and onto her beautiful golden-brown abs. I was so fucking horny I couldn't stand it anymore, so I shoved my left hand down my shorts and rubbed myself furiously. Watching Marta's beautiful freckled face twist up in ecstasy was more than enough to make me cum, but I wanted some hands-on lovin', even if it was from my own hand. As I shoved my arm back and forth inside Marta's juicy, slippery snatch, I played with my swollen clit, flicking it back and forth, my cunt gushing like a waterfall.

"I'm coming, baby, I'm coming," she groaned.

"Jesus Christ, so am I." My clit was harder than I could remember it being in a long time—way harder than it had ever got with Jenna. It was pounding, throbbing, taking me to a place I don't recall ever being.

Marta was breathing in short gasps that matched the rhythm of my own. Together we rode an orgasmic tidal wave that ended with us both screaming out, "Jesus fucking Christ!" It's amazing how limited the dyke vocabulary becomes during unbelievably mind-blowing sex.

"Now, that's what I call a perfect spike," Marta laughed. But we weren't done yet. "I want to taste you. I want to eat you out. I want to make you cum," she whispered in my ear after I had collapsed on top of her.

We switched places, then Marta pulled off my shorts and drenched underwear. She spread open my legs and buried her face into my pussy. I was unbelievably wet. "I think I'm going to need a snorkel," Marta laughed, which of course cracked me up. But not for long. Marta's furious, skillful tongue slurped on my throbbing clit, which had barely had time for a siesta since our last bout. I grabbed the back of her head and pushed her gently into my pussy as she stuck her tongue into my hot hole. I guided her in and out of me, her long, thick tongue going in as far as humanly possible then coming out to labor on my clit. My hips rose to meet her hardworking mouth. "You taste so good. You *are* so good," she said between licking and sucking. "Just like Julia promised."

"What?" I barely made out, as Marta's hot, wet tongue probed my hole.

"It doesn't matter," she said.

"Tell me," I groaned. "But don't stop what you're doing." Sure, I was curious, but I wasn't about to let a little conversation delay my gratification.

Marta replaced her tongue with three fingers. As she slid them quickly in and out, she looked me directly in the eyes, as my hips bucked in response. "Julia bought my plane ticket down here, sweetie. She said we'd make a perfect match. And I couldn't agree more."

"So this whole thing was a set-up?" My cunt was pounding so hard I could barely talk.

"That's right, darling," Marta grinned. "And in the morning I'm going to write a long, long thank-you letter to Priceline.com. Now be quiet and let me do my job." Marta went back down on me, her mouth sucking and licking and flicking my red-hot, pulsing clit, her hands grabbing and fondling my taut breasts. With my right hand I pushed her sweaty head in deeper, felt her nose and mouth and chin nudging up and down into my cunt; her near-black hair fell in waves over my thighs. This babe wasn't just an athlete—no, she was an artist, the lezzie Leonardo Da Vinci of cunt licking—sucking, biting, and eating me out like I was the freakin' Last Supper, until I could stand no more and cried out in waves of nearly unbearable pleasure.

So was I mad at Julia for tricking me into this? Hell, no. As the saying goes, that's what friends are for. And did I give a damn about Jenna? Fuck, no. That's what new lovers are for. And would I get Marta to move from Charlotte to Sarasota? Shit, yeah. That's what U-Hauls are for.

And that's just what happened.

Mulligan on the Green Trixi

Mulligan wasn't a professional golfer; she was a professional fan. Her obsession with the sport began the day she watched her grandfather, decked out in his plaid knickers and matching hat, send the ball flying 150 feet for a hole in one. An Eagle, her mother leaned over and whispered in her ear.

From then on she watched him tee off every Wednesday and Friday night with her father, who was a lesser golfer but a better man, some said. She, however, found her grandfather thoroughly more engaging than her father; he was charming, suave, worldly, intellectual, a little off-color. He played the saxophone. He had once danced with Marilyn Monroe. Everyone at the club called her grandfather "Jeepers" because they wondered where he'd gotten his peepers—deep blue eyes rimmed with spring green.

Jeepers promised to take Mulligan golfing on her 12th birthday. She didn't sleep for two days before the big event. Spent the evening practicing her swing with a sawed-off broomstick. Ironed her beige church-going pants. Polished her sunglasses.

Mulligan stood beside her grandfather, never doubting for a moment she would love golfing. She was wrong. Mulligan hated the sun beating down and the number of times it took her to hit the ball—the ball that never sailed off in the right direction. Never. Hated the tepid applause from amused older men sailing by in their buggies, tipping their light-colored caps, smiling their urbane mustached smiles.

She hated the sport as a participating athlete, but this never dulled her love for it as a fan. The greatest fan Gulfport, Mississippi, ever saw. The girl always game for fetching a few balls. The cute redhead who clapped for everyone no matter how well they did. The Irish lassie sent to fetch more scotch for Jeepers.

As a child, Mulligan would breathlessly watch each ball jettison off into space then curve delicately to earth with a small thud and a roll. For Mulligan, the swing to the arc to the gentle contact with earth represented the purest form of elegance and style.

Even as an adolescent, she knew she would meet her great love on the golf course. And since most of the club's golfers were either married men or lesbians, it was fortunate Mulligan found herself reckoning with a strange attraction to women—specifically those bold broads who toted their heavy bags on muscular shoulders as they did rounds of tequila with Jeepers. The women her mother called "lizards" because of their leathery, tanned skin.

"It just doesn't look attractive for women to be so hard," she'd say.

"Mom," Mulligan whined in defense, "they're *golfers.*"

"I think they're lizards."

During Mulligan's 18th birthday party at the clubhouse, one of the younger, more handsome lizards came up and gave her (another) polo shirt. Later that night, Mulligan tried on her shirt and found a note clothespinned to the collar: *Come to Auntie Mame's later tonight, and us girls will buy you a beer for your birthday. They won't card you since the rest of us are regulars. —TeeTee*

TeeTee's real name was Tonya Treed. She'd been golfing for ten years, since she'd turned 15 and her family had moved up from the South. TeeTee was thin with firm arms, a chronically sunburned nose, and short blond hair. She wore a baseball cap with two golf tees side by side.

Mulligan hardly spoke to TeeTee, just enough to know her face. TeeTee was the quietest girl in a group of five who prowled the greens and the bar, laughing loudly with the men. She'd asked Mulligan to borrow her suntan lotion once since they shared the same pale complexion—though what Mulligan took for a sunburn was actually TeeTee's scarlet blush.

Mulligan put on her new polo with a pair of faded Levi's and set off for Auntie Mame's down by the river. The only lesbian bar in Gulfport, or at least the only one she'd heard about.

"Hey, Mulligan!" Sarah yelled from the pool table, waving her back.

"Hey!" Mulligan smiled.

Sarah and Elizabeth had just celebrated their eighth anniversary, and, surprisingly, didn't look like each other. They worked hard to maintain their separate identities, even refusing to share golf clubs. Sarah had short graying hair in contrast to Elizabeth's black bob. Both were in excellent shape, but each chose to display it her own way—Sarah wore T-shirts tucked in to tight jeans while Elizabeth poured herself into tight sweaters with baggy pants.

TeeTee stood beside Sarah and Elizabeth looking dapper in her overalls and black short-sleeved turtleneck with Anne (also known as "Bomber" for her hard drives). Bomber never dated—men or women. She'd play matchmaker then go home to her 13 cats and three dogs, claiming there was simply no more room left on the bed for a human being.

Mulligan walked up to TeeTee, ready to thank her for

the invitation when Bomber intercepted, "Come up to the bar, Missy, and let me get you your first birthday beer."

TeeTee turned around and chalked her stick, wondering why Anne stepped up when she knew TeeTee had a crush on Mulligan. Not that Mulligan would probably ever go for her anyway...no one was even sure she was gay, except Bomber. "I know these things," Bomber said. "My asexual persona gives me clear objective sight into these types of issues."

TeeTee was so shy she'd never ask anyone out—after months of talking about how cute Mulligan was and debating her sexual orientation, Bomber finally wrote the note, signed TeeTee's name, and pinned it on Mulligan's polo shirt. Now it was time to come clean.

"Listen, Mulligan, I don't mean to make you feel strange, but I have to 'fess up," Bomber told her at the bar. "*I* asked you to come along tonight, not TeeTee. But I only asked because TeeTee never would. She's got a huge crush on you..."

Mulligan looked back at TeeTee. She'd never considered dating a specific woman, just mulled over why she sparked up every time an attractive woman asked her to caddy. She looked over: TeeTee was beautiful. Rough and gentle and patient and understated with a quiet laugh. Suddenly, Mulligan wondered how it would feel to kiss her.

"I...ahum...I've never dated a woman before. But...I would...I would date TeeTee."

"Perfect! Now, don't let on that you know, OK?"

"OK..." She took the glasses while Bomber grabbed the margarita pitcher, splashing some on the counter.

Mulligan handed everyone a glass, leaving TeeTee's for last. "We weren't sure whether you liked strawberry or plain margaritas, so we went with strawberry since Bomber knew Sarah and Elizabeth liked strawberry…ahum…I hope that's OK—" Mulligan cut herself off, realizing she was beginning to ramble. Her nervous habit.

"Great, thanks." TeeTee looked in the empty glass. "I love strawberry, actually."

"Good…I'll grab the pitcher."

Bomber winked at Mulligan as Mulligan took the pitcher to TeeTee in the far corner. As Mulligan poured, TeeTee accidentally stepped back into a pool cue and broke off the tip. Her face flared red. "Oh, gosh… I'm never very good at indoor sports…" she said, rubbing the blue chalk from the wall.

"You meaning drinking?" Mulligan laughed.

"Yeah." TeeTee relaxed. "At least I didn't spill…"

"Then your priorities are in the right place."

The evening moved on with three games of pool (Bomber ran the table) and four pitchers. Mulligan stood in the corner with TeeTee, cheering Bomber's games and talking about her 12th birthday with Jeepers.

"I was so excited that I never even considered I might like everything about the game except *playing* it," Mulligan laughed.

"Oh, I knew I was addicted from the moment I stepped on the green," TeeTee smiled. "The solitude of the sport really appealed to my nature, in a way. The focus."

"When's your favorite time to play?"

"Definitely at night," TeeTee told her.

"Maybe when we're done here you could take me down and impress me," Mulligan flirted, to her own surprise.

TeeTee blushed again but met her eyes. "Sure. Let's go."

Bomber and Elizabeth behaved casually as the couple

walked out, but Sarah nudged TeeTee until she thought she would faint from embarrassment.

"She's got a mean streak," Mulligan laughed.

"Oh—tell me," TeeTee sighed dramatically.

They walked down a long tree-lined street toward the gate with its huge black lettering spelling GCC for Gulfport Country Club. "Not a terribly original name," Mulligan said.

"Better than Hall of Pretension," TeeTee smiled.

Moist, warm Mississippi winds stirred around them as they made their way to a wooded area far from the die-hards still slicing away on the putting green. The silence was calming, welcoming. TeeTee pointed to a tree-filled spot darker than the rest of the well-lit course. "Let's go sit down."

The two forgot the lawns were watered every evening at sunset, so when they sat down on the grass their pants got soaked. "Oh, shit, I'm sorry," TeeTee bumbled.

"No problem."

"I frustrate myself. Such a klutz... Whatever. Let's just go."

"Hey, ho, slow down," Mulligan smiled.

"I didn't even realize you were coming tonight, and then Bomber told me she gave you a note, and then I took you here...but I'm just not prepared."

Then Mulligan kissed her. Simple as that.

To Mulligan's delight, TeeTee's confidence obviously lay in the sexual arena. She turned her over and kissed her passionately, moving to her earlobes. No shyness here. Mulligan felt TeeTee's breath on her neck, warming her despite the cold water on her back.

"Can I touch you?" TeeTee asked.

"Yes..."

Her hands moved slowly under Mulligan's polo as she bit gently on her throat. Mulligan bent her legs and pulled TeeTee's hips in to hers.

TeeTee leaned up on one hand and looked Mulligan in the eye as she pulled up her shirt and unsnapped the front clasp of her black bra revealing perfect pink nipples and freckled breasts. She maintained eye contact while her fingers brushed Mulligan's nipples, then she bent over to kiss them.

Mulligan lifted her hips unconsciously and pushed TeeTee's head down to let her know she wanted harder kisses, more sucking, biting. TeeTee responded by biting her just enough to cause the perfect mix of pain and pleasure.

The line of Mulligan's jeans rubbed her where she was most sensitive. She wanted TeeTee's hand there. Wanted to feel her fingers push inside her. Her mouth. Her tongue.

Mulligan brought TeeTee's hand down to rub along the seam. She kissed her stomach, then asked if she could undo her pants.

"Yes," Mulligan said. "You don't have to ask...everything's yes."

"Well, OK then." TeeTee popped Mulligan's top button and pulled down her zipper. She wiggled the denim down her hips then leaned back over her, burying her fingers in Mulligan's soft curls. She delicately spread her open to run her fingers along the wet inside. Teasing her opening, bumping her clit. Pushing her index finger inside... for just a moment.

Going this slowly made Mulligan want it faster. TeeTee sensed her need and responded by driving her fingers roughly inside her wet pussy. Mulligan sucked in a breath of air, surprised by the jolt that ran through her body.

TeeTee pulled out and rubbed Mulligan's swollen clit up and down until she joined in the rhythm. She kept her hand still while Mulligan found her own pace and took control. Mulligan gripped the cold, damp grass with her hands, all attention focused on the movement of her hips against TeeTee's fingers.

Within minutes, Mulligan held her breath, tipped her head back, and pressed TeeTee's finger down on her clit. TeeTee took over, moving in quick circles until Mulligan came hard and fast. She shivered, almost ready to go again.

Then they heard the rumbling and squeaking of a golf bag's wheels coming up on the ninth hole. TeeTee sat up. "Shit." She poked her head between the trees and saw Jeepers pulling Mrs. Chamberlain's bag.

He gestured toward their trees. Mulligan saw him wheeling her way and grabbed TeeTee's hand. They dashed off, hoping Jeepers and Mrs. Chamberlain hadn't seen them. They ran all the way back to the clubhouse then collapsed at the bar in a fit of laughter.

"My grandfather!"

"And Mrs. Chamberlain—oh, my god!"

TeeTee went over to the bar and bought them a beer. She set Mulligan's down in front of her then leaned over and whispered in her ear, "I want to finish what we started."

"So do I...but how about we have a date first?"

"OK...how about...ahum...I have these tickets for a weekend. The girls bought me... My birthday is next week—"

"Yes," Mulligan finally interrupted. "I'll go to Dinah Shore weekend with you."

"Did Bomber tell you?"

"Yeah... when you went up to get another round for us, she said she was trying to get you to take me."

"We'll have to buy her something nice...like a lady for herself," TeeTee laughed. They picked up their beers, toasted each other, then looked out across the course, wondering when they'd see Jeepers and Mrs. Chamberlain coming out from the trees.

Bull Rider Sacchi Green

Amsterdam.

Amster-god-fucking-*damn!*

Sin City of the '70s, still sizzling in the '80s. Cheap pot you could smoke in the coffeehouses, but that's not what lit my fire. Sex shows and leather-toy shops? Coming a whole lot closer—but what really ignited a slow burn low in my Levi's were stories of how the working girls displayed their wares behind lace-curtained windows. Something about the dissonance between elegance and raunch struck a chord. "Fine old buildings," ice maiden Anneke had told some of the Australian riders, with her Mona Lisa smile and a sidelong glance at me. "Many visitors tour the Red Light district just to view the…architecture."

Maybe I should have tried harder to figure out Anneke. A damn fine rider, in total control of herself and her mount, she was all blond and pink and white with cool, butter-wouldn't-melt-in-her-mouth self-possession. But a certain preppy princess with a long chestnut ponytail and a cute round ass—and delusions of being a world-class equestrienne—had been using up too much of my energy at the time.

That was all over now. With a vengeance. A fair share of it was mine, true; I still needed to drown my sorrows in whatever fleshpots I could find. I was not going to leave Europe without at least a taste of decadence.

But you don't get to taste much without a few guilders clinking in the pockets of your jeans. Which I didn't have.

Damn near didn't even have the jeans. First French tourist jerk-off to point at my ass and say, " 'Ow much?" came close to losing his business hand. "*Chienne! Pour les Levi's!*" he hissed, rubbing his numbed wrist.

"More than you've got!" I stepped away, and he scurried in front of me with a fistful of bills. "No way," I said, lengthening my stride until he dropped back. Before I made it across the Central Station plaza, I'd had two more offers, Spanish and Japanese, and damn sure would have taken one if I had any alternate covering for my BVDs. But after that fiasco at the equestrian tournament, I'd left behind everything except my hat, buckskin pants, and fringed jacket. And I'd pawned the leathers to raise my plane fare home. Too damn cheaply, if even torn jeans reeking of horses and stable muck were in this much demand.

Maybe the stable muck was the selling point. Authenticity. I could've made a fortune if I'd known enough to dirty more jeans! The question now was, could I parlay all that authenticity into getting laid? I had 24 hours before my flight to find out. And a conniving little preppie to purge from my system.

Oh, hell, there it went again, like a movie in my head. My jaw and fists clenched—and my clit too—as I sat on a bench at the edge of the square and spread a map across my knees. I lowered my head as though the names of streets, canals, and landmarks were all I saw.

She'd planned it from the start. All those weeks spent coaching her to signal the horse with her knees, to wrap her thighs, naked and moist, around my neck, to lift her tight little butt in rhythm with the horse's gait, to tilt her hips to the thrust of my demanding hand—and all along she'd known the moment would come.

She'd been about to come herself, which only made her moment better. I saw it in her eyes as they went from deep and velvety to glittering and triumphant. She focused on something over my shoulder. My fingers slowed, and she switched all her attention back to me. "Eat me, Toby! Eat me!" she commanded, pushing my head toward her pussy. The musk of sex and the rich aromas of hay and horses blended into a powerful aphrodisiac. I delayed a moment, inclined to make her beg; then she flicked her little pink tongue over her lips like a kitten licking drops of cream, and I forgot everything but getting my own mouth into her cream, and my own tongue deeply into where it would do the most good.

She had never wriggled with more abandon, never let her gasps and moans and ultimate shrieks rip so free. No faking it either. Her internal spasms surged right through her pussy into my mouth and hands and rocked me to my toes, but it was no tribute to my skill. When I came up for air I saw her eyes fixed again on someone behind me, and a look on her face like the proverbial cat who's deep-throated the canary.

Some instinct made me roll away just before his fist could connect. It's a wrench to shift from surging lust to fight-or-flight, but I made it fast enough to have ten feet and the business end of a hay fork between us before he could swing again. I recognized him from the picture she'd shown me. Charles, the fiancé. I almost felt sorry for him.

"You goddamn fucking dyke!" he sputtered at me, as much pain as rage in his voice.

"Oh, Chub, do you always have to state the obvious?" Miss Ponytail languorously brushed hay out of her chestnut hair. "Afraid you can't do as well as a stable hand?"

Stable hand. I swung the hay fork toward her and then back toward Chub's more physical threat.

I'd worked my way through the same elite Eastern women's college she was lounging through. Stable hand, stable manager, eventually assistant riding coach; what she called me didn't matter as much as the contempt in her tone.

"So, Chub," I said, "let me know if you need any more pointers." I hurled the fork just barely over his head into the bales of hay behind him, and got out of there fast before he could pick himself up off the floor.

Any sympathy evaporated late that night when he caught me alone in the barn and came at me with rage in his eyes and a serious bulge in his pants. Poor dumb bastard. I left him hurting so bad he wasn't going to have the means to please Miss Preppy anytime soon.

If I'd left it at that, I might still have been able to fly back to the States on the chartered plane with the rest of the equestrian team. If I hadn't charged into the Bitch Princess's room, pressed her face into the pillow, immobilized her with my knee between her shoulder blades, and taken my knife to that long chestnut hair until no fancy hairdresser was going to be able to conceal all the ragged gaps without cropping it even shorter than mine, the police and the International Equestrian Organization officials wouldn't have been called into it. But I did, and they were, and I barely got away ahead of arrest with my passport and leather duds and the clothes I'd been wearing to load the horses into the vans for the transport plane.

So here I was in Amsterdam. (I'd fed the chestnut hair strand by strand to the wind from the back of some Hungarian biker dude's motorcycle—he'd picked me up hitching on the outskirts of The Hague.) The breeze here in the city was light, smelling of canals and the ocean, but I folded my map and stood and ran my fingers through my hair and tried to imagine the hot scent of her expensive perfume and that greedy pussy being blown away over the North Sea.

Then I headed for the Walletjes Red Light District in search of replacement memories.

OK, decadence is a subjective concept. Packaged, health department–inspected sex doesn't do that much for me, and the cruising scene seemed to be—no surprise—mainly the boy-meets-boy variety. There had to at least be a women's bookstore somewhere; I can handle that scene, as long as I can steer the conversation to the better bits of Colette, just as I can coach show riding and could compete myself if I could afford a show-class horse, even though at heart I'm Western all the way. But literary foreplay, especially with language barriers, wasn't what I had in mind.

The ladies of the night weren't disappointing, exactly; the tall, elegant windows glowed with discreetly red-tinted light, and the flesh casually displayed was enticing enough. One brunette dressed only in a long white man's shirt saw my interest and treated me to a knowing smile over her shoulder as she straddled a chair and did a slow grind on its plumply upholstered seat. But a paying customer caught the vibes and knocked on her door. After a close look, he invited me to come in too; I declined. The window shade came down. I moved on.

The neighborhood provided plenty of rosy-fleshed occasions for fantasy, but none of the others quite did it for me. I began to have a sneaking suspicion that one particular pink and white and blond vision had been making my subconscious simmer. I sure as hell wasn't going to find her here, but I might know where I could. For all the good it would do me.

Anneke had always been civil but reserved. Once, when I'd helped her with an emergency repair in the tack room, she'd said, "Toby, you should be riding that fine horse, not her," with a nod of her head toward Miss Preppie.

"Could never afford it." I wrestled with multiple interpretations. Riding the horse instead of riding the girl?

"No, nor could I." Her trace of accent was tantalizing. "The brewing firm I work for keeps a show stable for...what is it in English? Public relations?"

"That's it," I said. "You work for them? I thought you must be family."

"No, I work summers in their Amsterdam clubs, as bookkeeper and assistant manager. The newest is a country-western bar on Warmoesstraat, all the rage, like that movie *Urban Cowboy*. They would go crazy for you there, Toby!"

Then she was gone, and like an idiot, I didn't follow up. Now it hit me hard just who I wanted to go crazy for me, just what smooth, white skin I wanted to raise a flush on, what cool, half-smiling lips I wanted to suck and bite until they were red and swollen and begging for more. And whose butter I wanted to melt in my mouth.

How hard could it be to find a country-western bar in Amsterdam? I even remembered the name of the street. Had she meant me to? Anneke had always been so collected, so focused on her riding. Maybe I'd been afraid to try anything.

The neon outline of a rodeo bull rider told me I'd found the right place. I hesitated in the doorway, well aware that I didn't have the means to buy a lady a beer, and even if I did, this might be the kind of place where a move like that could get me thrown out. Then again, the way the people inside were rigged out in wannabe Western gear, where could I get more mileage out of my battered hat and authentically work-worn (and pungent) denim vest and jeans?

It was early, but crowds were building. Behind the bar a large woman with a generous display of pillowy breasts scanned the room as she wiped the countertop. When her gaze crossed mine it moved on, stopped for a beat, then swung back.

Without looking away, she pulled a phone from under the counter and spoke briefly into it. *Oh, shit*, I thought. *Are the police here looking for me?* My "victims" couldn't have wanted that much publicity. Then a grin lit her round-cheeked face as she replaced the phone and beckoned to me. I might've resisted the good-humored gleam in her eyes, but the foaming stein of beer she offered was something else again. I hadn't had anything to eat in almost 24 hours, and nothing to drink but water from public fountains.

"On the house, honey." Her name tag read MARGARETHA, but her accent said New York. "You look like you might liven this place up. Ever ride one of those?"

I followed the jerk of her head. Through a wide archway I saw, rising above the sawdust on the floor like some futuristic mushroom, a mechanical bull just like the one Travolta and Winger ride in *Urban Cowboy*.

I wiped beer foam off my mouth. "You mean, does my ass live up to the advertising of my Levi's? Lady, you have no idea."

"Don't bet on it, darlin'." Her assessing look informed me one way or another, a good time could definitely be had. Much as I appreciate older women, though—hell, one saved me from fratricide—my hopes for something else grew. If it wasn't the police she'd called, who on this continent but Anneke would have described me to her?

"Yeah," I said, "I've ridden those, and the snorting, stomping, shitting versions too. For another beer and some of those hefty pretzels, I'd be glad to demonstrate."

"Wait a while." She refilled my stein and slid me a bowl of pretzels and cheese-flavored breadsticks, and I did my best not to stuff myself. Some things are better on a less-than-full stomach. Bull riding is only one of them.

"So, where are you from, Toby?" she asked, chatting me up while keeping a close eye on the door.

"Montana," I said. I hadn't told her my name.

"They let women ride bulls in rodeos there?" she asked.

"Not yet. Not officially. Except at small local shindigs where anything goes." I paid close attention to my beer and pretzels, not wanting to talk much about it. But there was no way I could keep from remembering the surge of wild triumph when I outrode them all, even my brother Ted—the pounding of my blood, the pressure building until I had to explode or die—and the revelation that, to achieve explosion, I needed to wrap myself around Cindy's full, smooth curves.

Back when we were 12, Cindy hadn't minded a little mutual exploration. She'd been away for a few years, though, and this time, as I tried to pull her close, she twisted away and ran around the grandstand to throw herself on Ted. Another revelation—that life was a bitch—seared me. However much I could work like a man, even beat the men at their own games, their rewards were officially off limits to me.

I was only 17 then, and the shock filled me with rage. I

leapt for my brother, and only the intervention of Miss Violet Montez, sultry lead singer for the intermission entertainment act, kept me from killing him.

"Hey, Tigrina, come with me." She pressed herself against me as Ted struggled to get up. "I have what you need. And what you don't even know you need." And she surely did, or close enough.

When I rode back to the ranch at daybreak, too drained to sort out the remnants of pleasure and pain and smoldering resentment, Daddy was waiting in the barn. He couldn't quite meet my eyes. "Looks like maybe you'd better go East to school the way your Mama always wanted."

"Looks like," I agreed. And that was that. Someday I'll find the words to tell him that it wasn't his fault. I'd never have survived being raised any other way. And how could he, after letting me know all my life I could do anything a man could do, tell me that the one thing I couldn't have was a woman of my own?

Besides, he'd have been wrong. Going to a women's college didn't make a lady of me, but I sure learned a lot about women.

Not that there isn't always more to learn.

Anneke came through the door and stood for a minute, cool as ever, with just a hint of defiance. "I'll be damned!" Margaretha muttered from behind the bar. "I knew you'd made an impression, but jeez!" From the dropped jaws and arrested strides of several waiters I got the feeling that they weren't used to seeing Anneke in tight, scant denim cutoffs and a gingham blouse molded to all the delectable curves not peeking out over her plunging neckline.

Body by Daisy Mae, face by Princess Grace. A divine dissonance, but what the hell was I supposed to do with it in a public place and a culture I didn't wholly understand?

I sure had to do something, though, with the surge of energy pounding through my body. "Maybe it's time for a ride," I growled and jerked my head toward the room with the bull.

"Good idea." Margaretha shoved some coins at me across the bar. "Go for it!" As I turned away, she grabbed my shoulder and swung me back. "Take it a little easy. She may not admit it, but she's new to this." She didn't mean the bull.

I set the controls on "extreme" and vaulted aboard the broad wooden back, my hat held high in the traditional free-arm gesture. It was a damn good thing the bull was mechanical; my body could handle all the twists and lurches without involving my brain. Matching wits with a live, wily, determined bull would've taken concentration I couldn't spare, with Anneke on my mind.

I was vaguely aware that a crowd had gathered, the music was "The Devil Went Down to Georgia," and Anneke was leaning against a nearby post watching with her Mona Lisa smile. Less vaguely, I realized I was going to be sore tomorrow—though nowhere near as sore as I'd like to be unless some vital moves were made. When my wooden mount slowed to a stop and the room held still, I tossed my hat toward Anneke, who caught it deftly and allowed her smile to widen. Then I shifted my ass backward to make room and held out a hand to her. With no hesitation she let me pull her up to straddle the bull.

Someone, maybe Margaretha, put more money in the machine and set it on "easy': The music changed to "Looking for Love in All the Wrong Places," and I was in the kind of trouble worth dreaming about.

Riding without stirrups can be an erotic experience all by itself. Riding with Anneke's ass pressed into me, kneading my crotch with every heave of the bull, was sublime torture. Her slim back against my breasts made them demand a whole lot more of my attention than they usually get, while her luscious breasts...I nuzzled my face against her neck and gazed over her shoulder at the rounded flesh gently bouncing and threatening to surge out of the low neckline. From my vantage point, glimpses of tender pink nipple came and went. Much as I wanted more, I didn't necessarily want to share.

"Your décolletage is slipping," I whispered into her ear. Instead of adjusting it, she turned her head so her smooth cheek curved against my lips.

"Help me, Toby," she murmured. "Hold me." And I was lost.

I cupped her breasts, gently at first, as the motion of the bull made them rise and fall and thrust against their thin gingham covering. Then I felt her back arch slightly, and her flesh press more demandingly into my hands. There was no way I could help moving my fingers across her firming nipples. I felt her soft gasp all the way down to my toes.

Her ass began to move against me independent of the bull's motion. My clit felt like it was trying to scorch a passage through my Levi's. My grip on her breasts tightened, and her nipples hardened and pulsed against my fingers as she leaned her head against my shoulder. "Toby," she breathed. "You are making me so sore!"

"Want me to stop?" I teased her tender earlobe with my teeth.

"No...don't stop...make me sorer still, please, Toby..."

How could I refuse? I unbuttoned her blouse at the waist

and slid my hands across her silky belly before filling them with the even silkier flesh of her breasts. Then I drove her to as much sweet, sore engorgement as hands alone could provide. My hungry mouth made do with the soft hollows and curves of her neck and shoulders, feeling the nearly soundless moans she couldn't suppress vibrate directly from her body into mine. Her pale hair was coming loose from its intricate chignon, so I pulled out the fastenings with my teeth and let the golden curtain fall across the marks my mouth left on her skin. Her hair gave off the faint, clean scent of herbs and roses.

I hadn't forgotten our audience, but I was beyond caring. During my first wild ride there'd been whoops and cheering, but when Anneke joined me the sounds had dwindled to a low hum, an almost communal moan. Somebody put more coins in the machine, and "Looking for Love in All the Wrong Places" was still playing.

My problem was the accelerating need to get right down to it in ways even permissive Amsterdam couldn't handle. Or, if it could, I couldn't.

"We have to get out of here," I growled against Anneke's cheek. She gave a slight nod.

"Soon," she said, with a shuddering sigh. "Help me turn." I admired her flair for showmanship as she swung one leg over the pommel, poised briefly in sidesaddle position, twisted so that her hands could brace against my shoulders, and pushed herself up and over until she was facing me astride.

OK. A little more for the paying customers. Just a little. My hat, now upside down on the floor, had become a target for a fair number of coins and bills.

I urged Anneke's legs up over my thighs and got a firm

grip on her waist. She leaned her head back as I savagely pressed my mouth into the hollow of her throat and let anger flicker through desire. New to this, was she? New to what? Performing with a woman? What had she done here with men?

My mouth moved down, and Anneke leaned farther back, both of us as balanced as if our moves had been choreographed and rehearsed a hundred times. I tore at her shirt with my teeth until the buttons let go and I could get at her arched belly. A collective sigh rose from the audience as the fabric slid aside to leave her round breasts and jutting, rose pink nipples naked. I knew what they wanted, but there was only just so much I could share.

She lay so far back now that her legs were around my hips and only my grip kept her upper body from sliding off the gently heaving bull. I probed my tongue into the ivory rosebud whorl of her navel as her thighs tightened and jerked.

My clit jerked too. I ran my mouth down to the waistband of her shorts and then over the zipper, biting down gently just where the seam pressed against her clit. The fabric was wet and getting wetter. Our musk rose like a tangible cloud, mixed with the scent of roses and the earthy reek of the stables.

I bit down harder, tugged at the thick seam, pressed it into her, and knew by the spasmodic thrusts of her hips I could make her come right now, right here. And knew I wasn't going to.

I may have a streak of exhibitionism as wide as the Montana sky, but some desires are too deep, too intense, too close to the limits of self-control for any but private performance. I pulled Anneke upright and kissed her long and hard, letting her feel the sharpness of my teeth. "There's an old showbiz saying," I said against her mouth, my voice harsher than intended. "Always leave 'em wanting more."

I swung us both to the floor and stood, still holding her in my arms until the ground stopped heaving under my feet. Her legs tightened around my waist, as her arms did around my neck, reminding me, for all the enticing tenderness of her flesh, that she was a world-class athlete. The dazed look in her blue eyes retreated slightly. "But Toby, what if *I* want more?"

"You'd damned well better want more. You're going to get it. But not here." I started toward the door, not knowing where I was going. Hands reached out as we passed. Some just stroked us, some stuffed money into my jeans.

Margaretha called out; Anneke turned, laughed, and caught the big old-fashioned key spinning toward her through the air. She shouted something in Dutch, and thrust the cold iron down inside the waistband of my BVDs. It slid, of course, much lower, producing new and interesting sensations when we ran hand in hand through the Amsterdam night.

The little houseboat rose and fell gently on the moonlit canal. Anneke went down the steps to the deck, turned, caught me by the hips, and burrowed her face into the crotch of my jeans. My legs nearly failed me.

"Mmm," she said, inhaling deeply. "I never thought to breathe anything as sweet as the smell of a horse. But mixed with the scent of a woman..." All her cool reserve had melted. She looked up at me with eyes darkened by night and arousal, and just a trace of laughter on lips still swollen from my kiss. "I never thought to touch a woman, either, until I had such dreams of you I thought I must go mad!"

I came down the last few steps and pressed her against the low door to the living quarters, trying desperately to feel in control of a dangerously reeling world. When I kissed her as gently as I could, her tongue came tentatively to mine and my clit lurched as though it, too, had been touched.

"But Toby," she whispered, turning her mouth away just enough to speak, "I must get the key! I must…is it all right?" She touched my crotch lightly, then drew her hand up along my zipper to my belt.

"Yes…" I managed to gasp. It wouldn't have been all right for anyone else. Even now, I couldn't let her slide her hand down into my pants before I had mine deeply in hers. It was too late for control—I knew I was going to lose it any second, going to come at the touch of her fingers on my throbbing, aching clit—but I'd be damned if I was going to come alone.

Experience counts for something. And Anneke wasn't wearing a belt. I had my whole hand curved around her pussy before she'd gotten farther than the waistband of my briefs. She gasped, and paused, as I worked my fingers between her folds, not penetrating yet—the night was still young—just gently massaging the increasing wetness and circling her clit with my thumb tip. She arched her hips forward, but her hand slid down over my mound, and in desperation to distract her—and myself—I lowered my mouth to one breast and licked at her pink nipple until it was hard and straining. Then I sucked her, hard and harder, biting a little, and she pressed herself deeper in to my mouth. Her gasping breaths turned into deep moans, but her hand still moved down and her fingers curved in imitation of mine.

I pressed my fingers deeper, moved my thumb faster, harder, demandingly against her clit, and her fingers moved too, tentatively, but more than enough to push me to the edge. The iron key, shoved back now between my ass cheeks, only intensified the sensations.

I had to cheat. I gripped her wrist with my free hand and raised my head. "Wait," I said against her lips. "Just feel, feel it all." Then I covered her mouth with mine and sucked and bit and probed and worked my whole hand back and forth in her slippery depths, spreading her juices up over her straining clit, stroking faster and faster until she spasmed against me and sobbed into my hungry mouth. I let her pull away enough to breathe.

"Toby," she gasped, "please, let me, I have to...let me touch you!" She struggled to move her hand against my grip.

I had to let her. And had to bury my face in her soft neck in a vain attempt to muffle the raw cries tearing through me on waves of explosive release.

She withdrew her hand, and the dripping key, slowly and sensuously. "Oh, yes," she sighed, "much, much better than the dreams. And there is more?"

"More," I assured her, still breathing hard. "All you can handle. This was just a taste."

She smiled wickedly and touched her tongue to the key. "A fine taste!" Then she turned, and the door swung open.

In the snug interior, lit by a hanging lantern, I opened her to pleasures she hadn't yet dreamed of. I took it a little easy, since she was, after all, new to this; then as her demand grew, she drove me to extremes. And invented new ones. Being with someone whose strength approached mine, who, like me, had as great a hunger to touch as to be touched, was a new and disconcerting experience.

By morning, when Margaretha stopped by with some

coffee and hot rolls and my hat filled with cash, we were both sore and exhausted. And as high as if we'd just won the gold.

"Take all this." I dumped the money on the bed between Anneke's splayed legs. "If my half is enough, could you get my leathers out of hock and send them to me? I'll find the pawn ticket…in a minute…if I ever manage to move…"

"Maybe I can find a way to deliver them in person." Anneke rolled over to straddle my thigh. "You won't mind, Toby, if I wear those snug trousers a bit, maybe ride in them? And think of you, and get them very, very wet?"

"We could send them back and forth," I said, "until they're seasoned enough to travel on their own. But in person would be a damn sight better." I found the energy to flip her over; maybe the coffee was kicking in. I nuzzled my face into the pale-gold fur adorning her finely seasoned pussy. "How wet did you have in mind?" Exhaustion forgotten, I was ready to ride again. And to be ridden.

Turned Out Kirsten Imani Kasai

I have a friend, Mel.

My kickboxing partner. Met in class, hit it off right away, and the rest, as they say, is history. Mel drives me crazy. I think she knows it too, though she feigns ignorance. We work out together twice a week, getting hot, sweaty, lathered. I love the sheen on her lips, cheeks flushed red, hair damp beneath her helmet, that fierce don't-fuck-with-me look in her eyes raising chills over my already tingling skin. She calls my name while we spar, egging me on: "Violet, Violet." Hissing through clenched teeth as she dances around me, gloves up in front of her face, walloping me with a strong kick and nearly toppling me. Often I end up on the mat, distracted and weak-kneed, lacking concentration, grappling for some short measure of restraint to reel in my fleeting self-respect. She likes to pound me and probably considers me a poor opponent.

Mel doesn't yet know I have a secret weapon (my tongue), doesn't realize she's baiting a tiger when she teases me in the locker room, peels off her wet clothes, drops them in a sweaty pile on the puddled, concrete floor, shakes out her long, dark hair (black or chocolate brown, depending on the light), and ducks under the jet of a steaming shower.

I watch, sometimes covertly, sometimes openly, unabashedly, my eyes narrowing to cold dark stars as water droplets halo her beautiful face. Mel doesn't know (or perhaps she's pretending again) that I watch her, that I covet the pleasure of mining the hot, pink cave of her mouth, winding myself around her like an amorous cat around the sugared tower of her body. See, Mel's a straight girl. But I know better. I know there's a tenuous pane of resistance, a delicate membrane to be punctured with deliberate force, or alternately dissolved beneath a torrent of sweet suggestion, that will woo her into submission, recognition. I dream of turning her out.

I shower a few stalls away, deep in my protective bubble with my gaze lowered as she soaps herself, white suds sliding over her hard, lithe body, foam obscuring her fine, upstanding little tits and slim, boyish hips. We turn off the water, exit laughing, making small talk. Watching. The gym is nearly empty. It's gorgeous outside. No one wants to be indoors breathing sweat-sock air. I hear Danny in the other room slinging equipment into the metal cage, locking up all the boxers' supplies. Waiting for us to finish up and leave. We dress, head for the mirror, still chatting; she brushes her hair up into a severe ponytail while I run careless fingers through my own short crop. I say it's a beautiful day, and we agree to get a beer. Neither of us has anywhere to go. It's hot and muggy out. I want to lick cherry vanilla ice cream from her taut navel, glide ice cubes across her jutting collarbone. We go to Clio's across the street; the transition from dusty, sun-drenched sidewalks to the cool, beer-funked must of the bar is startling but good. I like that tangy, almost pissy beer-smell in the air; it's portentously friendly, smoothly promising good things to come. I intend to take up the offer.

Mel and I take a corner booth. We're both hungry after our workout, but I have far more on my mind than burgers and fries. I like the way she drinks, leaning into it with gusto, relishing her cold pint, greedily licking foam from the corners of her mouth. Mel's the perfect combination of hard and soft, butch and femme. She can't wear slinky dresses and would surely break her neck in a pair of heels, but she looks shit hot in a pair of tight trousers and a man's undershirt. She's ripe with bravado, almost to the point of being a show-off as she leaps from the high dive, less concerned with form than making a big splash, like when she kicks my ass in the ring. I thrill to watch her rub on strawberry kiddie lip-gloss with her pinkie and marvel over her cooing, endless fascination with bubble bath and candy-scented soaps. She has a fetish for girly trinkets, crinkly, cellophane-wrapped sweets, stuffed toys. She smells good all the time.

Mel regards me with an expression I've never seen before. Her pretty golden green eyes glitter in the dim light.

"Violet," she says.

I nod, my throat suddenly dry, tight.

Beneath her jaw is a hollow of dancing shadows. Setting sun is electrifying the horizon, the bar filling up with noisy patrons clinking glasses, laughing low. Rowdies orbit the pool table.

"I have to go to the ladies'. Come with?"

Sure, I'll come with you.

We go to the back, pushing through ribbons of blaring disco, the dance floor filled with happy-hour oyster slurpers, giddily sucking down raw aphrodisiac half shells with lemon and Tabasco-stained fingers. Salt-crusted margarita glasses litter the bar; a cool breeze wafts in from the patio. The bathrooms are the kind where there's just one toilet and sink in a room, like somebody's house. The hall's dark, and Mel's singing along with the Commodores, her throaty voice hitting all the right notes. Once in, I turn my back, fidgeting in the mirror, waiting for her to finish, but I don't hear anything. I turn halfway round, Mel's hot stare sending chills down my neck, that same flat, unreadable expression she gets while plotting her strategy. Just before she decks me. I'm such a sucker, I like it.

"Yeah?" I say. Perfectly nonchalant, as if I have no clue.

"I've seen you, Violet, seen the way you look at me."

"Like I'm starving," I whisper.

She's surprised; maybe she thought I'd play her little party game, not cop to my attraction.

"Yeah," she laughs, unsure of herself. "Like you're going to eat me up."

"I'm going to eat you alive." And I pounce forward, unsettling her placid reserve. She stiffens. Her nipples rise like candy buttons under her shirt, and it pleases me. Immensely.

Mel once told me she wasn't interested in sex; a message relayed in the tone of voice one would use to say, "I don't care for blackberries" or "I like blue pens." I'd inquired why her so-fine self was yet unclaimed and she'd shrugged her shoulders. "Not into that." End of discussion. Maybe she doesn't like to get her hands dirty. Maybe she's never come before, except in that quick, fluttering, over-and-done-with way of some little rutting animal. Maybe she's never had a bone-jarring, grind-your-teeth, mind-altering explosion rock her fucking world, set it on edge and leave her feeling as though she's just swum the English Channel. I know how she fucks from the way she fights. Hard. Strategic, abandoning herself to the moment of the exchange, pulling no punches. It's why I want her, why I lust for her until the pain of my need requires a vibrating Band-Aid, why I'm now standing with my breasts just beginning to press up into her, where I can feel the heat radiate from her eager skin. Mel's having a hard time breathing.

"Did you want something, baby?' I ask, pressing harder. I'm about ready to come in my pants, she's got me going so, standing there with her back up against the graffitied wall, her red lips parted, ragged breaths moist on my neck. I say, "Damn it," grinding my body into her, liking that I'm bigger, a little softer, stronger than her, though I've never let on to my strength.

"Did you want something?" I ask again, pushing against her resistance, willing it to give way because she's pleading with me, her golden eyes molten, burning.

"Tell me," I prod, glad I'm packing tonight (I'd stayed behind, slipped into my strap-on while she booked ring time from Danny), my bare hips in baggy jeans grinding hers, my wet cunt riding her thigh, craving her virginal fingers in my hole. I want her so bad, but like in the ring, I must allow her lead. Mel not moving, perhaps considering.

"Thought not," and I draw back, make a move toward the door.

"Violet," she murmurs, her husky voice like raw silk against my flesh.

"Don't call something unless you want it to come," I warn from my post by the door. I can hear impatient, full-bladdered females whining on the other side.

"Come," she says.

I amble across the tiny room, luxuriating in her look of growing impatience, need, fear. I'm so hungry and she's like the last piece of cake; I don't know whether to devour her or savor her. Her lips tremble, her eyes are huge and glossy. She wants this. I step up to the plate, slide a thigh between hers. Cup her damp crotch in my hand, her pussy hot even through her clothes. Rubbing it, liking the feel of her. Someone bangs impatiently on the door.

"Guess she'll have to use the men's," I murmur, unzipping Mel's trousers. I slip my hand into the panties I watched her put on, deep into her syrupy slit, getting a feel for the lay of the land. Her ass quivers against the cold wall. I kneel, kneading her wet meat, stroking her clit growing hard between my fingers, slipping my tongue between her lips, sucking her clit, fucking her with my hand. I'm such a glutton, I went straight for the frosting. She tastes sweet. I come up licking my lips, raise her shirt, her belly so smooth and fine, her hard little breasts just like sour green apples in my mouth. Her mouth, at last warm and receptive, pliant under mine, her tongue a slippery red oyster I long to swallow.

Girls pound the door. "What are you doing in there?"

"Sorry, I'm sick," I answer through mouthfuls of Mel.

I wind her silky ponytail around my wrist, tugging her head back, her scalp pulled so taut it practically goes *ping!* I kiss her cheeks, lips, ears, bite the thin skin of her delicate neck, making Mel moan involuntarily. She struggles, but I've got her pinned against the bathroom wall. She gives up and simply surrenders herself to my ravishing, passively allowing me my fun. Which pisses me off. I want the fighter in her to emerge; I want to screw Mel's bitchy side. If she's going to act like a lump of dough, then I'm going to take advantage of it. I bite deeper, fastening my lips around a dollop of creamy skin, sucking hard enough to pop the capillaries. Mel groans, a low leonine rumble deep in her throat that speaks of something touched. Mel's finally moved. She makes a feeble attempt to push me off, but I'm ravenous, my mouth watering. I have to resist the urge to allow my teeth to meet through her skin, not because I have some vampire fantasy but because she'd be a peach to eat, summery, brightly sweet. I pull back, satisfied to see a wide trail of love bites mottling her throat and I chuckle as Mel rubs her sore neck. Glancing in the mirror above the sink, she gasps.

"Violet! Damn, look at my neck!"

"Looks good." I loosen her ponytail and her hair falls around her like a soft, fragrant curtain. One hand slides down to cup perfect little breasts growing warm and tightening under my palm. My other holds her bum, my fingers slowly stealing into the groove, finding her slick with desire.

Mel gets mad at my intrusive fingers, my firm grasp, the kisses liquefying her defenses.

"Mmm, finger-licking good," I murmur, curling a tongue around my wet fingers, laughing as she flushes bright tomato red, smooths her clothes and tries to catch her breath.

"I don't know about this," she asserts unconvincingly, fingering her bruised neck. "I told you I'm not into sex." She says, "I'm sorry, but I just don't feel anything." But her husky voice, her swimming, dark eyes give her away.

"You don't like it when I kiss you?"

Mel shrugs again; she's so cute when she's trying to be cool. "Sorry."

"Hmm," I muse. "You don't like it when I do this?" I grace her lovely mouth with a tender, lingering kiss. Mel shakes her head.

"You don't feel anything when I touch you?' Lifting my shirt, pressing my bare skin to hers, the heat delicious.

"When I taste you?" I flick my tongue over her hard nipples, teasing them between my teeth, coaxing out Mel's amazing purr.

"Nope. Nothing," she grunts.

Anchoring her hands over her head, I lick the crease beneath her arm, sucking that sensitive little sex organ, her pits a little cinnamony. I love the taste of clean sweat. Mel wheezes, "Violet, what are you doing to me?"

"Going to town, baby." She arches against me as I'm struggling to get my hand between her strong thighs. I push two fingers into her cunt, palpitating the rough, spongy flesh, then sliding forward to slick her hot come over her clit. I glide my fingers faster and faster in and out. Mel crumples in my arms. I have to support her, hold her body tightly to me as she rocks over my hand, clenching her thighs. I'm working magic here and Mel responds, stirring from passivity and lethargy to wild life, smothering me with her candy mouth, tugging my shirt over my head to get at my full breasts. God, she's rough! So delicious. Mel takes over, yanking my jeans down, no panties, no boxers, just me and my buddy Dick. Her eyes widen uncomprehendingly, watching me stroke my black rubber prong.

"It's all for you baby. Don't give up now."

Mel shoves me down onto the cold toilet, straddling me, kissing me everywhere, breasts grazing my cheeks, her hands all over me like some ardent octopus. I push a finger into her ass; she bucks and moans loudly, her cries ricocheting off the tiles.

Pulling her closer, her fragrant crotch on my face, my tongue working her big clit. She's getting violent, shaking me, bashing me against the toilet tank, but I won't stop. I know she's close to coming so I spread her labia, coaxing her down onto my dick. The base of my dick massages my clit with each thrust.

"I can't believe I'm letting you fuck me in a public toilet," she yells, orgasming loudly and wetly, thrashing on top of me. Mel grabs a fistful of hair and bangs my head against the tank, screaming. I've never been fucked so hard. I'm seeing stars. Mel wraps herself around me, squeezing my tit painfully and reaching down beneath my harness, finding my aching cunt with surprisingly skilled fingers.

"Mel, honey, I have to tell you something," I gasp, then I come so hard I think I might black out from the pleasure (if not from Mel's recent toilet tank abuse).

Mel really lets it rip, a howling death wail as she convulses on my lap.

"What's going on in there?" A man asks, hammering on the door. "Hey! Are you OK?" There's a fluster of key-finding activity going on in the hall. I lift Mel off my dick, her knees still shaking. I tuck myself back into my jeans, splash a little water on my face.

"I'll be right out!" I yell to the voices beyond the door.

"Hey," Mel whispers, buttoning her pants. "What did you want to tell me?"

"When's our next fight?"

"Monday. Why?"

"'Cause, sweetheart," I pause, admiring the rosy, satiated glow on her pretty cheeks. "I've been letting you win. See you Monday." I saunter out, just in time to see the bartender arrive with a jailer's ring of keys and a knowing grin.

Going Up Anne Seale

I heard a gunshot. It was Sunday afternoon at 3:13 by the tiny clock in the corner of my computer screen. I'd just been dealing with an E-mail from my ex-lover Joan.

"Darling LaVonda," Joan had written, "Robert is out of town for the next few days, and I want to be with you. When can I come over? I'll give you a call."

I lied—Joan wasn't as much of an ex-lover as I would have liked.

I hit the reply button and typed, "Darling Joan, if the only time you want to be with me is when your husband is out of town, don't bother." Before I could send it, my anger failed me, or maybe it couldn't compete with my libido. Anyway, I deleted the whole thing and was signing off AOL when I heard it: the gunshot.

I looked out the window, but the only unusual thing I saw was it had finally stopped raining. I was on my way to the other side of the house when both the phone and doorbell rang at the same time. I grabbed the wall phone in the kitchen.

It was Joan. "Sweetie, did you get my message? When can I come over?" She used her sexiest voice, causing a severe tickle in my nether regions. The doorbell rang again.

"Hold on, Joan. I'll be right back." I dropped the receiver, dashed across the living room and opened the door to find myself face-to-face with the grimiest woman I'd ever seen. Sodden hair hung in clumps around a face that was smudged with dirt. Her shirt was mud-spattered, and in only a few places were her blue jeans still blue. An industrial-size backpack was slung over her shoulder.

I checked to see if she was holding a gun. She wasn't. *Wait*, I thought, *Maybe this woman didn't fire the shot. Maybe she's the victim!* "My dear, are you all right?" I asked, scanning her body for blood.

"I think so," she said, glancing down to see what I was looking at.

"I heard a gunshot. I thought you..."

She laughed, showing teeth that could use a good brushing. "That wasn't a gunshot. It was Big Ornery backfiring." She pointed to a red Ford pickup that was dripping mud all over my driveway. "It's one of B.O.'s many impolite noises."

Miss Manners kicked in. "Well, how can I help you?"

She stuck out a hand. "My name is Maxie Pulliam. I'm looking for LaVonda Dew."

The hand was smeared with dirt. Miss Manners hesitated, but finally shook it. "I'm LaVonda Dew," I said. "Where on earth did you come by all that mud?"

"I've been climbing rocks in the foothills east of here," she said. "I was having a good time of it, too, until 24 hours of solid rainfall washed out my tent and mired the truck." She told me she'd hiked for miles and finally found a farmer who charged her a hundred bucks for a tow. By the time she made it to town, she was tired, dirty, and nearly broke.

"What I need is a hot shower and maybe a sandwich, and I'll be on my way home to Los Angeles. But I can't drive all that way like this."

"I see," I said, "and how did you happen to come to me?"

"I looked in a phone book for the word *gay*..."

"I'm listed under *gay*?!" I yelped.

She laughed again, and shifted her backpack to the other shoulder. "No, but I found the address of the Gay Alliance and stopped to ask if there were any good Samaritans in this town. A volunteer told me she was a friend of yours, and she was sure you'd help. She tried calling, but the line was busy."

"I was reading my E-mail," I said, then mentally kicked myself for having told this stranger I had a computer. Maybe I should mention my state-of-the-art stereo and antique clock while I was at it.

"So she gave me your address and I drove over," Maxie said. She couldn't remember the volunteer's name, which was too bad because I would have liked to throttle her.

"Come in, then." I sighed.

To Maxie's credit, she removed her boots before stepping on my carpet. I fetched a couple of towels and promised her a bite to eat after the shower. No way was she going to sit on any of my chairs in those pants.

I was measuring coffee into the Braun when I heard a strange beeping from the wall phone. I'd left Joan dangling! I grabbed it, clicked the button until I heard a dial tone, and punched in her number. She didn't pick up, even though I was sure she was sitting right next to it pouting. I ran to the den and fired up the Net. "Sorry, Joan," I typed, "I'm too busy at the moment to plan a get-together with you. There's a dirty woman upstairs taking a shower, and I need to think about what I'm going to do with her afterward." I clicked the "send" button with a great deal of satisfaction.

The coffee was smelling good by the time Maxie entered the kitchen. If it weren't for the crinkly green eyes, I wouldn't have believed she was the same person. I'd thought she was younger than I was, but now I could see the dark brown hair had gray in it, and the crinkles weren't confined to the eyes.

She wore clean Levi's topped by a faded lavender T-shirt that proclaimed LEZ IS MORE.

"What would you like to eat, Maxie?" I said, pouring her a cup of coffee. "I can make ham sandwiches or heat up a can of chicken noodle."

"Thanks, but I don't eat meat," she said. "Actually, I don't drink coffee either."

Ah, one of those kind of lesbians, I thought with distaste—the kind that brings tofu stir-fry to Alliance potlucks and turns up her nose at my Swedish meatballs. Well, she could starve, for all I cared. I poured the coffee back in the pot and rinsed the cup.

"Do you have a tea bag?" she asked.

"I do," I said coldly, "but it's real tea."

She smiled, showing teeth that now sparkled. "Real tea will be fine."

I softened a bit and retrieved her cup from the drainer. "I have peanut butter or I could fry some eggs...that is, if you eat eggs."

"Fried eggs would be wonderful!" she said, redeeming herself somewhat.

As I cooked, we shared coming-out stories, as lesbians tend to do. She said her first love was a fellow Girl Scout she'd met at summer camp when she was 11. They'd held hands for two weeks solid. She'd had longer but not necessarily more fulfilling relationships since then, but at the moment she was single.

My story was much different. I told her how I'd been married for 15 years before entering into an angst-ridden affair with Joan who had promised to leave her husband but never did. I left mine, however, and took a tiny apartment where Joan could visit me whenever she got horny. Nice deal for her, huh? My therapist thought so too.

I had since bought a house and joined lesbian groups of every kind, but I seemed unable to break my sexual ties with Joan. What can I say? She knew exactly what I liked. Just hearing her voice and knowing the breath that formed it was curling around that tongue and passing between those teeth made me moist.

I didn't tell Maxie all that, I simply said I had put some distance between Joan and myself but had found no one to replace her. I must have sounded sad because she put her hand over mine on the table and kept it there for a while.

By now we were eating the eggs with Italian bread toast and strawberry Smuckers. She changed the subject, telling me about rock climbing and how much she loved it. She even taught at a rock gym, whatever that was. Her climbing partner had recently moved to North Dakota, which is why Maxie had been out by herself, a no-no in the climbing world. "You know what, LaVonda? What I need is a new partner. Would you be interested in learning?" she asked.

"To climb? Oh, dear, no," I said quickly, thinking about my dislike of heights. "No, not at all. Not my thing." I was miffed when she didn't seem too disappointed.

I suggested to Maxie that she spend the night in my guest room and start back to L.A. in the morning. She said she'd love to but couldn't because she had to work the next day. We parted with a hug and a promise to keep in touch. She wasn't gone five minutes when I called Joan, who picked up this time and fortunately hadn't read my latest E-mail. "Get over here now," I said. When she arrived, we ran to the bed for some of the best sex we'd had in years. I didn't tell her I was pretending the hair on the fair head between my thighs was dark brown sprinkled with gray.

■ ■ ■

After a few weeks, Maxie called, inviting me to visit. I left for Los Angeles after work the following Friday, stopping for a burger on the way. I figured it might be the last piece of meat I would see for a couple of days.

Nearing the city, I took a wrong exit off the freeway and found myself on the way to San Bernardino. It took a while to get back on the original road, but I finally did, arriving at Maxie's apartment later than expected. She was relieved to see me and took me in her arms, planting a kiss right on my lips. I tried not to look too surprised.

We started in talking and didn't stop until after 2. I was a little disappointed when Maxie threw a pillow and quilt on the sofa for me.

At 7:30 A.M. she shook me awake, saying we needed to get over to the rock gym where she was teaching. I tried to burrow deeper into the cushions, but she would have none of it. In 30 minutes I was washed, dressed, and sitting in Big Ornery who, like Maxie, looked older without a coating of mud.

When we entered the gym, I couldn't believe my eyes. It looked as if the room had been built around the side of a mountain. I wanted to run outside to see if I had somehow missed the rest of it in the parking lot. Maxie told me it was a climbing wall. Small colorful handle-shapes were affixed to it here and there, and ropes and harnesses were piled nearby.

She told me to look things over while she ducked into the

locker room. Women straggled in and did some warm-ups.

Maxie came back wearing a tight black tank and bicycle shorts. She called the women together and lectured for a while about techniques and safety. When she got to the part about never, never climbing without a partner, she looked in my direction as if daring me to tell on her. I winked in complicity. Hopefully, she hadn't noticed I'd been staring at her well-muscled legs.

When she finished, the women paired up for climbing, and gathered in front of a part of the wall labeled TENDERFEET. In turn, one of each duo buckled herself into a harness attached to a sturdy rope that was threaded through a ring on the ceiling and held securely at the other end by her partner. Maxie told me if a climber lost her grip, the partner, called a "belayer," would hold on to the rope to keep her from plummeting to the bottom. I asked why, then, was there a thick mat at the foot of the wall? She grinned and told me, "Don't worry, it hardly ever happens."

My anxiety level lessened as I watched each climber go as far as she could and return to the ground without death or dismemberment. I even relaxed enough to join in the choruses of "Way to go!" and "Nice climb!"

When the lesson was over and everyone but Maxie and I had gone home, she smiled and said, "OK, it's our turn now." She rummaged in her backpack.

"Our turn to what?" I asked.

She held out a Spandex tank and shorts similar to the ones she had on. "Whose are those?" I said.

"They're mine, of course, but I'm loaning them to you."

"Oh, no," I said. "No, no, no. I told you, climbing is not my thing. I'm terrified of heights. I never stay above the third floor in hotels. Have you got the wrong person, woo-ee!"

"I don't think so."

" I'm bigger than you are. Those things'll never fit me."

"They stretch."

"Anyway, I'm hungry. I need some breakfast."

"You climb better on an empty stomach," she said, still holding out the clothes.

"I can't climb that wall, Maxie! My arms are weak. What if I slip? There I'll be, hanging in the air from that stupid rope like a puppet. And what if someone walks in and sees me? I couldn't bear it!"

Maxie crossed to the entrance and firmly turned the deadlock. "Nobody will see anything. But you won't slip."

"I won't?"

"You won't."

I was in a tizzy. My brain was still crying *No!* but something deep in me that obviously didn't have any sense at all was daring me to challenge that wall, see if I could defy gravity as those other women had. That something in me longed to experience the breathless anticipation I'd seen, the complete immersion in the task, the radiant exhilaration afterward.

Grabbing the tank and shorts with a grimace to let her know I wasn't happy about it, I trudged to the locker room to change, my stomach full of butterflies. When I emerged, Maxie had donned the harness and was offering me the other end of the rope. "I'll climb first. You can be my belayer," she said.

Grateful for the delay, I gathered the rope as I had seen the others do. Maxie leaped onto the wall, grabbing a handhold. She pulled herself up and moved from ledge to ledge in a zigzag fashion, sure-footed as a mountain goat. Sweat gleamed and ran, staining her shirt and shorts. The muscles on her arms and legs bulged and rippled. A thrill ran through me, and my tummy's butterflies flew farther down.

Maxie climbed all the way to the top then descended. On reaching the ground, she took the harness off and helped me into it, fastening it securely. Without comment I approached the wall, took hold of a red knobby thing and placed my right foot in a niche as I had seen the others do. I glanced back at Maxie, who nodded encouragingly.

I looked up. The wall seemed impossibly high—I wouldn't have been surprised to see an eagle peer back at me from one of the overhangs. I started to feel dizzy and decided looking up was a bad idea.

With an indelicate grunt, I pulled my body up and grabbed a higher handgrip, flailing my other foot around until it found support. In this manner, like a clumsy inchworm, I moved slowly upward, totally absorbed in the task of finding the next reachable handhold, the next safe place for a toe. "Nice going, LaVonda," I heard Maxie say.

I was less than a third of the way to the top when my body gave out. My limbs shook, and my face felt fiery red. Maxie told me to ease on down, saying that next time I could go higher but this was fine for today. I gratefully descended.

As I neared the floor, strong arms caught me around the waist. Maxie lowered me until I was sitting on the mat. Although my muscles shivered with fatigue, I was tremendously proud of myself.

Maxie held a bottle of some kind of fruit juice to my lips, and I drank it all—nothing had ever tasted better. She set the bottle aside and gently pushed me flat. She massaged my upper arms and shoulders and the fronts and sides of my legs. Then she turned me on my stomach and kneaded my entire backside. I was barely conscious.

When she'd rubbed the tremors away, her touch became lighter. Her hands caressed then patted lightly, rhythmically, on the fabric that was stretched taut over my buttocks and upper thighs. I kept my eyes closed, but now I was acutely awake. My body resonated with each fingertip as it landed on the black Spandex drum.

My legs were slowly drawn apart and the touches moved obliquely toward my crotch. It felt like tiny creatures, fairies maybe, were performing an intricate dance toward my center, and would never get there. When they finally did, my fluids started to run, drenching the fabric in my crotch, pooling on the plastic mat beneath me.

I moaned. The feathers became fingers again, insistent ones. They poked, teased, and rubbed, lightly at first, then harder and faster. The friction made the fabric hot. My lower half squirmed and thrust. Maxie stretched out beside me. She pressed her thighs against mine, and moved with me. I straightened against her, letting my head fall back on her shoulder. I was gasping. She gave a low laugh and brought a hand around, rubbing each breast in turn, squeezing nipples still encased in shiny black knit. Finally, she reached between my legs again and found me hard and wanting. She grabbed a handful of fabric and rubbed it into me. I exploded in a waterfall.

She held on until my breathing slowed, then whispered, "We need to go home, don't you think? Are you still hungry?"

"I am," I said, and we both knew it wasn't just for food.

We spent the rest of the day in her bed, raiding the fridge every once in a while. She fed me dishes I'd never had before—nutty hummus on whole-wheat crackers, creamy green pesto salad, oddly textured melon that tasted of ambrosia. I was in heaven.

On Sunday morning I was watching Maxie sexily make waffle batter—I'd come to consider her every movement sexy—when I suddenly realized that our lovemaking had been rather one-sided. The pattern was, she'd touch me or stroke me, or even look at me with one brow cocked, and I would roll over on my back, spreading everything like a hound dog begging for a scratch. After I'd been scratched, I would drift into a deeply relaxed sleep.

Maybe Maxie doesn't want to be the recipient of my caresses, I thought, then decided I didn't like that thought very much. I had to find out. Moving up behind her as she stood at the counter, I ran my hand lightly across her buttocks.

"Want to help, sweetie?" she asked. "Fetch the syrup. It's the cupboard next to the fridge."

I found the bottle and placed it on the counter, then pressed my body firmly against her back. "I'm really hungry," I said.

"The iron's almost hot. Won't be long now." She stirred the golden mixture.

I slid my hands around her waist and laid my cheek on hers. Looking down, I saw firm nipples outlined in the knit of the tank top. I picked up the syrup bottle, twisted the lid off, and poured syrup into the small valley between her breasts. I put my other hand down her shirt, smearing syrup on and around her breasts. "I'm really hungry," I said.

In one motion, Maxie turned off the waffle iron, pulled the shirt over her head, and turned to me. "So eat," she said.

I licked the syrup from both breasts, paying special attention to Maxie's pebbled nipples. She breathed faster.

GOING UP

Still holding the bottle, I pulled her to the floor and removed her shorts and satiny underwear. I poured syrup on the tightly curled pubic hair and licked most of it off. Some, however, had dripped into the V of her crotch. I went after it. She opened her thighs to accommodate me.

I applied another dollop of syrup, used my fingers to spread it, then removed it with great slurping noises. Maxie tossed her head from side to side and began to rotate her hips. They slid easily on the syrupy tiles. I lifted her buttocks and poured syrup into each depression I could find, going after it with my tongue in a sweet-toothed frenzy.

"LaVonda, here!" Maxie pulled her lips apart, revealing an erect clit. "Do it here."

I poured syrup on the tiny mountain and flicked at its base with the tip of my tongue, working my way up. After teasing the tip for a while, back to the base I went, slowly tickling round and round to the peak again. Maxie was grunting now and doing some serious pelvic thrusts. I sat up to look at her body. Each hip and leg muscle bulged—I could see the fibers and the way they intertwined. I studied them until Maxie gasped, "LaVonda!"

Pouring the last of the syrup on her clit, I took it in my mouth and sucked, rubbing my tongue back and forth against her hardness. "Almost!" she cried. I worked harder, and soon felt rhythmic pulses on my tongue. They went on and on as she keened in delight. Finally she took a great breath, and her hips splashed down into a puddle of syrup and fluids.

"How are you doing?" I asked, lying next to her on the sticky tiles.

"I think I just conquered Everest," she said. "Thank you, darling." She turned her face to mine. "How are you doing?"

I held up the empty syrup bottle. "To tell the truth, I feel a little queasy."

■ ■ ■

Joan phoned Monday afternoon as soon as I got home from work. "I tried to call you several times this weekend," she said shrilly. "Where were you?"

"In Los Angeles. I have a friend there," I said.

She was quiet for a while, then said in a lower, friendlier tone, "I've missed you. Why don't I come see you tonight?"

It was my turn to be quiet. I was waiting for the tickling and wetness, but they didn't come. I switched my thoughts to Maxie, her hard body, the teasing hands, the Spandex, the maple syrup. Moisture and butterflies came in a rush.

"Are you still there?" Joan asked.

"You know what, Joan? I'm not."

Spurred On Debra Hyde

Elizabeth Canford. That's what the return address on the card said. Elizabeth Canford. Not Mrs. Edgar Canford-Priess. Not Elizabeth Canford-Priess. Just Elizabeth Canford.

The words took my breath away and made my hands shake. Years had passed since I had last considered them. And seeing them now meant she'd made good on an old promise, a claim that if she ever lost the husband, she'd lose the hyphenation. True to form, Elizabeth kept her word.

For a few seconds I stood there holding the envelope. Conflicting emotions washed over me, from the excitement of seeing her name again, to the ecstasy I felt when I fell for her years ago, to the pain she caused when she ripped a hole through my heart. Then I remembered how she once clutched my cunt in her hand, how she whispered her lewd intentions, how she used to exercise those intentions. Like a kid going for a Christmas present, I tore open the envelope.

Inside there was a note card. I opened it. The words, in Elizabeth's florid script, made a hard lump form in my throat:

> *So the reunion's almost here. Twenty years.*
> *Can you believe it? I'm bringing my crop.*
> *Still got your spurs?*

Wow. The crop and spurs—she remembered them. I remembered what she did with them—it had made me love her forever.

SPURRED ON

The crop and spurs incident happened not long after Miss Wealthy, Wonderful, and Popular had first noticed me, Ms. Middle-Class Nobody. I'm not sure if I caught her eye because I was good in the saddle or good with girls, but by the time she met me in the barn, we'd been making eyes at each other for weeks already.

Elizabeth had just finished a riding lesson; I was about to start mine. She knew I'd be tacking up one of the college mounts, and she found me just as I was drawing the bridle over the horse's head. She came into the stall and snaked her arms around me from behind. Her lips were at my ear. No words yet, just a breathy nibble at what bit of earlobe peaked out from under my riding helmet.

"Not here," I pleaded. Visions of riding instructors catching me in mid orgasm raced through my head.

"Yes, here," Elizabeth insisted.

She came around front just as I slipped the reins out of the tangled mess I'd made of the bridle and the halter. That's when it happened: The reins snapped wildly through my hands and hit her square in the face. The slap of the leather against her fair skin mortified me, and as I saw red marks rise on her cheek, I gasped and begged forgiveness.

It was worse than spilling a drink on your date.

Elizabeth brought her hand up to the marks. A sly smile crossed her face. I just stood there shocked.

"Turn around and face the wall," she told me. I gulped, too stunned to move because I couldn't believe what I was hearing.

"Turn around and face the wall," she insisted.

I did as told. I faced the wall. I put myself in a spread-eagled stance; that's how I always envisioned it, but never with the rich smells of an old barn—the wooden walls, the fresh straw at my feet, my mount's horsy odor, the leather tack.

"Raise your right foot," Elizabeth ordered.

Again I did what she wanted. I felt her hands at my ankle, working the strap of my spur loose. Her hand snaked up to my crotch and pushed my hips away from the wall. She placed the nub of my spur against my clit, resting it between the stall's wall and me. Elizabeth's ingenuity was so unexpected, so tantalizing my heart raced.

"Keep it there. If you let it drop, I'll make you so late for class Ms. Harwich will glower at you the whole lesson."

What came next changed my life. With the spur anchored between my crotch and the wall, I was a ready target. Elizabeth took her crop and brought it down across my ass. Ecstasy bolted through me, and I moaned as the pain blazed hot as lightning.

It was every bit as wonderful as I'd imagined.

As were the other 11 strokes she levied against me, and when it was over, I caught the spur in my hand as I turned to find Elizabeth soothing my mount. Poor gelding, he knew what the sound of the crop meant and had spooked. Elizabeth cooed and comforted him, and once he settled down, she looked at me and said, "You'd better get to class."

I'm sure she saw my gratitude and amazement as she handed me the reins. This time I handled them carefully as I hurried off.

Later that night, before I fell asleep in her arms, she took that same spur and rubbed it against my clit until I came.

Yeah, that moment changed my life. Hell, that year, my junior year, Elizabeth changed my life. I had transferred to Marion College—the Mount Holyoke of the Midwest—to major in equestrian studies. Once I got there, I found myself in another world. I felt like a fish out of water. For starters, the rest of the junior class had been there since day one; I was the only transfer. Even worse, I was just about the only middle-class kid there, and my presence was funded by scholarships and financial aid schemes. Everyone else came from money, wealth made either in industry (with horses on the side) or in horses (with stock and bonds on the side). Whereas I was lucky to have a decent saddle and school mounts to borrow for lessons, my peers drove luxury cars and boarded their own horses at the school.

By all outward appearances, Elizabeth was wealthy. She drove a Benz sports coupe, rode a well-schooled gelding, and had a generous monthly allowance to cover her every whim. Her mother even flew the family's Cessna to bring Elizabeth home for various family functions, one of which was an annual visit to their accountant. At 20, Elizabeth had enough personal wealth to warrant filing for taxes.

But she was different than the other rich girls. She didn't care about status, and played pool and downed beer without putting on airs that she was slumming. She never went to the school-sponsored mixers with the men's colleges. Meeting Mr. My Moneybags Are Bigger Than Yours didn't matter to her.

Instead she did what any sensible college lesbian did, circa 1980: She stayed in on a Saturday night and played her Janis Ian albums, waiting for somebody to notice.

I noticed.

Funny, but after that the first time we lay in each other's arms that evening, I told her I thought she'd never notice me. She giggled and said, "Who could ignore you when you're jumping a horse?" She grabbed my ass for emphasis, then waxed serious for a moment. "I thought no one would ever notice me—really notice me, you know? You'd think there'd be a few more lesbians at a girls college."

Perhaps there were, but Elizabeth and I only had eyes for each other.

In fact, when I knocked on Elizabeth's door later that day, she was waiting for me. She reached out, grabbed me by the back of the head and pulled me in, shutting the door behind us. She pushed me face-first up against the nearest wall and pressed into me. Her hot breath raged against my neck, the sound of it, fury in my ear.

"So when I whipped you with my crop—did that make you wet?"

God, did it. Just her asking made me wet all over again and robbed me of speech.

"Did it?" she repeated.

"Yes."

"How wet? Tell me."

"I was slippery in the saddle."

Elizabeth laughed in my ear. "Oh, I doubt it was that bad. But next time…" She paused and nibbled at my neck. "Next time you ride that wet, I want you to remove your panties afterward and put them in my mailbox in the student union."

With that she bit me in the neck. Pain flared and I cried out and squirmed. But Elizabeth pressed in harder, refusing to give me pause until she'd left a mark. My skin pulsed as her teeth left me and the pain burned, then faded like a flame robbed of fuel.

Elizabeth grabbed me by the hair again and dragged me away from the wall. With her free hand she undressed me. As she unbuttoned my shirt, she interrogated me. Apparently, she preferred to learn about me over sex, not coffee.

"You dress like a boy a lot. Are you butch?" She pulled open my shirt, and the air, just cool of tepid, hit my breasts. My nipples went hard. The shirt slipped from my shoulders and down to my elbows. I felt exposed, on display, physically and psychically.

I gulped. How could I answer her? I wasn't a big-boned butch, nor did I have any muscles to throw around. My height and weight were average, and my hair was short not because I saw myself as butch, but because stringy, straight hair looked best short. I was athletic and tomboyish, but only when it came to horses. And even though I was a natural-born bottom, I wasn't at all femme. I didn't go in for makeup or dresses or anything feminine. I didn't read *Cosmo* or *People* magazine. I didn't even like disco. I was caught between two images and had yet to define myself.

"Which is it?"

"Neither. I'm neither."

Elizabeth caressed my right breast, admiring its contour. She cupped it in her hand, then squeezed it as if she were assessing a piece of... She circled its nipple with her fingers, then pinched it lightly. It felt beautiful, so beautiful a moan escaped my lips.

"True. You're not exactly butch. And you're nowhere near femme," she observed. "But you're always in jeans and button-downs, so it's hard to know."

She let go of my hair and my breast. "Get undressed," she ordered casually.

Though I hesitated when she interrogated me, I didn't when she commanded me. I shed my shirt, kicked my shoes off, and fumbled out of my pants. As I pulled them off, I noticed Elizabeth had fixed her eyes on my pussy. She sat on her bed, and her gaze rose to meet mine. They smoldered blue and transfixed me. "Come over here and lie down." Captivated, I complied.

She pushed my legs apart and brushed my pubic hair aside, exposing my cunt lips and clit.

"Yeah, you look kind of butch. Kind of. Like a baby butch waiting to grow up."

Her finger caressed my clit, and it immediately responded. Elizabeth noticed, and she leaned down to kiss me. Her lips were soft, full, but assertive and hungry, and they devoured me. They curried my appetite, elicited my hunger, even as they took sustenance from me. Finally, when her tongue shot into my mouth to find mine, I rose toward orgasm. I pushed my clit harder into her finger. I rubbed against it, urgent for that wild moment.

Suddenly she broke our kiss and asked, "So am I butch or femme?"

God, there I was, just about to come, and she pulled away to ask me that? I answered her, not with words, but with hurried hips, hips intent on diverting her away from her ill-timed question and back to my orgasm.

But Elizabeth wanted words, not action. She smacked my cunt with her hand, sending a sharp sting across my clit. I yelped while my cunt throbbed in wicked delight.

"I asked you a question, girl. I expect an answer."

Elizabeth's eyes blazed. She meant business. I whimpered even as I marveled at her.

Another smack struck me; more pain coursed through me.

"Femme or butch?"

Oh, man. Did I really have to answer? I looked at Elizabeth, at all she was. Her long, wavy blond hair. Her smoldering eyes, petite nose, prominent cheekbones, full luscious lips. She was porcelain made human. I gazed over her body—statuesque, stout but not heavy. She was Grecian in her beauty, too shapely for butch and too sturdy for femme. She was as clearly femme as I was butch.

Elizabeth was something else, I decided. She was an Amazon. I told her so, and she laughed delightedly then resumed smacking and rubbing my clit, torturing me with her touch. Pain and pleasure rippled through me, coaxed me, claimed me, and then I came. I exploded in her grip.

Yes, she was an Amazon, and I worshiped her. I worshiped her every time she parted her legs and exposed the sweet slit that rested there. I worshiped her when I lapped her juices, made plentiful by my attentive tongue, when I pushed my fingers into her tight hole, when I nudged her clit awake. I worshiped her when she took in three of my fingers then urged me to push a fourth up her ass, when she rocked on my hand as I sucked and bit her tits, when I brought her to one shattering, shuddering orgasm after another. I even prayed—literally prayed—when I stuck my panties in her mailbox.

Remembering all this, I knew I still worshiped her, despite myself. Despite our history.

I had to set history aside and get to work, which meant putting Elizabeth's note down and leaving for the stable. Since college, I'd spent most of my years teaching equestrian skills to rich country club kids. Connecticut Cunt Club kids, I joked with my dyke friends. Although it was sometimes rewarding, it continued that old battle: middle-class me versus upper-crust them. Always the hired help, never the upper echelon.

Elizabeth's note dredged up bitter memories. As my

day wore on, watching girls post to a trot, and sit to a canter, toes up, heel down all the way, I grew more and more agitated. My mind mumbled, *Just like her, to assume you're single and willing to come back. Just like her to presume.*

Except she presumed right, damn her.

And what about how she dumped you? I asked myself. Memories of Elizabeth the week of graduation flooded me. "I can't tell them," she'd said, astounded that I didn't get it. "They expect me to get married. I've been engaged for two years."

Two years and she never even told me? She hadn't even had enough poor manners to show me the ring? I was astounded.

But she had had a plan: I could come West and work at the family stable, manage it, school the mounts, maybe even learn the equine flesh trade of thoroughbred hunter-jumpers. No thanks, I'd decided. I wasn't about to live in the shadow of her family and their straight expectations, under the false fluffy cloud of her husband and marriage. No way would I sit on the sidelines of her closeted life. Instead, I spent my senior year in abject misery, graduated, then fled to England to escape my pain and earn accreditation from the Royal Academy of Equestrian Studies. By the time I burned my way through their expert-making training, I'd purged Elizabeth from my system. Or so I thought. Because for every bitter argument I could muster, an erotic memory came back in rebuttal.

As I schooled a rich man's mount on the flat in the late afternoon, I realized I hadn't really escaped anything. I'd simply gotten over the worst of it and moved on, leaving my past with Elizabeth as one big loose end. I realized I needed closure, and I needed it so badly I was willing to endure anything to settle the score.

While I worked the horse through a series of figure eights, I remembered the sting of the crop, the cold feel of its handle as it fucked me. I remembered Elizabeth when she toyed with me like that, putting me through erotic paces every bit as structured as what I did with horses. I remembered her focus, her concentration, her wry smile that said she got off on doing whatever she wanted to me.

As I worked my horse into a sweat, I worked myself into an emotional lather, a state of erotic tension and acknowledgement that could be resolved one way and one way only. Later that night, I answered Elizabeth's note with an affirmative all my own. I didn't use words, pleasant or resentful. I didn't use memories, warm or otherwise.

I simply pulled off my underwear and slipped them into a mailer.

If Elizabeth remembers the crop and spurs, then she'll remember my panties in her mailbox, waiting there. And if she remembers the panties, then she'll know I'm waiting for her now, ready to forgive the past and consider the future. I hope she's done the same.

The Fencing Tournament Sarah b Wiseman

We were heading up to the capital city for the largest women's fencing tournament of the year, and *The Mask of Zorro* was the chosen film for the bus ride. I got comfortable and looked forward to a weekend of great fencing, along with some quality time with the horribly repressed, homophobic, and sexphobic women on my team.

Unfortunately, unlike softball, fencing isn't a popular dyke sport, though it should be. I love fencing. I love the anonymity behind our masks, the sound of blades touching as they play for control, the rush that comes when the blade bends clear against someone in a direct hit, and I love the ache that bending in the *en garde* position puts in my thighs—the same one that comes from hours of fucking.

Except for a few who played cards at the back, most of my teammates stared intently at the six televisions lining the bus. And across the aisle from me, Stephanie sat knitting away at a sweater. I watched her knit for a few minutes. Every few rows she would sweep her long hair behind her only to have it fall in front and interfere with her knitting again. My eyes lingered on the pink-and-blue striped sweater she wore and how nicely it clung to her breasts...until she noticed me looking. I grinned.

"Did you make that sweater you're wearing?" I asked.

"Yeah. Two years ago I did most of it on the bus ride to a tournament in Quebec."

"Good way to pass the time," I said, making sure to keep my eyes on the seat in front of me.

She giggled and went back to her knitting. I put back my seat, slid my Walkman into a pocket of my cargo pants, and tried to relax.

Aside from the scene where Zorro ridiculously and thrillingly disrobes the heroine with his sword, I didn't watch the film. I kept to my music and thought about how frustrating it had been spending so much time with the team preparing for the last few tournaments. I hadn't had time to have sex in months, and I was in dire need of some girl-on-girl action. A One Inch Punch song blared through my earphones as I rested. "I am a pretty piece of flesh / I will split you in two," the words went. I let my mind wander and fell into a sexy reverie. In it I fooled around with an aggressive Francophone whose ass I'd just whipped in an intense fencing bout.

The bout started with me sending her enough lunges to keep her coming back for more and ended with a smooth *flèche* that caught her, literally and sweetly, off guard. I could barely see her face as we fenced, but even before she took off her mask to shake my hand at the end of the bout, I knew what she wanted. And before we left the fencing strip she was taking me off guard. She threw her mask to the floor and came toward me.

"You deserve a little talking to for coming at me with that last *flèche*," she said, giving me a long kiss.

"What is it you have to say?" I asked as I pulled away.

We were both hot and sweaty from the match, and her short hair glistened as I moved my hand through it.

"Your ass looks great in those knickers," she said.

I fondled her ass in the middle of the strip, and before I knew it she started to unzip my *lame*...

THE FENCING TOURNAMENT

When I was finally startled out of my fantasy, the bus had approached the hotel where we were staying for the weekend. I looked around to see if anyone could tell I'd just had a wet dream. Fortunately, my teammates were focused on getting their stuff together. I tried to shake the dream away and think about the reality of my situation: Our accommodations for the weekend worried me. Last time we were away for a tournament the women I ended up sharing a room with watched *Jerry Springer, Married With Children* and a nail-care infomercial for hours, and I had to negotiate my space in a bed with a chick who seemed to think my queerness would rub off on her in the night. This time the arrangements were the same: four to a room, two to a bed. Needless to say, I wasn't thrilled.

But when we got to our hotel I discovered there was a mix-up and I had a room all to myself. Relieved, I made my way up to Suite 339. When I opened the door, a thrill ran through me. The two big empty beds just begged to be filled with some anonymous dyke's fantasies. I closed the door, unpacked my sword and equipment, then moved my hand between my legs and started to apply pressure.

I didn't even have time for a quickie before I heard a knock at the door. Stephanie had found out about the extra bed in my room and had come to claim it. I didn't protest, just sadly gave up the idea of this room being a little sexual haven away from the rest of the team. I figured Stephanie would be as good a roommate as any. She was shy and giggly and seemed sweet. We could always talk about fencing. And at least I had a bed all to myself.

I put my stuff on one side of the room and decided to see if I could find a queer bar in the government town we were staying in.

"I'm going out to grab a beer. I'll be back later," I told Stephanie.

"Oh, I'll come too," she said.

Shit, I wasn't expecting this. How was I going to explain this? I wasn't sure who on the team knew I was a dyke, and coming out to Stephanie right then didn't seem like a great idea.

"Well, actually I'm, well, I guess, um, I think I just want to be alone," I finally blurted out.

She seemed naïve enough to believe me and took my explanation at face value. I was thankful. But I was also curious what she would think if she came out with me. I imagined her shock at the sights to see in any given queer bar: queens, kings, leather boys, leather girls…

Still, I headed out on my own and found a little bar with a strikingly hot butch bartender, who had arms to die for. I watched her while she poured drinks for a few minutes, then decided to have a beer and a game of pool. A little cruising would do me good, I figured. But for some reason I couldn't stop imagining what Stephanie's reaction to the place would be. Maybe she'd just giggle. Maybe she'd walk in and immediately fall for the bartender. I found myself imagining that possibility—the bartender flirting a bit by flashing her and then later on, Stephanie grabbing her ass as she walked by us with drinks. Or Stephanie grabbing the nape of the bartender's neck, leaning her against a wall and kissing her hard. Or better yet Stephanie pulling out the tie she often used to keep her hair up and binding the bartender's hands behind her back, only to walk away after whispering in her ear all the things she planned to do to her after closing time.

I pictured them both in fencing garb: Stephanie unzips

THE FENCING TOURNAMENT

the bartender's body *lame* and slides her hands in to hot skin. Once her muscled arms are exposed, she pulls down the bartender's fencing suspenders, pushes her onto her knees, and gives her gentle and gradually more powerful whacks on her ass with a sword. The bartender's biceps flex each time she's struck. And each time Stephanie asks in her sweet girly voice, "Does that feel good?" the bartender responds with a plea for more.

When I finished off my beer, I walked back to the hotel playing various Stephanie-bartender scenarios over and over in my head. Once in a while I even filled in for the bartender. I've never been one to fall for, or even fantasize about, straight girls. Especially naïve giggly straight girls. But here I was getting all wet over Stephanie. Knowing she'd be in the hotel room when I got back made me nervous; the last thing I wanted was to let her in on my little secret.

Once I got inside our room I noticed Stephanie's underwear on my bed. A pair of women's white cotton briefs. I heard the shower running. My mind automatically flipped back to my fantasies involving Stephanie in all stages of undress. Then I thought about all the panty sniffers in the world, and I had a sudden urge to take a whiff of Steph's panties. When she came out of the bathroom fully clothed I was still standing there staring at her underwear. She looked at me looking at them and then, after what seemed like a bit too casual pause, giggled, picked them up, and laid them on her side of the room.

I laughed to myself with uncertainty and decided to get ready for bed. It crossed my mind that Steph might be toying with me, but I figured it was probably just an extension of my fantasies.

When I pulled down the sheets I discovered a fake velour

blanket under the gaudy cover of the bed. I pointed it out to Steph. She laughed, and to my surprise, brought her bags over to my bed and sat down. She pulled out a box of hot chicken wings left over from dinner.

"I'm starving," she said, tossing her dark hair behind her back and looking at me in a way that seemed expectant. "Aren't you?" She patted the velour where she wanted me to sit. Suddenly Steph didn't seem so shy. I guessed this might be a long night after all.

We sat cross-legged on the bed facing each other while we ate.

"So, uh, how long have you been, uh, coming out to fencing tournaments?" I prompted her, hoping that if I asked the right questions, she'd tell me she was questioning her sexuality or something.

Without a pause she said, "About seven years," and went back to her chicken. Then when she looked up at me she giggled. "Oh, you're dripping," she said. "Let me get that for you." She used her napkin to carefully catch the grease dribbling down my chin.

I still couldn't tell if she was flirting or not. Either way, being stuck all night with this giggly straight girl in a hotel room with velour bed sheets was beginning to have a great deal of appeal. The sound of her sucking away, pulling the chicken off the bone, and licking the grease from her chin and lips made me even hornier for her than my fantasies had.

When we finished eating, Steph lay back on the bed and sighed. She was becoming more attractive by the second, with legs wrapped in smooth denim and a seductive bulge of exposed skin between her jeans and T-shirt. I noticed she was watching me watch her.

THE FENCING TOURNAMENT

When I caught her eye she smirked slightly and said, "Hey, I've got a little treat for us."

She riffled through a bad and brought out a small bottle of rum. She took a big swig then passed it to me.

"So you have a wild side, do you?" I asked before I took a sip of my own. I was surprised; she seemed like such a good girl.

"Well, you should have been at the practice last year where a few of us showed up a bit tipsy. We were tripping over our footwork, but our bladework was as fun as sword fighting in the movies."

We passed the bottle back and forth until it was empty, telling each other fencing stories and jokes. Pretty soon we were both giggling out loud. I fell onto the bed laughing, and as we quieted down, I put my head on her stomach. As we relaxed, our heavy breathing grew rhythmic. My breath was making her midriff damp. Seeing the little bulge of bare flesh so close to me made me want to run my fingers across it. As I lay there I considered whether I'd been wrong about Steph's naïveté. I still wasn't sure. I told myself not to think nasty thoughts at a moment that could be perfectly platonic to her.

But as I got up, Stephanie put one hand on my head and the other against my lips. Gently her fingers worked their way into my mouth. My tongue raced toward them. My pulse sped up with shock and pleasure. I sucked, rolling my tongue around each finger, sucking hard and soft. I imagined her clit between my lips as I sucked.

Steph took her fingers from my mouth and trailed their wetness across the naked inch of her belly. Then she tucked her thumb between her jeans and her skin. I felt her pulse speed up through her stomach. I reached out my tongue and licked her belly. She giggled as she opened the top button of her jeans, unzipped the zipper, and combed her fingers through her exposed, reddish pubes. No underwear. The hairs on my own belly raised. I wanted to say something, but all that came out was a moan.

She pushed her fingers down through her pubic hair and moved them in a motion that showed me her clit was wanting and her cunt was wet. I tried to lift my head up to look at her face, but she held my head against her stomach as her fingers moved. So I watched them move, slow yet anxious, around and around. Then Steph dragged her fingers up across her now naked triangle and back into my mouth. I sucked her juice from her fingers one by one, moaning loudly the whole time. I could hardly stop there, I wanted her so badly. I wanted to put my mouth where her fingers had come from. My own cunt was slick and quivering. I tried to move toward hers, but again she held my head down.

Steph pulled her fingers from my mouth and pushed them back into her soft mound. She held me tight and made me watch her as she fucked herself. Her denim-covered thighs struggled, and she clenched as her fingers dove deep into her cunt and then came back up to her clit, moving faster, into a rhythm with her hips. Her breaths shortened and so did mine. I knew she was coming when she gripped my hair and pulled my face up to hers. Our bodies moved together as I watched her ache into orgasm. She became frantic. My fingers slid up under her T-shirt and tweaked her nipple in time to her breaths. She came louder. She pushed me onto my back, tightened her legs around my thigh, and pressed her lips firmly to mine, shrieking into me.

Slowly Steph's breathing slowed. She laid her head on

my breasts, and I stroked her hair. Relaxed, but still hot with shock, I couldn't help laughing out loud.

"So what do you think of all those unzipped fencing uniforms between bouts on tournament days?" I ventured.

Steph giggled a while, then brought her face up to mine. "You mean how they show off hot skin and sweaty sports bras?" she said as she unbuttoned my shirt. "Pretty damn fine." Her fingers were sticky from her cunt juice as they trailed along the edge of my bra.

"So I guess you're not straight," I laughed again, watching her unbutton me.

She got up from the bed, her jeans still partly open, and smiled. "I've been fucking women since I was 16." Then, in a more serious tone, she commanded, "Take your clothes off."

Naïve straight girl turned experienced dyke top. Who knew? I undressed for her slowly.

When I was done, she instructed me to lie on my back and not move. I relished her orders and smiled as she picked up my fencing sword from where I'd set it against the wall. She laid the cold blade across my sweaty body, its tip at my neck and its bell tucked up against my crotch. Then she knelt on the bed and without touching me anywhere else, took my nipples into her mouth one at a time and sucked them until they were sore and wanting more. The sensation of her lips on my nipples and the thin metal along the length of my torso surged to my cunt. I felt ecstatic already. I tried not to move as she took her mouth away from my breasts.

Standing in front of me again, she lifted the sword away from my body, holding it by its grip.

"I've been wanting to fuck you for a while now," she said with an adoring, proud smile. She spread my legs with the blade, dragging it up my thigh and sliding it along my wet cunt. Then she traced circles all around my body with its tip wet with me. My nipples ached as she circled them. I closed my eyes and throbbed.

She stopped moving the blade, and I felt her lie against me on the bed. My eyes opened just as she leaned in and kissed me softly. The kiss released me. I kissed her back, and she let me push against her, flip her over, move my hands under her T-shirt, pull her jeans down to the floor. With one hand I fondled her breast, and with the other I picked up the sword by the blade and pressed the leather of its thick and firm French grip against her thigh.

"And if I'd only known about you…" I said, moving the grip up her leg closer and closer to her cunt.

She moaned into my ear then suddenly pushed me back onto my back. She straddled me, and I dropped the sword.

"What would you have done?" she asked as she moved her hand behind her and laid it on my naked thigh, spreading my legs apart.

"I would have watched you…" I said.

She slid her fingers along my cunt and watched my reaction. My breath started, and my eyes closed.

"I would have paid attention," I continued, "to your pacing…" She started moving her fingers slowly back and forth against my clit. "And the way you moved your blade," I moaned.

"What else?" she asked, clutching my breast with her free hand.

Restraining myself, I managed, "You would have known I was watching."

Her fingers pushed harder against my clit and moved faster. My breath quickened and my hips rose, lifting Steph with them. She didn't stop what she was doing. I struggled under her weight, panting hard, and came quickly. She moved her hand to my neck, caressing my face with her fingers.

Eventually she lay beside me and laughed for a long time. I kissed her neck and stomach while she giggled and held her hands together above her head until she quieted.

"*Etes-vous prêtes?*" I asked.

She grinned at me in anticipation.

For the rest of the night, like blades, we played against each other's bodies for control, and the next day our thighs were aching long before the tournament began.

Naiad M. Christian

Her arms were packed tight with lead. Her legs burned from the inside out. Her eyes boiled in their own salty juices. A heavy drumbeat shook her shoulders. The water was cement.

It was 1:30 A.M. Sage simply wasn't going to get any faster.

For something like the last five times, she hadn't climbed out of the pool, she'd hauled herself out like some kind of accident victim. This last time, she'd slipped and fell on her ass heading back to the starter's block.

Face it, kid, Sage thought. *It's time to pack it in.*

Still, it was hard. Joanne's eyes, voice, hands-on-hips posture, and bowl-cut blond hair, looked down on her aches and pains with a silent, accusing, *That's not an attitude that wins*.

Only after she realized she had started to stagger and limp did she slip the determination Joanne had infused in her. Sage wasn't getting any faster and, if she kept it up, she was only going to injure herself. Badly.

The need for sleep suddenly reached up—past Sage's throbbing shoulders and legs, past the burn and the pull and the ache—and smacked her across the eyes. As if they'd been filled with stones, her lids seriously drooped and sagged. The pool, a mini-Olympic in the YMCA basement, started to flutter and fuzz. Sleep wasn't just around the corner, Sage realized. It was sitting on her chest and smothering her with a pillow.

Despite the orchestra of aches and strains and pulls and sprains, she managed to haul her butt off the starter's block and drag herself toward the showers, hypnotized by thoughts of her hide-a-bed.

Joanne strolled alongside her. Even though she was almost half a foot shorter than Sage, she walked a good deal slower (and was in Chicago for a national fitness convention) Joanne managed to be always above and ahead of her—looking down at Sage's 5 feet 11 inches with a distant air of more than faint disapproval. Sage owed a lot to her sandy-haired coach: her fifth place standing at Nationals last year, her quickening lap time, her muscle-mass ratio, her breathing rhythm, and her singing muscles when she fell into the groove and the water wasn't water anymore, but air, and she flew rather than swam. She owed Joanne a lot, absolutely. But aching and tired and weak and wobbly, she just wished she'd leave her alone.

You won't make it thinking like that. You have to keep pushing: Stop pushing and you won't make it. Don't think of it as pain. Think of it as something to push through, that's all. Something to pass by and leave in your wake. Something to get beyond.

Fine, Joanne, fine. Terrific, she thought, walking slowly and steadily on the tensed coils of her exhausted muscles, *but can't I just sleep for a while?*

Only you can win. Only you—your muscles, your lungs, your legs, your arms—can win. Her projection of Joanne walked in front of her, sternly pulling her along.

I'll do it, I'll do it. Sage stopped for a second to wheeze in breaths laced with the sting of chlorine, lungs flaming and abraded from holding her breath too long. The Y's mini-Olympic surged and lapped in the background, settling down, it seemed, for its own calm sleep. Overhead, buzzing fluorescents burned her already scalded eyes with hesitant flashes. The Jacuzzi seemed a million miles away and completely uphill. *I'll do it for you, Joanne.*

Somehow she made it. In some ways it was worse than swimming those endless laps; harder because she felt alien to the land now, suited to water alone. She stopped again at the lockers to laugh a bit to herself: *Leave me alone, Joanne. Just let me rest here and work my gills a bit...*

The problem was that Sage owed Joanne so much. So much that Sage was starting to believe she was only real to Joanne when she was in the water, pulling herself, kicking herself through the thick coolness. Even when they fucked, it wasn't quite real somehow. No matter the passion (at first) and the skill (acquired over time), she only seemed to be really alive in the water—to both herself and her coach.

"I'll do it, I'll do it," she told the locker, fogging its cold metal door with her overheated breath. The problem was that it had felt so damn good when she saw her standing at Nationals last year, when everyone started using that word, "hopeful." It was magical—the hesitant, flashing smile on Joanne's face. That was worth it.

The lip of the tub. The churning water. "It all comes back to you, though..." she told the churning bubbles. The liquid was calling her back, welcoming Sage home.

Slowly, she flipped her arms and shoulders out of her one-piece. Once past her strong hips, the red suit dropped heavy and wet, with a more than slightly disgusting *plop!* on the chill concrete floor.

Carefully, so as not to let her enthusiasm trip her up—literally—she flipped the starter switch for the jets and climbed in. The water was hot, and it felt great. Its hard pounding was the key to her locked-up muscles.

The kneading water reminded her of Joanne when she smiled and touched her with her proud hands. But unlike Joanne, the jets just kept on coming—no pause for a stern lecture, a tip about performance, or a slight frown with the implied, *You could do better*—in the pool or in bed.

Now, that night, it was just Sage and the water.

The Jacuzzi was just the right temperature, hot enough to seem like a heavy wet blanket around her legs, chest, and arms. The bubbles played about her limbs, tickling up and around her thighs, toes, and armpits. This merrily churning cauldron of rambunctious sensation, its warmth and its pure, undiluted wetness was like a rambling chorus of different feelings.

Eyes half-closed, head tilted back against the chewed rubber headrest, Sage let the bubbles bash their little atmospheric brains out against her concrete muscles, letting the choir of hot, chilly (where the air of the pool room brushed against her wet skin), hard, soft, tingling, smoothing, painful (right foot next to a scalding water jet) sensations melt her muscles away.

Water: Enemy. Opponent. Obstacle. Still, it felt really, really good.

Water is heavy. Lying on the ground or trickling from a pitcher, it doesn't seem so. But if you have to push your way through it with all your burning, cramping, twisting muscles, and the best you can do is match someone leisurely trotting alongside the pool ("You can always do better, Sage—"), it could seem like granite. Flowing steel.

Way too fucking heavy. But in the tub, heated and pushed around by the little jets and the thrumming motor of the pump, this water was…playful. Eager. Energetic. Not stubborn and steadfast, but frisky and flirting.

Yeah, flirting. No doubt about that. Maybe it was because her muscles were unwinding in the pounding, steaming pool, or maybe it was because Joanne had just been too busy (traveling, trying to drum up sponsors) for her over the last the two months. Sage ached…everywhere. The water was doing a very, very good job of soothing, of loosening. Her body let go of its pain and her mind.

She floated in the water. It still lapped and bashed its fluid against her, but it wasn't such an uphill climb: She was closer to water now than the stone she had been when she first stumbled out of the big pool. It had taken a while, but now she was as fluid as the water in the tub. She began to have a hard time telling where the water stopped and her own skin began.

Melting…

Her body temperature rose to that of the steaming pool. For a while it was the only real delineator between the water and Sage: The temperature differential between solid (her) and liquid (the pool) had formed a kind of ghostly bag for her mind to drift within, a bag of her slightly cooler body temperature. But as she loosened more and more—and the heat within her rose—that barrier finally fell away.

Sage was very, very wet.

It was a kind of wetness beyond anything that might happen between her legs: The water went through her. She became more liquid than flesh. Sage tilted her head back all the way and closed her eyes against the burning, flashing intensity of the florescent lights. She let her body lift up slightly in the bubbling water while her arms and legs floated naturally apart.

Her rival, water, was getting very…friendly with her. The bubbles floated up and around her firm, hard body and burst as the churning underwater jets pushed firmly against her muscles, making them less like the iron Joanne wanted and more like the softness Sage missed.

Sage didn't miss this softness when she smashed, crawled, and pushed her determined strength through the water (as Joanne snapped the stopwatch and nodded). She didn't miss it when her power gave her that edge, when the point of focus at a particular moment of the race told her she was it.

Sage missed the softness in her own body when people mistook her for a drag queen. Not a big hurt, but a sting nonetheless. Somewhere beneath her strong, fast exterior was girl who wanted to be pretty and flirted with. And if she couldn't be—well, there was always getting faster. At least if she got faster, Joanne would nod to her—want her.

Now though, in the whirlpool, she was soft. She was liquid.

Hello, daughter, the pool seemed to say with its bubbles, froth, and foam.

The water was a warm embrace, a hot presence. So warm and heavy it felt like…well, something like a woman: a frisky, affectionate woman who wanted to play with her, to feel her and be felt by her. It squirmed and lapped and pushed and pulled at her. *Play with me, play with me!*

Affectionate, yes. Very affectionate.

But there was something else. Playful, yes. But also respectful. Comforting. Motherly. Greater, more powerful than Sage was (floods, tidal waves, pounding rain…) but it smiled at her, knew her, respected her, loved her?

Maybe…

But it was definitely wet. Very wet. Almost as wet as she was. It's sometimes hard, Sage knew, to tell wet from wet when you're swimming. Sometimes you can't feel it behind the pumping muscles, the straining arms, the race; but it was still there: coming out in an explosive horny end when the adrenaline wore off, as Joanne had found out several times. Once, after a regional championship (third place), she had pulled Joanne into a storage room and ripped off her swimsuit and Joanne's jeans in a purring whirl of hands, teeth, and even toes. She had shoved her face into Joanne's crotch, her cunt, then and there, crouching amid brooms and mops and the stronger than usual smell of industrial disinfectant till her own juice dribbled down her leg and between her toes. Very wet.

Very wet in the pool too.

Her excitement was there, she calmly realized. A good kind of horniness, the kind that rolls rather than roars up. A slow, progressive wetting of the pussy, a tightening of the asshole, a crinkling of the nipples. Not a physical climb, so much as an ascension.

What was really great about it, she realized with a slight smile, was that she didn't want to fuck or lick...anything. Didn't really want a mouth or a pair of hands. Nah, she liked the water just fine. Very fine.

And it certainly seemed to worship her.

The energetic, frisky bubbles played with and around her nipples, racing down the track of her spine, effervescent hoards on her delicate asshole, then up up up between her parted pussy lips—a gentle tapping on her hard clit. The water kneaded her thighs and back, boiled around her breasts, and gently stroked her sides.

Her breasts had never been big, but after years of training,

Sage had become quite...streamlined. Still, flattened and muscular, her tits were still tits—and they felt wonderful in the playful waters. Her nipples were normally pretty big, but the action of the pool made them huge: dark pink islands rising from tropical waters. She almost started stroking and pulling them but stopped, putting her hand back into the warm liquid. It didn't really seem necessary. She was more than halfway, she knew, to the end result anyway.

It was going to be so good, she felt. She didn't want to rush it with the same things she did when she masturbated: rubbing feverishly at her clit to get some sleep. This was hot—this was going to be special.

This was going to be sacred.

The water was wonderful. It lapped and surged against her clit like no tongue ever had. Slowly, Sage let herself sink in till her head was slightly off the headrest, her body was in contact with the bottom of the pool, and her clit was in the sights of one of the jets.

Oh, boy—

The jet was hers and hers alone. It seemed to focus just on her cunt with a kind of insane concentration. Sage felt like the single-minded object of worship of the most dedicated of cunt lickers. More than ever, the water was there for her, to comfort her, to melt her muscles, and to tickle more than a little of her fancy. Now even her areolae, darkened beaches around the hard hills of her throbbing nipples, poked up out of the water. Seeing them, seeing the intensity of them and the wonderful ache of them, Sage giggled, then sighed as the water jet tickled her just right.

The water was like a constant bout of foreplay with someone who knew exactly where you wanted it, how much you wanted, and when to stop—which wasn't going to be until Sage screamed out and smiled a big wide smile.

Which wasn't far off, she realized. Now, more than ever, she ached to put a hand between her legs and help the bubbles and the water along with a few quick strikes to her clit. She wanted—oh god, did Sage want—to put her hands up to her strong, flat tits and twirl and pull at her nipples.

But the water was too damned good. She wanted it to last and last and last. She wanted its attention on her never to waiver, never to get bored or criticize. It was single-mindedly pushing her up and up toward a tremendous orgasm—and it was glorious.

Her clit was pulsing a beat or two faster than her own racing heart. The throb of her nipples was a kind of surging ripple.

A huge wave of excitement began at her tingling toes, raced up her liquid legs, churned against her cunt and clit, licked at her tits and nipples, and splashed like kisses at her mouth. The wave of sensation rocked back and forth, back and forth: thighs, cunt, tummy, tits, and back and forth and back and forth. It was coming and she couldn't stop it. She didn't want to stop it. It came from her rival, her enemy, her partner—and now her lover, her goddess—and she let it come. For her. Just. For. Her.

It was like a first come, a virgin come.

The fire started in her cunt and clit, raced to her nipples, around her tummy, down to her asshole, and up and through her to her lips and mouth.

Sage groaned. Her orgasm surged through her like a crashing wave.

The room was quiet. Just the sound of the tub's pump, the sputter of the lights, and Sage's heavy breathing.

Man, was she wet.

Loose and relaxed, unknotted and surprisingly wide awake, she got out of the Jacuzzi, stretched her long, strong body in a series of quick moves, then retrieved her street clothes from her locker.

Warm and dry, she hoisted her gym bag and started for the doors, the street, the city, and her tiny apartment. But she stopped, between the edge of the pool and the door to bend down and stir the water a bit, feeling its immensity, its firmness and its weight.

I'll be back, Sage thought, *for you.*

No, she added, standing and smiling, *for me.*

Sports Dyke Dawn Dougherty

There is this very clear but invisible line in every aerobics class that separates the people taking it.

The line runs through the middle of the class, dividing the women at the front of the room from those in the back. The line is based in part according to how much one's tits bounce. The closer she is to the front of the room, the more likely her breasts are well supported by a combination of the proper sports bra and supple pectoral muscles. The farther from the aerobics instructor, the more likely she is to be wearing a large, white cotton T-shirt, tits swinging in circles like a stripper trying to get her tassels in sync. I fall in the latter category. At the moment, I am pretending to box an imaginary opponent in the last row of class at the L Street Community Center in South Boston. I don't own a sports bra.

It's Monday night at 6:30, which means I am taking Tom's Combo Impact II class. This, in and of itself, is enough to put me into a blinding rage since I have no idea what the fuck "Combo Impact II" means. All I know is there are women with thighs that could crack walnuts screaming with orgasmic glee at Tom's instruction: "Now jump up and down on your left foot!"

I am in a rotten mood.

In this particular class, for some reason that completely escapes me, people love to shout and hoot and holler as well. Every time Tom changes from jumping up and down on one foot to jumping up and down on the other, a bevy of women in the front row let out a Herculean cheer. Apparently being up front means you're fucking annoying too.

If you know anything about Boston, you may be wondering what the hell a dyke like me is doing working out here anyway. South Boston is a community known for rioting to keep black folks from being bussed into white schools in the '70s, and for going to court to keep gay folks out of its precious St. Patrick's Day parade (a holiday on which the gym closes) in the '90s. My first St. Patrick's Day in Boston I ventured to a bus stop close to Southie (as South Boston is affectionately known). A group of 20-something drunk boys all wore T-shirts that said SOUTH BOSTON ST. PATRICK'S DAY PARADE: THIS AIN'T PROVINCETOWN. I decided Southie wasn't a place where I needed to spend a lot of time. But here it is almost six years later, and I'm shaking my ass to an incredibly frenetic remix of a Spice Girls song in the heart of Irish Catholic Boston where the rent, for the most part, fits my budget.

I hate working out.

I am not a get-high-on-life, rock-climbing, sports-loving dyke who lives for the game. I am the human equivalent of veal. Or at least I used to be. I'm now in my fourth month of membership at the L Street Community Center and am frankly astonished at my commitment to this grubby excuse for a gym. A friend recommended that I check L Street out, and at $50 for a full year membership (I paid the extra $20, and they threw in all the aerobics my arteries could handle) that even I couldn't pass it up.

I'm presently jumping up and down on my right foot (a move I am sure Tom picked based solely on its ability to move tits) and am growing angrier by the minute. That's usually how it works for me. I spend the entire time cursing inside my head at the stupid people taking the class and the moron teaching it and the bastard who designed the underwear stuck so far up my ass I may never get it out. In about five minutes I'll be on top of a bell tower mowing down the entire class with an automatic weapon. I can just see tomorrow's paper, "'She was a quiet girl who hopped in the back of class,' remarked her aerobics instructor. The instructor survived a bullet wound to the left testicle."

As my mental tirade continues, the class cheers again. We're now pretending to jump rope. I turn to the woman next to me and ask, "What's with all the yelling?"

"I don't know," she says. "It's not like this is fun." We give each other a conspiratory smirk and go back to the drudgery. The class, however, is more than I can bear, and 15 minutes before it ends I grab my water bottle and leave, trying to summon my best "fuck you all this class sucks" swagger.

In the quiet coolness of the hall, I contemplate the complete mental patient I have become.

I walk down the hall past signs for a smoking cessation workshop and Junior Alligator swim sign-ups. I stop in the lobby and check out a massive mural called *The South Boston Sports Hall of Fame*. In between the painted faces and green shamrocks are the names of all the famous athletes Southie has spawned. I scan the lists looking for someone famous, thinking maybe Tiger Woods or Lisa Leslie (the only athletes I know) spent a few summers in Southie. Apparently not. The wall is filled with names like Flynn, O'Hara, Shea, and Cunningham, and somehow I doubt any of them are pitching for the majors at the moment.

I head into the locker room and plop my ass down with a thud. I lie back and stretch the whole way across the bench and let out a long, frustrated sigh.

"That doesn't sound good."

I look up at a woman on the other side of the room.

"Sorry," I say. "I thought I was alone."

"Oh, you're not bothering me. You just sound like you're in a little pain is all."

She's cute. About my height and wearing a pair of biking shorts and a sports bra. Definitely front row material.

"Not exactly pain," I answer. "I just took a tough class and wasn't quite stretched out enough." I don't care if she believes me or not. It isn't any of her fucking business why I am in pain. She probably took four of Tom's classes in a row.

"Yeah, I don't think the instructors here do a real good job of warming their classes up." She pulls a white T-shirt over her head. "Plus they do a lot of jerky movements too early in the class."

I turn my head to get a better look at her.

"I've given up on aerobics and step classes," she says. "Now I just do the treadmill and lift weights."

"Good idea." I'm not sure what I am supposed to say next. I like anybody who bitches about working out.

"You should try yoga. It'll loosen up those achy muscles."

So that's her angle. Get me to stick my foot behind my head and end up in traction. A tiny voice inside my head tells me that maybe I'm a bit too cynical. I brush it aside.

"Yoga isn't my thing." I sit up and open my locker.

"Have you tried it here?"

"No, I took a class a few years ago, and the instructor was bizarre. She talked about third-eye energy and made us all chant." I peel off my sweaty socks. "Plus my ex used to take a lot of yoga classes, and that alone makes me want to steer clear."

She laughs out loud, which surprises me. "Well, I've done this class for a long time, and there's no chanting." She slips into her sneakers, and I wonder if she got that my ex is a woman.

"Nice to talk to you," she says. "There's a yoga class starting in the dance studio now if you're interested."

I tell her goodbye, and as she walks away I check out her ass. Maybe she'd consider taking up aerobics again so I could stand behind her.

I slam my locker shut, and the sound reverberates throughout the empty room. My calf muscles ache, and I'm looking forward to taking a hot bath when I get home.

As I pass the dance studio, I stop to look through the window. She's there, sitting in the front of the class. Shit! She's the instructor. Me and my big mouth. Just my luck: The first person who says hello in four months, I insult what she does for a living.

She looks up and sees me at the window. She waves for me to come in, but I shake my head. She waves again, this time with a stern "get in here" look on her face. Well, that's what I thought it looked like. Maybe it was just wishful thinking, this chick wanting me.

I stand there for a minute holding my breath. It would be rude to turn her down. Especially after she was so nice and all. Plus I'm guaranteed not to get in her pants if I don't at least try the class. I've done worse things than yoga to get a girl horizontal.

I go in, put my gym bag in the corner, and take a seat on the floor. We start out with our legs crossed, relaxing and breathing. Not so bad. I can definitely use a few deep breaths now and then.

"We take our shoes off to do yoga." Her voice is soft from her place in the front row.

I open my eyes and look around. Sure enough, everyone is barefoot. Plus they are all sitting on mats. I quietly slide off my shoes and go over to fetch a mat from the corner. As I grab it all the other mats fall over and make loud slapping sounds on the floor.

Christ. I am the fucking Lucille Ball of spiritual enlightenment.

No one moves as I sit back down on the floor and recross my legs. I'm still cracking my toes and chewing on a hangnail when she ends the meditation and moves into a series of stretches. She'll first demonstrate a pose, then move around the room to help people.

There are six women and two men in the class. About half of the students have brought their own mats, and I'm pretty sure everyone is wearing natural fibers. They all take deep elongated breaths as they hold each pose. I try to follow suit.

She's gotten us into one position called "downward dog" when she comes over and stands behind me. I'm on my hands and knees with my butt up in the air trying to keep my arms from shaking.

"This looks great," she says. I'm more than a little nervous with her standing directly behind my very available ass. I hope I don't have any holes in my sweats. "It's OK that your arms are shaking."

She moves around to the front of me and places the heels of her hands at the base of my spine. Then she presses down and pushes out, causing my back to arch and my ass to push out farther. My arms stop shaking and I let out a groan. "Good job," she whispers.

This isn't yoga—this is porno.

She touches me three more times before class is over, more times than she touched anyone else because I counted. Two times she touched Mr. I-Don't-Wear-Deodorant and everyone else just once. We were doing some spinal twist thing on the floor, and she put one hand on my hip and the other on my shoulder and pushed in opposing directions. I felt like hot taffy being pulled apart. "Great," she said, her voice like honey. The next time we were doing something called a triangle pose, and she put her hands around my extended hand and gently pulled my arm. I gained two inches as she stretched me. She didn't say anything that time. This last time, at the end of class, we're pretending to be corpses, just lying there relaxing. At some point I hear her above my head. "Is it OK if I touch you?" I nod. She places both of her warm hands under my neck, lifts my head, and pulls slowly. My head extends out of my neck and shoulders. Then she places the heel of her hands on my shoulders and presses down. The movements create all this space in my neck and shoulders I hadn't known was there. It makes the relaxing part a lot easier, and I actually do what I'm told and picture my breath going in and out of my nose for the rest of the meditation.

At the end she asks us all to sit up. Then she says that the light in her honors the light in us, and bows her head down. Everyone else bows, so I do too, and then everyone silently puts away their mats. I just stretch out and sit there. This isn't at all like aerobics. I actually like it.

"Well, what do you think?"

I smile sheepishly. "That was a great class. Nothing at all like I thought."

"I'm glad you liked it."

"Listen," I start. "If I was a jerk before I'm sorry. I tend to speak before—"

She cuts me off. "Don't worry about it." She has long arms and legs and looks like a dancer. But more solid.

"How come I've never seen you before?" I ask. "I've been coming here for months."

"I guess you should have tried yoga sooner, huh?"

She's definitely hitting on me. She has this little come-hither look that is totally an invitation. I'm planning what to cook her for breakfast when a muscle dyke with short hair walks into the studio.

"Hi, honey." Breakfast just got a little more complicated.

"This is my girlfriend," she says. The girlfriend introduces herself as Lou, which I'm sure is short for something like Louise or Mary, and gives me an "I'm the dyke in charge" handshake. The yoga instructor tells me her name is Kelly. She introduces me to Lou as one of her students, which feels kind of funny since I've only taken one class.

While we chat for a while about the gym and other mundane stuff, I'm checking out both of them. Kelly isn't exactly femme but standing next to Lou she may as well have a ball gown on. Lou screams dyke from across the room. I'm surprised I haven't seen her before, but guess it's because she can bench press a horse and works out in the free-weight section at the other side of the building. I wonder if any of the men give her a hard time. Probably not.

"Do you guys wanna take a sauna?" Kelly asks.

My ears perk up. I thought the gym was closing.

"Tonight?" Lou asks.

"Yeah." Kelly turns to me. "It'll do your muscles a world of good after aerobics and yoga." My body does ache. They're both looking at me.

"Sure, but aren't they closing?" I ask.

Kelly picks up her mat and puts it in the pile in the corner. "I have a key to the building."

This is when I realize something else is going on. She starts to move differently, more snake-like or something. She flicks off the light and says she'll meet us in there. The entire time she wears something between a smile and a smirk on her face, and when she looks at me she drops her chin and pretends to be all serious.

Kelly walks off down the hall, leaving Lou and me standing outside the studio.

"She's got a great ass, doesn't she?"

I nod, worried Lou will rip my head off if I actually say yes.

"You took aerobics today?" she asks. I nodded again. "Well, then we should shower before we get into the sauna. There's nothin' worse than sweatin' on top of old sweat." I figure Lou is an expert in this area, so I follow her into the locker room.

Everyone else has gone. The lights are off in the aerobics studio and the halls, and with the exception of a few emergency lights, the place is dark. I hear Kelly's voice saying goodbye to someone, but it's far away and muffled.

I feel awkward getting naked in front of Lou. She's a large woman. Probably three inches taller than I am with massive biceps and small round breasts. Something about her quiet naked presence as we shower next to each other makes her seem larger than life. She slicks back her half inch of hair and runs her face under the stream of water. Kelly is nowhere to be found.

"So, do we...have to wear bathing suits in the sauna?"

"Nope." She doesn't even look at me as she runs a bar of soap down her leg. "Nobody's here but us."

An even mixture of nerves and excitement swims around in my stomach. We finish our showers at the same time and walk dripping wet down the hallway to the brown wooden sauna door. A sign on the front reads, WARNING: IF YOU HAVE A COMMUNICABLE DISEASE, PLEASE DO NOT USE THIS SAUNA! That doesn't inspire a lot of confidence in me. The sign doesn't seem to bother Lou, who opens up the door and walks in. With slight hesitation I follow her.

The room is small, dark, and desert hot. A red light in the ceiling gives the whole place a Dante's *Inferno* feel. Lou sits on one of the two benches and leans against the wall, legs spread like she's at a baseball game. She groans and stretches her hands over her head. With her arms up, her breasts disappear. I sit on the other bench, keeping my arms and legs as close to my body as possible. The heat feels good, and I feel beads of sweat forming on my forehead.

Lou doesn't say or ask me anything. We just sit there naked—she sprawled comfortably open and I wound tight as a vintage wristwatch. I hear the shower start and feel relieved that Kelly will soon be joining us. At one point I look up and Lou is staring at me. I get the feeling she likes making me nervous. She smiles, and we each give a kind of chin up nod. I am now officially in a 1974 prison porno with Lou the burly guard from Cell Block C about to dole out my punishment. It's a little surreal.

Thankfully the shower turns off, and I hear Kelly's bare feet on the wet tile as she heads for the sauna. The door opens and lets in a blast of cool air. Kelly steps in and closes the door. She's completely naked and the presence of a third set of breasts in the cramped space heightens the tension. Lou has her eyes closed and lets out a breathy, "Hey, babe," as Kelly sits next to her. They are simultaneously an odd and perfectly matched couple.

"Everyone's gone," Kelly reassures me. "This heat feels great." Sweat pours down my forehead.

We all sit there silently. They both close their eyes, and I stare at the places where their bodies meet. My eyes keep darting up to see if they're watching me. Kelly's pea-sized hard nipples look lost on her breasts. My eyes settle on her crotch, and the way the black hairs curl around each other. I must have stared too long because when I look up Lou is watching me. I panic.

She laughs, but in a way that doesn't make a sound. More of a shoulder shrug and a release breath. I cock my head to the side quickly as if to say, *Oops, you caught me*, and feign a smile. She leans forward, and I think this must be the point where she disembowels me. But instead she takes Kelly's arm and pulls her to her feet. Then Lou stretches out on the bench, and Kelly looks at me, smiling, with wide eyes. She steps up over the bench, spreads her lips open, and lowers herself down onto Lou's waiting mouth. As easy and nonchalant as pickin' daisies, she's got her pussy on her girlfriend's face two feet away from me. I nearly have a heart attack.

"Shit," I say, sitting up straight. They never miss a beat. I wonder if Kelly assumed Lou and I had talked about this while she was gone. You know, setting it up and making sure I was OK with everything. On second thought, I'm sure Kelly knows Lou didn't say a word.

Surprisingly, my entire body relaxes. My legs spread, my shoulders lower. Knowing I'm not going to be killed, but instead am getting to watch these two fuck is the highlight of my day. My week. OK, my year.

Lou is hard at work. Her hands are on Kelly's ass, and her knees are bent. I can't see any part of her face but her forehead. Her lips and tongue spread Kelly's cunt, and she sucks and pulls and plays with her clit. Kelly's knees push into the wooden bench, and Lou brings her head up to meet her body. She has strong neck muscles, and the veins stick out with each movement of her mouth or tongue. The room grows hotter, and I feel light-headed.

Lou takes her time, and the whole experience enters a time warp. I can smell Kelly's cunt and the longer they are at it, the more we all sweat. Drops run down her back into her ass. Her hair is tied back and the strands cling to her neck. She moans and runs her cunt back and forth over Lou's face. Lou knows exactly what she's doing, and when Kelly comes, Lou grabs the top of her ass and pulls her down into her face. She arches her back up off the bench to take in everything she can get. Kelly lets her full weight collapse onto Lou's face, and her nails scratch the sauna walls.

Kelly stays on top of her for a minute catching her breath. I hear Lou say, "Nice." When Kelly stands, everything below Lou's eyes are glistening wet. She sits up and wipes her mouth with her palm. My cunt aches.

Nobody says anything as Kelly comes over and asks me to scootch forward a little. Then she swings her left leg around me and sits on the bench behind me, straddling my body. Our bodies slide easily over each other. Her pubic hair touches the skin at the top of my ass. She puts her chin on the base of my neck and runs it over my shoulder and down the top of my right arm.

She reaches around and puts her hand at the top of my

chest and slides it down over my nipple, cups my breast, and squeezes it up. She holds it there and then does the same with the left. Then she runs her hands down my torso to the insides of my thighs and spreads my legs. She takes her legs and hooks them around my knees so I'm pinned to her body with my legs spread wide open, her tits pressing against my back. She takes my elbows and pulls my arms back to rest on the wood bench. Lou sits watching the whole scene. Sweaty and wet, Kelly runs her hands over me, starting under my chin and ending at my calves.

Once I'm all set up, it's Lou who gets between my legs. I look down and see the top of her head just beneath my stomach as she runs her tongue up and down over my clit. Kelly says, "You got it, babe," in the same voice she used in yoga class. "Come on, baby," she whispers in my ear as she watches her girlfriend eating me out. Lou's face disappears. Her arms are wrapped around both our bodies, and she pulls us closer. Kelly lifts her feet up and brings both sets of our legs down on Lou's back. We may as well have had oil poured over the top of us, the way we slide and slip over each other's bodies. I can't figure out where mine ends and Kelly's begins. The heat is making me dizzy. I could come in a second, but Lou keeps backing off. She'll zoom in and circle my clit, then slip her tongue down to my ass, then back up again. Our bodies move in unison. It lasts a long, long time, and I grow hotter and sweatier and dizzier. I need to come and suspect Lou is fucking with me and I want to beg her to stop moving her tongue away. All the while Kelly says, "All right, babe, you got it," in my ear, and I'm not exactly sure who she's talking to.

Then I'm coming, yelling, "Yes! Yes! Yes!" and both of them are pinning me down. Our legs squeeze around Lou's head as we thrash around. Then things get murky. I'm feeling incredibly woozy like I'm going to pass out. Then I guess I do. Through it all there's a rush of cool air, and Kelly says, "You'll be OK," and hands me something to drink.

The next clear memory is of me sitting on the dirty floor outside the sauna. "You gotta watch how much time you spend in there," Lou says, with more than a little humor in her voice.

Kelly is holding a sports drink and telling me I'll feel fine in a few minutes. The locker room is dark, and the sight of our three naked bodies brings me back to reality. I mutter something about Lou being right and stand up feeling acutely embarrassed.

We shower together. Well, Kelly and I do. I soap her breasts under the cool water, and she runs her hands over me. Lou watches. When we're done, she sits naked on the bench and has a cigarette, which I think is kind of odd. She didn't strike me as a smoker. Maybe I spooked her by passing out, but then again, maybe she has knocked out hundreds of girls the same way.

We get dressed and leave without a lot of pleasantries. Between aerobics, yoga, the sauna, sex, and passing out, I can barely lift my arms to drive.

■ ■ ■

My friends are all amazed by my transformation. "Are you going to the gym again? God, you're always working out!" When I show them my new sports bra they demand to know what's gotten into me. I just smile and say, "I've finally found a gym that satisfies all my needs."

Touchdown Ren Bisson

It was a horrendous separation. Somehow Gracie had finagled both cats and the dog from me, and she kept the apartment we had shared for two years—the one I had done all of the cosmetic work on to make it as nice as it was. She told me that since the breakup was entirely my fault because I refused to change my annoying behaviors, it was only fair that she get the pets and the apartment. Regardless, I quickly moved out to get away from her henpecking, but after a short time I realized I really missed the dog.

Since it was June and all the college kids had moved back home for the summer, I found an apartment fairly easily. It was a relatively small place, but it had an incredible bedroom skylight that made me feel like I was in a planetarium. I set up my futon under it, and at night I'd watch for a falling star to wish upon.

As the summer quickly passed, I realized I'd done nothing but work and mope around. But one day I ran into my friend Jane, who I used to play flag football with, and she invited me to play with the Wildcats again. Gracie had forced to me to quit playing, saying she thought it made me too manly and that she didn't appreciate my being so touchy-feely with other women. As if pulling a flag off someone is sexual contact. So when Jane asked me to play again, I jumped at the chance. She told me practice was scheduled for Saturday at 1 o'clock.

I woke up Saturday morning with a smile on my face,

looking forward to getting back in shape, not to mention being around all those buff, sweaty women. I rummaged through a box in my closet and found my old Wildcats jersey and my cleats. I tried them on, and the cleats still fit fine, but I was grateful my jersey used to be big on me because it was none too loose now. Hopefully football season would help me take off a few extra pounds. I ate a light lunch, packed a water bottle, and headed to the field.

When I arrived at exactly 1 P.M., most of the players were stretching, tossing the football, or catching up with each other. I only recognized about four women from the old team. They all said hello to me as I walked on the field. Jane wasn't there yet, but Sally, our faithful quarterback, welcomed me back with a big bear hug. She told me Jane was probably still at Jake's Sporting Goods (our team sponsor), picking up our new flags and uniforms. We were lucky enough to have a sponsor, but it kind of sucked because they selected our uniforms, and we didn't have a choice of color or style—which made us walking billboards for the store. We couldn't even have our names on the back of our jerseys because JAKE'S SPORTING GOODS was stitched across the back—like no one would also notice it on the front. At least our uniforms were red and not some hideous color, and we got new ones every year—which was fortunate for us, because by the end of each season most of them were completely ripped and stained.

"Hey, Lance, are you ready for the 2 o'clock scrimmage?" Sally asked me.

"Shit, Jane didn't mention that. Sure, I guess, but I don't know any of the plays you guys use now."

"The plays haven't changed much," Sally said. "We have a coupla new ones, and we've changed the names of some, but I'll help you out. You still want to play running back, don't you?"

"It's the only position I know," I told her.

"Good. We've missed you, buddy."

Sally summoned the team and introduced me. She told them I used to play and that I was damn good too, and she said this was the only reason they were allowing such a late addition to the team. They'd been practicing for a month already, and the season was starting next Saturday.

Jane finally arrived, apologetic for being late. Nobody seemed to mind since she was bearing gifts. She passed around the bag of flags and said she was going to hand out our uniforms. We got to at least pick the number we wanted, and, so there'd be no confusion, Jane had made a list. Since I had absolutely no seniority on the team, I'd be stuck with whatever jersey was left over.

"Hey, Lance, look! You're lucky number 69," Jane grinned.

Everyone laughed and slapped me on the back. I played along but was embarrassed about being the butt of any joke. Not to mention that Marcia, the woman who took my old number, was my least favorite person on the team. My last year playing was her first year on the team, and she did more whining and complaining than playing. She was such a princess that we all called her Queenie behind her back. Sally had told me back then that Queenie had a crush on me, and I thought it was a crock of shit, but now I was wondering. Not only did she have my number, but she sat next to me as Jane handed out the jerseys and was acting all goofy and flirty toward me.

Jane and Sally led us in warm-ups, then told everyone what position they'd be playing. Right away we began practicing offensive and defensive drills. Sally ran almost every play to orient me, and I picked up the new plays quickly. It was just like riding a bike.

The other team showed up at about 1:45, and when I found out who they were, I was pissed: the Prides, who were infamous for their dirty tactics and roughhousing. They won the league almost every year—not because they were good, but because they scared the crap out of everyone and intimidated other teams to the point of creating so much fear and anxiety that they couldn't defend themselves. The sad thing is, they'd make it to the state tournament every year but lose because they didn't know how to play by the rules. It pissed our team off to no end since each season we beat them at least 50% of the time.

As we started the scrimmage, without referees, we all hoped we'd finish the day with our bones and spinal cords intact. I checked out the other team and noticed a lot of new players. Perhaps this was a sign that they wouldn't be up to their usual tricks. Unfortunately, I noticed that my ex's ex was still playing for them, and I knew she had never let it go that Gracie had left her for me. Hopefully by now she knew we were over. The girls on our team all called her Brute because she did more tackling than flag-grabbing, muscling other players around like they were rag dolls.

I got my answer the first time I carried the ball. Brute hit me so hard that it flew out of my hands and I got the wind knocked out of me. The two team captains exchanged words, and we were given five yards from the point of the foul and first down. I was just hoping I'd be able to get out of bed in the morning. Sally ran me again, and this play was far more interesting. As I was running, trying to avoid a player I'd never seen before, she grabbed my ass instead of my flag. After the play was over, the player smirked and said, "Sorry about that," with a wink and a devilish grin. I was kind of shocked, but I forgot about it until my next play. This time she grabbed my crotch and again apologized. Her teammates started ragging on her, making comments like, "Why don't you just ask her out?" and "Oh, real subtle, Allie." At least now I knew her name.

During halftime I checked her out, and she was looking at me too. Damn, she was a hottie, with long blond hair and a curvaceous body. Her hair was pulled back in a ponytail, and she stood with her hand on her hips as if she were in charge. I for one knew I could stand her bossing me around a bit.

The rest of the game was a blur, except for Allie and me flirting. I wasn't playing it up too big, though. You know, playing hard to get.

After the game, Jane gave us our schedule for the season. Our first game was against none other than the Prides. I was secretly happy about this, since I figured by next week I might be able to get up the nerve to ask Allie out and maybe find out a little more about her. After being around all these hot women, I was extra aware of how lonely I was and was definitely aching for some stimulating contact.

We had practice two times that week. I asked around, but nobody knew Allie very well. The only thing Sally found out was that she was new in town and was definitely single. That's all I needed to know.

Saturday's game was intense, and Allie didn't pull many of the flirting antics she had the week before. As a matter of fact, Queenie flirted a lot more than Allie and even offered me my old jersey back if I would 69 with her. Allie did smile after a few plays and she even said "Good run" to me once, but the energy was definitely different, and I lost my nerve to ask her out.

We ended up winning the game by a small margin, mostly due to really good refereeing. The Prides weren't playing as dirty as usual, and we all hoped it would stay that way. Even Brute kept her trap shut, which surprised us all. Before we left, Jane gave us next week's practice schedule and told us all to join her that evening at the local gay bar, Magnolia's, for Retro Night.

After I got in my pickup, I noticed a note under my wiper blade. I grabbed it, looking around to see if anyone was watching. To my disappointment, I spotted Queenie waiting for me to look up so she could wave goodbye. I opened the note, which read: *Hey, number 69, do you want to have a good time? If so, meet me here at the field at midnight tonight on the bleachers. I promise you won't regret it or ever forget it. Guess who?*

I was in awe but wasn't sure who had written it. Queenie or Allie? I was leaning toward Queenie after her earlier 69 reference and the different energy Allie had put out today. If it was Queenie, I really didn't want to go there; I wasn't attracted to her at all. But if by some small chance it was Allie, well, then I guess I'd have to show. If it was Queenie, though, I'd let her know how I felt and hopefully we could put it behind us.

Later that night I got spruced up and headed for Magnolia's, where I met up with the Wildcats. Journey and Toto were blaring alternately on the speakers, so when the clock struck 11:30, I didn't have to make much of an excuse to leave and head for the football field. "This music isn't really my thing," I told my teammates. "And I'm tired anyway." Thankfully, they didn't put up much of a protest.

As I drove to the field, a nearly full moon and extraordinarily bright stars lit up the sky. It was warm for an early September night, and I was growing more and more excited at the prospect of my admirer being Allie.

I arrived at midnight on the dot. I looked around for cars and people, but the place was deserted. Even though I knew this could be some kind of prank, I was willing to risk it. As I approached the bleachers I spotted a note taped to the bleachers with the number 69 written on it. I opened it: *Thanks for coming. Sit and relax. I'll be right with you.* I leaned back, placing my hands on the bleacher behind me, and looked up at the sky. The view was even better out here than through the skylight in my bedroom. I couldn't admire it for long, though, because before I knew it someone grabbed my hands from behind, braced my leaning body, and handcuffed me to the runner behind my seat. I was startled, not knowing whether to be frightened or excited. I looked around but didn't see anyone. "Hey, what's going on here?" I yelled. All I got in response was, "Shhh, don't speak." I was partly relieved, because it wasn't Queenie's voice, but I wasn't sure if it was Allie's because I hadn't talked to her that much.

I sat there for at least a couple of minutes before I heard someone come down from the top of the bleachers. I wondered how the hell she'd gotten up there without me hearing her. I turned around to look, and there was Allie in the moonlight, wearing only her Prides jersey. I sighed in relief and at the hormonal rush flooding my body. She sauntered over to me, then straddled me so that I knew in no uncertain terms that she wasn't wearing underwear. I couldn't believe this: I was used to being the top, the one in control, and now here I was, handcuffed and at this woman's mercy. Allie, still straddling me, looked at me and waited a moment before she spoke. "Hey, gorgeous, you OK with this arrangement?" she asked in a taunting tone.

I nodded. "Yes, ma'am."

"Good," she said. "Then don't say another word." With that she dropped and kissed me passionately, then worked my shirt up so she could sit on my bare skin. We kissed some more as she rubbed herself against my stomach. Lifting her shirt, she put her breast to my mouth. I teased her erect nipple until she demanded, "Harder!" I immediately obeyed. Allie groaned in approval, and before I knew it she undid my pants and pulled them down to my ankles. She went back to kissing me, then grabbed the bleacher on both sides behind me and thrust her swollen, wet clit into mine over and over. She looked like she was about come, but then she stopped. "You first," she said.

I was so turned on that my come was running down my crack onto the bleacher. With her hot, agile tongue, she kissed me some more before working her tongue down my body. She kissed, licked, and bit every inch of me before finally reaching my pulsing clit. She breathed on it and licked around it, teasing me. I almost came right there. I was on fire, burning for her to finish what she'd started. She entered me with two fingers as she put her tongue on my hot spot. I moaned so loudly I felt the bleacher shake beneath me. When her fingers found my G spot, I had absolutely no self-control, and before I knew it I was ejaculating so fiercely that I soaked the front of her jersey.

Allie looked at me with a self-satisfied grin as I tried to catch my breath. She kissed me again, working her way up over my face. Her scent was all over me, sweet and delicious. She straddled me so that her clit was inches from my mouth, then teased me, quickly touching down on me and lifting off again. I wanted my mouth on her so bad it hurt. After what seemed an eternity, she jumped off me and giggled a little. "What the...?" I sputtered.

"I'm leaving," she smiled. "My mama told me to always leave 'em wanting more."

I was flabbergasted. Allie jumped off the bleacher, went behind me, and unlocked one handcuff, put the key in my hand for me to unlock the other one myself, and before I knew it she was gone.

I freed my other wrist and pulled up my pants. I was extremely flustered, but I had a permanent grin on my face. I spent the entire ride home replaying the event over and over in my mind.

When I got home I decided to take a hot shower. Before getting in, I caught a glimpse of myself in the mirror and noticed some bruises on my chest and torso. I wasn't sure whether they were from today's game or tonight's escapade. Either way, they made me smile.

As soon as I got out of the shower, I heard a knock at my front door. After throwing on some boxers and a T-shirt, I grabbed my softball bat, cautiously approached the door, and looked through the peephole. Immediately I recognized the silhouette in the hallway.

When I eagerly opened the door, Allie said, "So do you want some more?"

I led her into my bedroom. Even though the lights were out, the entire room was illuminated by the moonlight pouring through my skylight. Handing me a bag, Allie said, "Here's a little something for you to wear." Then she asked if she could use my bathroom.

After I showed her the way, I opened the bag and was more than happy to comply with her request. Inside was an eight-inch silicone dick with a leather harness. Of course, I had my own dildo, but it certainly wasn't as large as this one. After I had it right where I wanted it, I put my boxers back on. The bulge in my shorts was enormous, and I felt my clit getting as erect as the cock itself. I sat myself in my reading chair while I waited for Allie to return.

My jaw dropped when I saw her. She had sprayed whipped cream around her breasts and over her pussy. I'd tasted whipped cream in my time but never on a dish like Allie.

"I want every drop gone before you can have me," she demanded.

I got up from my chair and licked the cream off her breast then kissed her with a mouth full of the stuff. She directed me back to work, and I ate her up as if I hadn't eaten in weeks. With little grunts and groans, she let me know I was doing a good job, and just when I thought I'd devoured it all, she pointed to a spot I'd missed. While I was on my knees taking care of the last of it, she pulled me up to her mouth and kissed me. Then she grabbed my ass and pushed me into her, rubbing herself against my cock. It wasn't long before she took it out of my boxers and began sliding herself back and forth on it while we stood there in the moonlight. My clit was throbbing; this woman was so fucking hot I thought I was going to explode.

"Fuck me now!" Allie commanded, digging her nails into my back. She bent over my reading chair, using the arms to stabilize herself. "From behind!" she ordered. I entered her gently, not wanting to hurt her with my mammoth cock. She groaned in pleasure as I slid the dick in; it didn't take long before she took in all eight inches. In, out, in, out, in, out:

Allie and I were in perfect sync with each gentle thrust before she pulled away and ordered me to sit in the chair. She positioned herself in front of me, with her back to me, and maneuvered the dildo inside her; we rode at her pace. She pulled my hands up and placed them to her breasts. Her sexual energy was so fucking hot I was melting. I found the perfect angle to pound her hard and fast. With the base of the dildo rubbing against my clit, in no time I came right there on the chair, nearly soaking the cushion.

Working her magic, Allie put one hand to her clit and within seconds she was screaming "I'm coming!" loud enough to wake up the entire neighborhood. Then she got off me and led me to the bed, where we lay panting for a while before she rolled on top of me and slid up to straddle my face. There was no teasing her: She was on top and definitely in charge. As I feverishly licked her swollen clit, she leaned back and dug her fingers into my thighs as she wiggled around. Again she let the neighborhood know she was coming.

Sweaty and disheveled, Allie dismounted me and lay beside me. We were both exhausted.

"Thanks for the good time," she smiled.

"No, thank *you*," I grinned back.

She kissed me then got up and quickly got dressed. "Sorry I gotta run," she said, "but I have to be at work in a few hours."

"Oh, yeah? What do you do for a living?"

"Public service." She bent over and kissed me then started to head out.

"Hey, wait, you forgot your bag," I told her.

"Keep it. You'll be needing it again soon." And with that, she left.

I looked at my clock: 4 A.M. Thank god I didn't have to be anywhere soon.

When I got up around noon I could hardly move. All that football and sex had wiped me out. I took a shower and got dressed, a bit saddened that I had to wash Allie's sweet scent off me.

After last night's workout, I was starving, so I went to the kitchen only to discover my refrigerator was empty; I had to go shopping.

Daydreaming on the way, I noticed—much to my dismay—blue lights flashing in my rearview mirror, so I pulled over. I was bending over looking for my registration when I heard a familiar voice: "Don't bother looking for anything, Miss. You're under arrest."

I looked up and saw Allie's face with its usual smirk. "I'll be by at 4:30 to frisk you."

"Public service, huh?" I laughed.

"Be ready to assume the position." Without another word she walked back to her squad car.

Yahoo for the women in blue!

Blue Ball Passion Shannon McDonnell

I knew I was in trouble when Abbie's first serve scorched the floor an inch past the red line. I managed one faltering step in the ball's direction before it was too late. Ace. Just like that I was down 1–0.

Even if I hadn't been thinking about those smoldering eyes of hers, even if I hadn't been eyeing those finely sculpted legs, I could never have returned that serve.

My confidence deflated like a pricked balloon. It didn't matter that I'd won my first three racquetball games of the day, dispatching my opponents with relative ease. Abbie wasn't anything like them. She was better—much better. And it was going to take all my concentration to keep her from sending me off to the losers' bracket.

Concentration was going to be a problem. This woman had my head spinning.

Let's get one thing straight. I'd always considered myself basically hetero, even though I did try the other side a few times at U.C. Santa Barbara. Experimenting and all that. And I found out girls could be a lot of fun between the sheets. But that was two years and a few relationships ago—all with guys. Once you're out of school, you start playing it safe. At least I did.

Yet here was Abbie, tall, lithe, stunning. And here was I, distracted, damp between my legs.

I moved a few steps closer to the line where it met the pitted left wall. Abbie glanced back at me, bent at the waist, bounced quickly on the balls of her feet, and whacked the ball.

This time she hit a soft wall-hugger high up on the right side of the court. It was the complete opposite of her first serve, and it tied me up. I tried to snare the ball with a snap of the wrist but succeeded only in banging my racquet hard against the wall. Another point for Abbie. I was definitely in trouble.

I had been getting a drink at the water fountain in the hall before the match, still high on my three consecutive victories. Then, turning away from the fountain, I bumped right into her. She was a few inches taller than me and a couple of years older, with an athlete's body and those mysterious, gray-green eyes.

"Sorry," I said.

She nodded, then looked at me for a long moment—wondering why I was staring at her, I suppose. Then, with a pointed look at the fountain, she said, "Do you mind?"

"Oh! Sorry," I repeated, and stepped out of her way. I started to head back to the court to get some stretching in. Well, I thought about going back. My body opted to stay put.

So I watched her, as discreetly as possible, while she stooped and drank. The little stream of water splashed softly on her full lips. I was at the Y a couple of times a week, trying to stay in shape on the treadmills or playing racquetball. But I had never seen her around before. I noted her snug white tank top, green nylon shorts, and Nike court shoes. Her straight, straw-colored hair hung just to her shoulders and was wet at her temples. She held an Ektelon racquet lightly in her gloved hand.

"You're playing in the tourney," I blurted.

She straightened and turned, fixing me again with those

captivating peepers. "Yeah." She wiped the water from her lips. "How have you been doing?"

That threw me. "Oh, have we met before?"

For the first time she cracked a small smile. "No, I meant, how are you doing in the tournament?"

"Oh!" I tried to cover my embarrassment, but my face burned. "Um, pretty well. Three-oh. I mean, I've won three straight. Not to brag or anything." *Oh, for God's sake.*

I pushed on. "What about you?"

"Same." She brushed that aside quickly with an introduction. "I'm Abbie."

"Hi. I'm Jil. With one L," I said, and winced.

She just nodded, a small grin still turning up the corners of her mouth. "I watched part of your game last hour. You're good."

"Thanks." I stood there stupidly, suddenly wishing I had worn my other gym outfit—the one my last boyfriend said looked "crazy" on me.

She broke the silence. "Well, nice to meet you, Jil with one L. Guess I'll be seeing you in a few minutes."

I should have seen this coming, but I wasn't thinking straight. "You will?"

Abbie was already halfway down the hall, carrying herself with smooth, confident strides. "Yeah," she called over her shoulder. "I'm your next opponent."

It wasn't until she had piled up seven straight points that I managed to get lucky, flailing at the ball in desperation and sending it directly into the forward right corner. Now it was my turn to serve, and I couldn't wait to show Abbie a few tricks of my own. But my turn between the red lines was brief. Abbie was simply stronger and quicker.

Game over, Jil.

Only it wasn't. Abbie may have been up 7–0, but it still takes 15 points to win. The spectators at the window began to drift off, no doubt expecting the athletic girl in the green shorts to coast to victory against the outmatched, shortish, ponytailed brunette.

Somehow it didn't happen that way.

I scratched and clawed my way back into the game. My first point came on a mistake by Abbie. Then I scored three more on a series of hard-fought rallies that left us both breathless. I discovered a few cracks in her game. Power and agility were on her side, but I had more experience. I adapted to her game, and she no longer ran roughshod over me.

But I was still fighting an uphill battle, on two fronts. My attraction to Abbie was pummeling me, and I didn't want to fight it. I wanted to surrender.

I came all the way back to tie Abbie at ten, but in the end, the persistent and growing urge to get physical with Abbie was my downfall. Maneuvering for a kill shot, she collided with me in the center of the court, our chests heaving, arms instinctively thrown around one another.

"Damn it!" She gazed into my eyes, making no move to extricate herself.

"My fault," I said, excruciatingly conscious of her sweet breath falling on my cheek in rapid little bursts, her sweat-dampened shirt pressed against mine, her crotch riding my right thigh.

"You OK?"

"Yeah. You?"

"Fine."

Awkwardly we separated, but something passed between us in that collision, something transmitted and received. I saw it flicker across her face as she pulled away from me. I couldn't repress a slight shudder. My tongue felt thick in my mouth.

Repeating the point due to my unintentional interference (or was it?), Abbie proceeded to take full advantage of my renewed imbalance. Five more minutes and it was over. I had lost, 15-11, but my ego wasn't smarting like it should have been. The game wasn't uppermost in my mind.

So off I went to the losers' bracket, still thinking about Abbie, resentful of whoever would share her court now, share her time, share her. I romped to victory over my next foe, a spindly schoolmarm type who played like a beginner.

Then I was free for a while. I grabbed a sandwich at the market across the street, hurried back through the rain, and spent a solitary half-hour in the Y's crummy lounge. I kept an eye out for Abbie, but she never appeared.

Back in the racquetball wing, a small crowd had gathered outside one of the window courts. I shouldered my way closer and looked inside.

It was her, of course. She had her opponent, a girl of 17 or 18, running back and forth, up and back, just trying to stay alive. Abbie put her away with an unreturnable shot into the corner.

"What's the score?" I asked one of the gawkers.

"The tall one's ahead, 10–6."

Just then, Abbie saw me; I noted her double take with pleasure. Perhaps I really had made an impression. Then she gave me a sly wink, so quick and so natural I don't think I would have noticed if I hadn't been looking right at her. I smiled and looked at my shoes, embarrassed.

Abbie returned to her game and I drifted away to consult the wins and losses chart. Abbie was leading the winners' bracket, and so far my only loss was to her. We each had one game left today, after which most of the players would be finished. A few would return tomorrow to battle it out for first and second place prizes—a can of racquetballs, probably, or your picture on the bulletin board. I hadn't bothered to check.

But there was a chance Abbie and I would play again.

I squeaked by my final opponent of the day. Five wins and one loss, not bad. That meant I'd be back tomorrow. I showered, changed, and headed for the chart feeling pleasantly tired.

Abbie was there, alone, still in her gym clothes. She looked a little droopy. Her last match must've been tough. She turned at my approach, and I saw the shadow of a grin on her face.

"There you are," she said.

"Hi." I tried to sound cool and nonchalant. "So? Where do we stand?"

"See for yourself." She took a half step sideways and I moved close to her, pretending to be solely interested in the chart.

Abbie—her last name was Zymaski, I saw—had finished Day One of the tourney at 5–1. Same record as mine. The teenager had come back to beat her.

Tomorrow's schedule was posted beside the standings. There was only one game listed: ABBIE ZYMASKI VS. JILL JONES.

"What is this?" I stammered.

"They gave you an extra L," she said.

"I see that. But why are we the only two people left in the tourney?"

"We have the best two records. One loss apiece. No one else has fewer than two. They're all out of it."

I felt woozy. "So..."

"So, it's just you and me, Jil." Then she definitely smiled at me, a sexy, entrancing smile, and I began to feel hot.

"I've got to take a shower and get out of here," she said. "See you tomorrow at 10. Don't be late—I don't want to win by forfeit." She gave my hand a squeeze.

I watched her disappear into the women's locker room and fought the urge to follow her. Now she would be stripping off her shirt, now her sports bra...her shorts next...now her underwear...stepping into the shower.

I rubbed my temples, amused and startled by my own case of raging hormones. And all over a chick! It was crazy.

Sunday dawned cold, gray, and wet. A steady rain against my window woke me from a dream about Abbie in which we lay together on a windy bluff, exploring each other's bodies. I didn't want the dream to end, but suddenly I was fearful of being late. I shot a glance at the bedside clock and was relieved to find I had plenty of time to get to the Y. Time enough, in fact, to return to those dreams of Abbie. I rolled over on my stomach with my hand under my hips.

I'm not one of those phonies who pretends she never masturbates. I closed my eyes, and this time it was special. It wasn't my hand touching, parting my lips, setting off sparks like a live wire at my clit; it was Abbie's. And it was Abbie's hand reaching up to my breasts, squeezing them, pinching my nipples lightly.

It didn't take me long. I let out a scream as I came, grateful for once that I lived alone.

Abbie was already on the court warming up when I arrived. "Hey," she said, a bit cautiously. She wore gray shorts and a sleeveless blue T-shirt dark with sweat around the neckline.

"Hi," I said, suddenly shy.

We hit the ball around in silence for a few minutes until the door opened behind us and the Y's pimply-faced racquetball director popped his head in. "Good morning. Abbie and Jil?"

Abbie snared the ball and turned to face him. "Yeah."

"OK, it's down to the two of you," he said, as if we didn't know. "Winner takes home this classy championship shirt." He held out a bright red T-shirt bearing a large, ugly YMCA logo in the middle of the front. He turned it around and I saw the words RACQUETBALL CHAMPION and the date in white block letters. It was hideous.

"Good luck," the kid said, and started to duck out of the room.

"Wait a minute." Abbie grabbed a handful of his shirt. He looked at her, surprised and a little scared. "Her name has one L—Jil, with one L. Got it? Now fix it."

The guy nodded hastily, eyes wide, and Abbie let go of his shirt. He bolted from the room and the door swung closed.

"Thanks," I said.

Abbie bounced the ball against the floor. "I can't let you take home that beautiful shirt today, Jil. I've got to have it."

"No way. It's mine," I replied. "I'll wear it proudly through the streets."

I felt better with the tension broken and even managed to ignore the gawkers outside the window. But ignoring my attraction to Abbie would not be possible, and I gave up trying.

She won first serve and took up a position between the

red lines. Her trim behind curved gracefully in her close-fitting shorts. I felt a jolt of excitement pass through me.

Then her serve careened toward me, hard and fast. I protected my face with my racquet and watched as the blue blur shot back to the forward wall, low and unreturnable.

"Lucky," I murmured, taking the ball from her outstretched hand. She gave me a quick swat on the ass.

Abbie regained control in short order and jumped out in front, running off three unanswered points. But I stopped her before she could bury me. I must have learned something from our game the day before, because I found myself holding my own. It was the hardest, most exhausting, most fun racquetball game I'd ever played.

The score reached 14–13 in my favor, and I had a chance to finish it. My hair kept falling in my eyes, but I didn't care. I had to win. I didn't want to say goodbye to Abbie, and I was convinced my winning would somehow keep us together. I would represent a challenge to her, someone worth playing again. At least that's how I hoped it would turn out.

My serve forced Abbie to hit an easy lob back at the front wall, and I took advantage of it, stinging the ball with all the strength I had left. It shot from the front wall to the back on a fly and went sailing toward the front again. Abbie could not catch up to it, and the game was over.

We met in the center of the court, Abbie putting those long arms around me in a warm, wet hug—holding me a little longer than most casual opponents. I returned the hug with just as much feeling.

A few of the spectators broke into a slightly mocking applause as we left the court. Poor losers. "Great game," someone said. The director thrust the revolting T-shirt into my hand, muttered, "Congratulations," then disappeared.

These things happened on the periphery of my consciousness. I was mainly aware of Abbie's presence at my side as we headed for the locker room.

"Nice game, Jil," she said as the small crowd dispersed. "You're really something."

I smiled and watched the stained carpet pass beneath our cross-trainers. "It could have gone either way," I said. "I mean, just look at yesterday's game. It's not even fair that I'm the so-called champion. We each won a game."

Abbie flashed me that little smile of hers. "It's OK. Besides, I can tell how much you wanted that shirt."

We came to my locker, and Abbie lingered. I hunted furiously for something to say, something that would keep the day alive.

"Well, see you around," she said.

"Wait!" I blurted. "You want to have lunch or something?"

She stopped and considered me for a moment. Then she seemed to reach a decision. "After I shower. Meet you back here?"

I tried not to look too relieved. "Sure."

She nodded and headed for her own locker, stripping off her shirt as she went. I watched her, acutely aware that we were not alone; another girl was dressing nearby, and I heard one of the showers going.

With a sigh I peeled off my sweat-soaked clothes, stuffed them in my gym bag and stepped into the nearest shower stall. Five minutes later I turned off the water, stepped out, grabbed a towel, and began to dry my body. I looked up in time to see Abbie's naked backside retreat from view as she walked casually toward her locker. I noticed a small, dark tattoo just above her right buttock. Instantly I was madly curious to see it up close, to know what it was.

Careful, Jil, you're staring.

I had just pulled on my purple sweater and buttoned my favorite pair of jeans when Abbie showed up. She had one hand stuck in the pocket of her loose-fitting cargo pants and the other holding the strap of her sports bag. Her flannel shirt was untucked and unbuttoned over a white T-shirt.

I drove. At her suggestion we went to Luigi's, just a few blocks from the Y. I think she would have walked, but the rain was coming down in buckets now and neither of us had an umbrella.

We slipped into opposite sides of a booth and shared a veggie pesto pizza. Abbie ordered a hard cider, and at my questioning look, ordered me one too.

She sat back and regarded me over the top of her glass. "So, how did you get to be so good at racquetball?"

I was munching away on pizza; I hadn't realized how hungry I was. "I have a couple of older brothers who play. They got me into it when I was a kid."

She nodded. "They must be pretty good too."

Just sitting with her, feeling her gaze on me, sensing the tension mount—it got to me. I was anxious for something to happen.

"Leonard—he's the oldest—he doesn't play much any more. Too busy with his family and work." I tasted the cider; it was deliciously crisp. "Billy and I still play each other now and then. He lives up in Berling Heights." I put down my glass. "What about you? I was sailing along yesterday till I ran into you. Where did you learn the game?"

Abbie shrugged. "I used to live in Oregon; racquetball's big there. I like tennis too."

That was a bit oblique. "I haven't seen you at the Y before," I said.

"I just joined a few weeks ago."

We ate in silence for a few minutes. A Tori Amos tune was playing.

Abbie tipped her glass to her lips, finished her cider, then put the glass down slowly. Her eyes shifted from the glass to me. "Best two out of three?" she said, sounding strange.

Sometimes I'm a little slow. "What?"

"Look," she said, "you got that glorious championship shirt today, fair and square. But we're still even at one game apiece. How about playing the tiebreaker, just for ourselves?"

For the first time, it seemed like Abbie was hanging on my reply. She was trying to sound casual, but she had put herself at risk. She needn't have worried.

"Now?" I stammered.

She shrugged again. "Why not?"

With a sweaty palm I pulled a few bills from my purse and laid them on the table. "Let's go," I said.

Neither of us spoke as I drove us back to the Y. My mind was racing, my body on autopilot. It was one of those experiences where you can't remember stopping at traffic lights, making turns, or doing anything at all to drive yourself from point A to point B—but somehow you arrive.

The girl at the front desk told us we could use whichever court we wanted, but we had less than an hour left; the Y closed early on Sundays.

Abbie walked quickly through the deserted halls. I followed her into the last court on the row, number six, a windowless box with a peephole in the door. Some important detail nagged at the back of my mind, but I was so worked up I couldn't see it.

I closed the door behind me and turned toward Abbie, who stood in the center of the court. That's when it hit me. Giggling with nervous energy, I looked down at my jeans, sweater and flats. "Uh, Abbie, I think we forgot a few things—a ball, racquets, gym clothes..."

"To hell with the game," she said, her voice so full of emotion she was practically inarticulate. With two quick steps she was on me, hands gripping my shoulders, lips pressed to mine.

I was surprised for half a second, but then the floodgates opened and I was free. I opened my mouth to Abbie's eager tongue and tasted the tart sweetness of hard apple cider.

With scarcely a thought to our surroundings, we fumbled at each other's clothing. I had to break off the kiss to pull my sweater over my head. Abbie took the sweater from me and tossed it away, immediately seeking my mouth again. She was dangerous. Her hands found the clasp of my bra, ripped it open, and flung it aside. I managed to get her shirt off and unbutton her pants, but her undershirt resisted; Abbie stopped stroking my back just long enough to whip the garment off.

"You're driving me insane," she said huskily, "but I wasn't sure you would..."

I tore at her bra; Abbie's fervor had rubbed off on me. "I wanted you the moment you aced me yesterday," I said, breathless.

She guided me down to the polished yellow floorboards.

On my back, I looked up at Abbie as she crouched over me on all fours like a possessive animal.

Abbie's mouth found my nipples, already hard and begging for attention. She sucked them between her teeth, biting but not hurting, and my back rose up off the floor. She left a wet trail around my nipples and down my stomach, stopping at my jeans. Overhead, the florescent lights in the ceiling made me squint. Abbie unbuttoned my pants and tugged them down past my hips.

"Abbie..." I breathed. "Do you think this is a good idea? I mean, what if someone checks in here..."

"Don't worry," she said. "No one will."

If she was willing to take the chance, so was I.

It was very strange, having nothing to look at but the plain, scarred white walls and ceiling of the racquetball court as Abbie went down on me. With the first touch of her hands on my vagina I yelped and tried to move my legs farther apart for her. But in Abbie's haste, she had left my jeans and underwear bunched around my ankles. She stopped a moment to pull each pant leg over my shoes, then the underwear, and I heard my clothes fall in a distant part of the court with a soft thump.

The floor was hard and smooth under by body. Abbie returned to my swollen sex, pulling my lips apart to better expose my clit. The next several minutes were incredible. I hadn't been touched and licked so expertly in years. My hands reached out wildly for something to hold on to, finally settling in Abbie's soft, tawny hair. It didn't take long for her to bring me to my first orgasm, and then a second—which is unusual for me.

She climbed back up and lay on top of me, her small breasts pressed against my full ones. I tasted myself on her lips and tongue, and enjoyed the sensation of the smooth, hairless skin of her face and chest against me.

"Oh…I'd almost forgotten," I said as she nuzzled me. She gave me a sly grin, and impulsively I hugged her tight. She lay atop me another minute or two while we made out like high school kids.

Suddenly I realized Abbie still had her pants on, and she was dying for release. "No fair, one of us dressed and one not," I said playfully. Abbie's hair fell over my eyes as she wriggled out of her pants. I went to grab her underwear, but my fingers felt only skin.

"Surprise," she whispered with smoldering passion. "I don't wear any." In a quick, expert move, Abbie swung around so her legs were on either side of my head. Her tattoo, I now saw, was a little green dragon, paused in an eternal crawl from her right cheek toward her lower back.

"I love this," I said, petting the dragon.

Abbie wiggled back a bit so her ace was positioned directly over my patch. My gazed moved from the dragon to her pretty cunt, just begging for attention. A thatch of straw-colored hair tapered to a point just above her clean-shaven lips.

"It's been a while, I warned her apologetically.

"Use your instincts," Abbie said, and the next second, as if to lead by example, she put her head down and kissed my hot spot again.

I had only to stick my tongue out to taste Abbie's soft pink flesh. She responded immediately with a little jerk backward. She spread her legs wider and her little rosebud popped into view. I flicked my tongue across it, back and forth, pleased with Abbie's increasingly ardent reactions. My hands wandered over her ass and down the sides of her thighs. She felt so soft and smooth yet had a firm, athletic suppleness I envied.

Overcome by a fever of excitement, I licked and sucked Abbie's clit with a fervor I had never known. Her little anus was winking at me, so I lifted my mouth and licked there too.

Abbie cried out and the sound reverberated through the court. She writhed on top of me, her vagina squirming against my tongue. I felt her hands grab my ankles and squeeze tightly, as if she were holding on for dear life. Her body went rigid, and with a long, low moan she came, wetting my face with her juice. Finally she went limp. I felt her warm, quickened breath on my inner thigh.

In the ensuing calm, I lay still and looked around as best I could. Our clothes were strewn all over the place. I smiled at the thought of what we had just done on a YMCA racquetball court. Somewhere outside the door, the staff prepared to close up. Tomorrow, unsuspecting people would come in here to work up a little sweat of their own—but not like we did.

I was just beginning to think we ought to get dressed when we plunged into darkness.

"What the hell?" Abbie jerked up onto her knees and elbows.

"They're locking up. Time to go!"

She rolled off me, and we jumped to our feet. As reality washed over us, I became keenly aware of my nakedness.

A single emergency light came on overhead. In its feeble glow we groped around frantically for our clothes and dressed quickly. Despite the urgency of our situation, I couldn't help laughing at the absurdity.

Abbie found the door handle and cautiously pulled the

door open. The hallway was dim, lit only by an emergency light and a few skylights.

"Come on!" she whispered, and we beat a hasty path to the locker room, seeing no one. Only then did we stop and take a good look at ourselves.

Abbie had her T-shirt on, but those were my jeans she was wearing. They were too small for her; she had left the fly open to get them to her waist. She held my underpants in her hand.

I had dressed myself in her cargo pants and flannel shirt. In my hand were both our bras. Solemnly, I handed over her bra, and she gave me my panties. Then I burst into laughter, and to my delight, Abbie did too. Her armor had cracked for the first time, but hopefully not for the last.

We sorted out the rest of our clothes and two minutes later, much to the surprise of the cleaning crew in the lobby, we ran outside. The rain had lessened to a gentle drizzle and the clouds were breaking up in the West. "You know what this means, don't you," I said, as we headed for the parking lot.

"We have to play again," Abbie replied.

"Yep," I said, smiling up at the sky. "Because we still don't have a two-out-of-three winner."

Roller Ball Thomas S. Roche

The Battlin' Bombers slowly skated into the locker room. Their pretty faces were sad with defeat and purple-blue with bruises; their skintight stretch uniforms were torn and dirty. Normally the Bombers would have taken pleasure in the fact that their opponents, the Screamin' Mimis, didn't look much better—but today was a special case. Today their captain's wager hung glumly over their heads as they filed into the dark chamber that stank of female sweat. Jenny Blake led the way, her teammates staring daggers into the back of her jersey. Jenny's soul was sinking. If she hadn't made that stupid bet, the team would have nothing to look forward to but a cramped overnight bus ride back to Minneapolis. Now they'd be lucky if they slept at all.

"Well, well, well," chortled Frankie Petrocelli, captain of the Mimis, as she stood in front of Jenny and grinned. Her lithe body was stripped below the waist, her legs slightly spread so Jenny could see her pussy, even smell its sharpness over the dank odor of the locker room. She still wore her roller-skates and her jersey, splattered with Jenny's blood from their encounter against the railing. "If it isn't the losers. Well, girls, you ready to make good on your captain's gamble?"

The Bombers shifted nervously. They had all gone pale.

Though the bleeding had stopped, Jenny's eyebrow still throbbed. "Don't include them," she said hastily. "It was my bet. You and me, Frankie."

"Ha! As I recall, it was your team against my team, just like on the rink. Only this time those kneepads of yours will get put to some real good use. Wasn't that the bet, Jen? Don't you remember?"

Gap-toothed grins on their lusty faces, the other Mimis crowded in close behind their captain, savoring the thought of taking sexual revenge on their nemesis, a team that had crushed them so many times before it had nearly broken their spirit. Most of the Mimis were already stripped down and ready to be serviced, some completely nude, some wearing only their skates; others had taken off their pants but left their jerseys on.

"Let them go," said Jenny. "I'll take care of you."

"What?" The pleasure on Frankie's face was obvious.

"I'll take care of you, Frankie. I'll fulfill my end of the bet."

"Ha! And what about my girls?"

Jenny dropped her eyes. "Them too," she said.

The Bombers began to whisper among themselves in horror.

Frankie grinned.

"You'd service all my girls just to protect yours?"

"That's right," said Jenny. "Every last one of them."

"Right here, in the locker room? Right now? On your knees, Jen?"

Jenny nodded dejectedly.

Frankie's laugh was harsh. "What do you think, girls?"

Big Lady Boom Boom stroked herself, her legs slightly spread as she hungrily eyed Tammi Black, a mean spitfire of a girl who had given Lady Boom the knee more than once. "I dunno, Frankie, I've been lookin' forward to seeing that bitch Tammi on her knees."

"From what I hear, that doesn't take much doing," laughed Frankie. Tammi blushed, her face angry as she realized her reputation preceded her. "All right!" shouted Frankie. "I'll agree to let you take care of the bet yourself—on one condition. Your girls have to watch."

Jenny's eyes went wide, and the whispers behind her grew louder. The deal didn't seem fair, but what could she do? She'd made the bet with Frankie, and now her teammates were on the line. If she didn't fulfill her end of the wager, they'd all have to pay the price.

Even as Jenny felt a quivering humiliation in her belly, there was also a certain excitement. Hadn't she and Frankie done exactly this, that long-ago weekend at the National Roller Derby Finals, when they'd put away a six-pack of Schmutz beer and tumbled into the hotel bed together? They'd never spoken of it since—but the incident was never far from Jenny's mind.

Jenny met Frankie's eyes, and in that instant she knew the truth. Frankie would take so much more pleasure in this than just the satisfaction of having beaten a rival in the rink. There was hunger in her eyes but also—Jenny could have sworn—a certain tenderness. Or was she just imagining things?

Jenny's heart welled up, and in a single throb of her hungry cunt she dropped her eyes, humiliation giving way to an embarrassed eagerness.

She nodded.

"Then it's settled." Frankie looked at the Bombers. "Girls, get comfortable. You're gonna be here a while." She turned to her own team. "And you girls—line up!"

There were evil chuckles among the Mimis as the Bombers crowded nervously together and prepared to watch. To Jenny's surprise, she could have sworn she saw vague smiles on the faces of several Bombers as the Mimis selected their places in line behind their captain.

Jenny reached down and checked her kneepads. She'd be needing them.

First, Frankie skated over and sat at the edge of the bench. "Off with the jersey," she said. "You want me to get rug burn on my thighs?"

Jenny thought about protesting, but she was already hot. Besides, what did it matter if she knelt there fully clothed or half-naked? Obediently she took hold of her sweaty, filthy jersey and lifted it over her head, revealing the swell of her breasts in the tight white sports bra. Her nipples were plainly evident through the light material. Jenny only had a moment to wonder why her nipples were so hard before she realized Frankie had noticed. Then they got harder—much harder—as Frankie's gaze roved over them.

Frankie grinned wolfishly and licked her lips. Then she spread her legs.

The Mimis all crowded in to get a better look. Jenny kicked off and skated over to Frankie. Executing a skid, she dropped to her knees in front of her, her kneepads cushioning her descent.

Frankie chuckled cruelly, reaching down with one hand to roughly tweak Jenny's nipples through her sports bra. "If I didn't know better, Jen, I'd think you were going to enjoy this as much as I am." Frankie's other hand snaked into Jenny's mousy brown hair, grasping the clip that held her ponytail and unfastening it. She shook out Jenny's hair, then took hold of it firmly.

Jenny looked up, half angrily, half desperately, and saw the heat in Frankie's eyes.

"And nothing would please me more," said Frankie, so quietly that the other girls couldn't hear. She took hold of that mousy brown hair and pushed Jenny's face roughly into her crotch.

Jenny was surprised how easy it was to let her tongue slide out and work its way into Frankie's moist cleft. Frankie's crotch was ripe with the sweat of a long match, and God forbid she might have showered before taking her pleasure with the rival captain. But to Jenny's surprise, she didn't recoil from the sharp taste; rather, she found herself pressing deeper into it, tongue burrowing between Frankie's swollen pussy lips and into her hole.

A raucous cheer went up from the Mimis as Jenny ate Frankie out, followed by a matching series of despairing mumbles as the Bombers saw their leader taken down a peg. *Am I failing my team?* Jenny wondered. *No*, she told herself, *just teaching them to make good on their bets.*

With a start, Jenny tasted the tangy gush of Frankie's pussy juice as Frankie let out a low moan of pleasure. Jenny licked deeper, working the tip of her tongue an inch into Frankie's body as she lapped up the sharp nectar. *God, I don't remember it tasting this good the first time*, Jenny thought. She recalled the long hours she'd spent in Frankie's sweat-reeking hotel bed, her face buried between these very thighs, lapping at this very cunt. Her senses dulled by Schmutz beer, she'd been unable to stop herself from pleasuring Frankie again and again as her nude Roller Derby rival twisted and writhed on the bed. Back then the taste had been barely noticeable—mild, even. Now it was overwhelming and seemed to fill every corner of her consciousness as she drove her tongue rhythmically into the squirming captain's entrance, coaxing moans and whimpers from her. Frankie's hand gripped Jenny's hair, giving Jenny a strange sense of comfort. However humiliating it was to be forced to service the enemy captain in front of her team, Jenny knew there was no way Frankie was going to let her off the hook—she'd be on her knees till an orgasm careened out of every Screamin' Mimi in this locker room.

But for now it was Frankie who was owed...and how! Demandingly, she pulled Jenny's hair to guide that eager mouth up one fraction of an inch into position over her swollen, throbbing clit. Jenny obediently licked it.

Frankie let out a sigh of satisfaction and her team cheered, shouting, "Suck it, Bomber!" and "Eat that pussy, Jen!" She heard a couple of nasty "lesbo" comments, but Jenny felt a surge of wicked pleasure knowing she was going to service every last one of those women before the stadium closed for the evening. That should change their tune! For now she slipped her hands under Frankie's thighs and lifted her slightly, pulling her body hard against her own so she could lick and suck her pulsing clit with more gusto.

Every few seconds she'd let her tongue dip down into the sopping tightness of Frankie's pussy, filling her mouth with that succulent tang. As Jenny serviced her, Frankie reached down and caressed Jenny's firm breasts, pinching her nipples to bring forth a gasp now and then. *If my nipples are this hard*, Jenny wondered with a lascivious rush, *just how wet is my pussy?*

Her body responded to the pleasure of eating Frankie again after all these months. As she squirmed and rubbed her thighs together, her juices soaked the polyester fabric. Jenny desperately wanted to reach down and touch her pussy, rub herself as she pleasured Frankie, but that would be too humiliating, too exposing in front of her team. She couldn't possibly reveal that she was enjoying this, could she?

Then Jenny heard a gasp behind her. Surprised, she lifted her face from Frankie's crotch to glance over her shoulder. What she saw sent a bolt of lightning through her spine, and made her head spin.

Tammi Black had her tights off and was spread wide on a spare bench while Brenda Shaughnessy knelt between her thighs. Delores McGovern had Shirley Jorgensen up against the wall, hands working under Shirl's jersey as the two of them kissed hungrily. Celeste Sweeney, Meg Polowski, and Geraldine DeFazio were wrapped up in a greedy threesome on the floor at the edge of the shower, their clothes bunched in improbable configurations as their hands and mouths avidly sought each other's bodies. Little Lucy Spunkmeier, the youngest girl on the team at 19, was propped alone against a wall with her pants around her knees. Her hand worked in slow circles between her legs as she caressed her ample breasts and she watched the scene with utter fascination.

How the hell did something like this happen? Jenny wondered. *How come it never happened before?*

But a quick glance up from Frankie's crotch assured Jenny the Mimis were no less carried away. Though they seemed to be saving themselves for her attentions, they were helping each other strip down for the privilege, and their side of the locker room was a sea of sweat-glistening female flesh.

"Hey!" snapped Frankie as she gripped Jenny's hair and pushed her face back into her glistening crotch. "Don't have second thoughts now that you've started an orgy, bimbo!" And Jenny didn't. She surrendered to her hunger as she worked her tongue up and down Frankie's clit. Frankie's moans rose in volume, and now that Jenny knew her team would be anything but horrified to see her enjoying herself, her fate was sealed. As she tongued Frankie's clit, she undid her belt, pulled her pants down just far enough to get her hand wedged between her legs, and pressed her fingers into her own softness. *Yep, I'm wet, all right.* She worked one finger into her hole and rubbed her clit up and down in time with her tongue strokes on Frankie's. They were going to come together, or damn close. Jenny felt like their clits were one, merged in the surging hunger that flowed between them. Jenny felt her clit explode with pleasure. Her orgasm shuddered through her body as Frankie let out a wail. Jenny didn't let that throbbing clit go for one instant as the two of them came together. Jenny went off so hard her ears rang. Frankie gently stroked her hair. Soft sucking sounds and cries of ecstasy echoed in the locker room as the Bombers trysted fervently behind her.

Suddenly, a cry went up as the Mimis scrambled to get back in line.

"Me next!"

"No, me!"

"I was first!"

"No, I was, bitch!"

Still holding Jenny's hair, Frankie pulled her head back and bent forward to kiss her. She licked the thick tang of her own juice from Jenny's lips. So quietly that the other Mimis couldn't hear it, Frankie whispered: "You do my girls right, and I'll make you happy."

You already have, Jenny wanted to say, but that was way too corny for a Roller Derby queen—even a losing one—so she just nodded as Frankie's thighs disappeared from around her face.

Another Mimi replaced them, and Jenny Blake went back to work.

■ ■ ■

Crashed out in her underwear on the bus later as the Wisconsin moon blazed overhead, Jenny rubbed her aching jaw. Her clit and pussy throbbed with overuse. She had lost count at a dozen orgasms, and that was only on the sixth Mimi. She didn't think she'd ever come so much, and she'd certainly never eaten so much pussy. But while the whole time she would have preferred Frankie's pussy to those of the Mimis, it was Frankie's beguiling whisper in her ear that drove Jenny to new enthusiasm in servicing the rival team. Every sound of encouragement she heard made Jenny want to do the job that much better.

Luckily, it was a sleeper bus, so there was a bunk for each Bomber, except for Celeste and Meg, who didn't mind doubling up (and Jenny noticed that Gerry's bunk had mysteriously become vacant).

Jenny sneaked a hand down her panties and touched the sore flesh of her pussy, gingerly stroking herself with mingled pain and pleasure. Could she have gone on? When she'd finally finished off the last Mimi (with an orgasm that almost made the skater box Jenny's ears), Jenny found herself wishing there were more for her to service, or more girls in general—like maybe her own team, say—to compensate them for the humiliation of having lost. But the Battlin' Bombers had soundly seen to each others' physical needs, and, surprisingly enough, to those of the few Screamin' Mimis who hadn't been content with Jenny's ardent tongue. Strangely, the two teams, so vicious on the skating rink, were bizarrely tender to each other among those locker room benches. It was downright touching, and it wouldn't have been out of the question for Jenny to think up an inspirational motto about sportsmanship if she hadn't been too busy eating jock pussy at the time.

Now, it hardly seemed worth the effort to think up a pithy saying when all Jenny wanted to do was lie there and stroke herself, thinking about Frankie's clit on her tongue, Frankie's thighs against her cheeks, Frankie's tender whisper into her ear. She could feel her pussy juicing and her clit getting hard again, the accompanying burn mingled with a desperate desire to push herself further.

The bus ground to a halt. Testily, Jenny climbed down from her bunk and quickly pulled on her sweaty jersey, tugging it down past her crotch so she was at least passably decent. The bus driver, after all, was a nun.

"Sister Evelyn?" Jenny stuck her head into the cab of the bus as the cowled sister opened the door.

"Looks like someone's in trouble," said Sister Evelyn, pointing to the silver-white bus parked on the side of the highway and the crowd of jersey-clad young women waving at them.

■ ■ ■

There really wasn't enough room for a second team on the Bomber bus, but it really wasn't surprising that most of the Bombers were quick to pipe up about not minding to make room. When Jenny heard a few wicked comments about how the Mimis were going to have to "pay for the ride," she knew that sore pussy of hers wasn't going to get much rest on the way back to Minneapolis.

"All right," she sighed. "Double up!"

The bus wasn't rest room equipped, so Jenny called for a bathroom break and went behind a bush herself. By the time she returned to the bus, the girls were all nestled back in their bunks, two and three to a berth. *Damn*, she thought, *it must be cramped in there.* The giggling sounds coming from the curtained bunks didn't do much to convince her otherwise.

Her eyes still hadn't adjusted to the dark on the bus, so she'd already shucked her jersey and climbed into her own bunk before she felt the warmth of flesh pressing against her, felt the hard kiss on her lips, felt the hand sliding up her tight cotton tank top, smelled the familiar sweat that made her overworked pussy feel an infusion of new life.

"Nice work in there tonight," whispered Frankie.

Jenny moaned as she wriggled out of her shirt. Frankie tugged down her panties and worked herself around until she could lie naked with her thighs spread around Jenny's face.

"Thanks," said Jenny softly. "Do you have any idea how tough it is to get these girls to throw a game?"

Frankie reached down to caress Jenny's face, and slipped her fingers between Jenny's lips. Jenny gagged on the faint taste and smell of gasoline.

"Probably almost as hard as it is to get a fuel valve propped open without anyone noticing," she said, and her mouth descended between Jenny's spread legs.

Yeah, well, I guess I'll find that out next season, Jenny wanted to say, but she was too busy moaning. And then her mouth was full.

Contributors

J.L. Belrose's stories have appeared in the anthologies *Queer View Mirror, Pillow Talk II, Skin Deep, Best Women's Erotica, Uniform Sex, Set in Stone, Herotica 7,* and *Hot and Bothered 3*. She lives in Ontario, Canada, and has done some dogsledding but really prefers piling herself and her dogs into a pickup.

Ren Bisson lives in Northampton, Massachusetts, where she works in the mental health field. She plays in the National Women's Football League (NWFL) for the Connecticut Crush and loves sports, especially downhill mountain biking. She has also written a lesbian novel called *Goodnough Dike* published through iUniverse.com, under the name R.J. Bisson, available at the usual big online stores.

Bridget Bufford's work has appeared in *Pillow Talk II, The Coming-Out Newsletter*, and in the online publication *Erotasy* (www.erotasy.com). Her story "Working Out" is excerpted from *Minus One*, a novel in progress.

M. Christian's stories can be found in anthologies such as *Friction, Best Gay Erotica, Best Lesbian Erotica*, and more than 100 other books and magazines. The editor of various anthologies, including *The Burning Pen, Guilty Pleasures*, and *Rough Stuff 1 & 2* (with Simon Sheppard), Christian is also the author of *Dirty Words* (Alyson, 2001) and *Speaking Parts* (forthcoming from Alyson).

Dawn Dougherty is a very unsporty femme dyke writer living outside of Boston. Her work has appeared in *Best Lesbian Erotica 1999* and *2000*, and *Zaftig*. In her spare time she fights crime, and belly dances.

Sacchi Green leads multiple lives in western Massachusetts, the mountains of New Hampshire, and her libidinous imagination. Some of the fantasies she's wrestled into story form can be read in *Best Women's Erotica 2001* and *2002*, *Best Lesbian Erotica 1999, 2000*, and *2001*, and the anthologies *Set in Stone, Zaftig, Best Transgendered Erotica*, and *More Technosex*.

Laurel Hayworth lives in Tampa, Florida, where she has worked for 11 years mixing drinks at a lesbian-frequented sports bar. She's terrible at beach volleyball but plays a fierce game of ski ball. This is her first published story.

Long ago, **Debra Hyde** accidentally struck her riding instructor with her reins, much like the protagonist in her story. Unfortunately, the event didn't lead to a torrid affair. Incidents like it, though, have inspired her erotic fiction. Her most current work can be found in *Noirotica 4, Erotic Travel Tales, Herotica 7*, and *The Mammoth Book of Best New Erotica*. She also tracks sexuality news at her online Web log, *Pursed Lips* (www.pursedlips.com).

Kirsten Imani Kasai is an artist, writer, and mother living in California. Her fiction has appeared in *Libido, On Our Backs, Whorezine*, and the poetry anthology *Pierian Spring*. Her current artistic focus is an examination of sacred archetypes expressed through modern celebrity culture. In 2001 she debuted her novel *Flesh Hell* at the Fourth Annual Sex Worker's Art Show in Olympia, Washington. "Turned Out" was inspired by the totally delish Sporty Spice. Read more at www.paganholiday.tv.

Rosalind Christine Lloyd's work has appeared in many anthologies, including *Best American Erotica 2001, Pillow Talk II, Hot & Bothered II, Skin Deep, Set in Stone, Faster Pussycats* as well as the erotic literature Web sites *Kuma* and *Amoret*. A native New Yorker and Harlem resident, she shares her domicile with her very significant other and two unruly felines, Suga and Nile. She's currently obsessing over her first novel.

Computer geek by day and writer by night, **Catherine Lundoff** lives in Minneapolis with her fabulous girlfriend. Her short stories have appeared in anthologies such as *Best Lesbian Erotica 1999* and *2001, Electric, Zaftig,* and *Set in Stone: Butch-on-Butch Erotica*.

Shannon McDonnell is a freelance writer whose favorite topics are baseball, science fiction, and sex—not necessarily in that order. Her erotic fiction has appeared in the magazines *18* (formerly *BabyFace*) and *Penthouse Variations*. She has also contributed to *Starlog, Boys' Life, Arizona Highways,* the *Washington Post,* and others. McDonnell lives in Phoenix, Arizona.

Gina Ranalli has contributed fiction to several anthologies, including *Pillow Talk II, Dykes With Baggage,* and *Set in Stone*. She lives in Oregon.

Thomas S. Roche's books include the *Noirotica* series of erotic crime-noir anthologies and the short story collection *Dark Matter*. His writing has appeared in the *Best American Erotica* series, the *Best Gay Erotica* series, and the *Mammoth Book of Erotica* series. He is the marketing manager at San Francisco's Good Vibrations and is at work on a series of crime novels. Visit him at www.thomasroche.com.

Anne Seale is a creator of lesbian songs and stories who has performed on many gay stages, including the Lesbian National Conference, singing tunes from her tape *Sex For Breakfast*. Her stories have appeared in *Set in Stone, Dykes With Baggage, Pillow Talk I* and *II, Lip Service, Love Shook My Heart, Hot and Bothered, The Ghost of Carmen Miranda, Wilma Loves Betty, Harrington Lesbian Fiction Quarterly*, and other journals and anthologies.

Trixi is the editor of *Faster Pussycats*. People say she can make a mean dirty martini and a nice clean getaway.

A devout Martina Navratilova fan since 1981, **Yolanda Wallace** is still trying to recover from Martina's unexpected loss to Conchita Martinez in the 1994 Wimbledon finals. She can be found licking her wounds in various sports bars in Savannah, Georgia. If not there, she can be spotted on the sidelines, in the stands, or in front of her TV whenever two or more women are gathered in the name of sport.

Sarah b Wiseman lives in Kingston, Ontario, Canada. Her erotica appears in *Faster Pussycats* and *Hot & Bothered 3*. She encourages more dykes to take up fencing!